Two Quests

IN AN AGE OF UNCERTAIN SPIRITS

PATRICK CONLEY

author**HOUSE**®

AuthorHouse™
1663 Liberty Drive
Bloomington, IN 47403
www.authorhouse.com
Phone: 833-262-8899

Published by AuthorHouse 07/28/2022

ISBN: 978-1-6655-6691-9 (sc)
ISBN: 978-1-6655-6690-2 (e)

Print information available on the last page.

CONTENTS

'67 Ford Mustang: The Long Drives

A Foreword & A Forewarning... ix
Money Blues 1
Journey to Hell... 9
Negotiating New Perspectives 17
Negotiating New Perspectives on the Homefront 25
Calling in for Reinforcements 31
Gaining New Insights: Chimayo.. 39
Facing New Problems.. 47
Heading South 57
Balancing all the Ledgers 69

The Oracle of Here

A Foreword & A Forewarning... 77
Luke.. 79
Rachel 87
Lou 95
Phil 103
Buck... 111
Zamir... 119
Leila 127
Cassie...135
Karen & Cameron 143
David..149

Rachel 155
Amanda 163
Tom 169
Lou, Revisited 175
Luke and Rachel 183
Simon 191

'67 FORD MUSTANG: THE LONG DRIVES

A FOREWORD & A FOREWARNING

All characters in this book are fictitious; accordingly, anyone looking for resemblances to living or deceased persons will be disappointed. Fiction allows us an escape from reality and a retreat from the mundane even as it teases us, if only momentarily, that this world of letters is real. However, if the characters and situations remain as flights of imagination, perhaps the stories themselves may provide some element of truth.

MONEY BLUES

———

Oh, I'd have a job all right—in six weeks. But the paychecks had stopped; the bills hadn't. My car couldn't do much more than ten miles an hour as it rumbled and rattled and bumped along. Fortunately, Bill's home and auto repair shop was only three blocks away. Bill worked wonders with cars, but he was retired and took on only a dozen or so long-time customers. "There's got to be some advantage to getting old," he'd tell us. His arthritic hands didn't work as nimbly as they used to, but his mind was as finely tuned as an Indie car's. He even had some of the latest computerized diagnostic equipment. "Yeah, I kept up over the years," he'd boast in a low-key way. "Still, most of the time all I gotta do is listen to that engine purr or sputter and I'd have the problem all figured out. Well, at least most of the time I would. I gotta admit, though, that this new technology is pretty amazing. But you still got to know how to handle a wrench, if you know what I mean." I did, sort of. If I really knew how to handle a wrench, I'd do the job myself, but in my heart of hearts I knew I'd screw it up. Besides, Bill did the work for half the price, sometimes even less, than the big repair shops would charge. But he wanted to be paid in cash, He said he'd redo any job needed redoing, but in the twenty years I've done business with him I've never known him to have to redo any work. He prided himself on getting it done right the first time. And he did.

As for me, I was still working on getting it right. Amanda and I had two children, one a senior in high school, the other an eighth grader eager to start high school. The older one, Amy, needed some help with her tuition next year. To save money, she'd go to the local university. She had already taken the ACT and the SAT and would take them again in two weeks. "I'm not that far off from getting some scholarship money," she kept reminding herself. She wanted to be a nurse like her mother. The eighth grader, Tom, had already majored in skepticism. As a young boy of six, he had put his trust in Mom and Dad and Sister. Now, no more. If we asked him to clean his room, he'd just claim in protest, "Why? It'll just get dirty again."" One day, his mother Amanda called his bluff. "Yeah, you're right Tom. Just wear the same underwear, pants, shirt, and socks to school tomorrow." His eyes opened wide when he heard his mom's retort, but true to his early adolescent skepticism he boasted that he'd go to school all right, dirty clothes and all. He did. But, when he almost slinked home the next day, he quietly slipped off his dirty clothes, tossed them in the washing machine, went upstairs, and tidied up his room. It wouldn't be fair to say that he really cleaned it. He more or less just picked up the eyesores and disposed of them. Amanda accounted this a minor victory in the ongoing skirmish. I'm not sure exactly how Tom regarded it, but his new nickname at school—"Stinky"-- stuck for an eternity (that is, in middle school time. By the next week, his classmates had moved on to torment their next victim).

My broken down car was giving me enough torment. True, Bill would do the job for half what some of the big repair shops would charge, and he'd do it right. But I had to pay him in cash, and lately cash was in short supply. When I described the problem to him over the phone, he said he couldn't provide me an exact estimate but that he guessed the whole repair, parts and labor, would probably be in the $500-$650 range. I wanted to groan but checked myself. Bill wouldn't cheat me—that I knew. And the old Ford had over 150,000 miles on it, so we had gotten our money's worth out of it. But right now there wasn't enough money to replace it. A new car was out of the question, and even used cars commanded a price that new cars used to. Amy needed money for school, and Tom was coveting that new pair of soccer cleats that some of his teammates were sporting. He would get some new cleats as he had outgrown his old ones, but he'd have to be satisfied with a pair a lot less pricey than the one his friends were wearing. Christmas loomed only a month away, but I was no Santa Claus. We'd nurse the old Ford along as long as we possibly could. Since I wasn't currently working, we weren't in immediate need of transportation, but that situation would end in a few weeks, I hoped.

I finally reached Bill's place, his three car garage that served as both garage and repair shop. "Yeah, I could hear ya comin' about a block away, maybe more. Come on, pull her in and let's take a look." Although I suspected that Bill had a premonition of what was wrong, he still took out his new, computerized diagnostic tool. Apparently, it revealed to him what he had already known. "Just what I thought, Joe. Look here." I gazed over his shoulder, his long grey hair almost hanging in my eyes. "You need a new timing chain and a new water pump at least, but you and Amanda have kept up the old Ford, so the core of the engine sounds good. It still got some more miles in it for you. But, just to be sure, we'd better check out the radiator and all, just to be sure. Anyways, right now it looks as if the whole job will cost you a lot closer to $400 than to $600. I know you're a little short on cash right now, so if you need to make payments, no problem. I won't charge ya interest or nothin' like that. Ya want me to drive ya back home?"

"Thanks, Bill, but it's only three blocks. It's not raining or anything, so I'll just walk." As I started back, I wondered whether the whole neighborhood knew that I was out of work. Next thing they'll be sending over food baskets to us except it wouldn't be baskets. If anybody sent anything, it'd be casseroles. Like most neighborhoods now, people waved to each other but didn't say much.

Instead, a few residents served as the local news watch for anyone who would read their posts in an internet discussion forum. Three years ago, when Amanda had breast cancer and had to undergo a double mastectomy, the neighborhood posters geared up in action and soon our kitchen was stuffed with casserole dishes. To tell the truth, I did appreciate the unsolicited charity. Dinner became one less thing I had to deal with. Amanda needed all the help she could at home and I still had to keep my job and tend to the household duties and help Amanda recover in any way I could. The chemo treatments weren't fun for Amanda, but she did need a ride and I was the one who drove her. Amy was still over a year away from getting her license, and even if she had been able to drive, I wouldn't feel comfortable with a newly licensed driver facing not only the dangers of the road but also the distractions of dealing with a nauseous passenger retching into a puke bag as the car headed home. But, the generosity of people we didn't even know comforted us—although for the following year none of us wanted to eat another casserole dish after the superabundance of mac and cheese variations, some with ham, some with chicken, some with various vegetables, but all with heavy, thick, gooey cheeses. I gained five pounds in the process. Amanda had anticipated the potential weight gain and contented herself with small portions. Tom and Amy still had adolescent metabolisms that burned the calories. As for me, I just gained weight and dealt with having to buckle my pants a notch looser.

The next day I got a call from Bill. "I got some good news for ya. The whole bill amounted to less than $400, $390 exactly."

"Great, when can I pick it up?"

"Tomorrow around noon."

"Great, that will give me time to go to the bank and pick up the cash."

"Ya know you can make payments if ya need to."

"Thanks, but I can cover this one." Even though I said that, I swallowed hard, fully realizing that we couldn't handle one more big bill.

"I got some more good news for ya."

"What's that?"

"Ya know that old guy—even older than me—who lives in that old mansion with an even older wooden barn in the back?"

"Everybody has heard of him, but I don't know anyone who has spoken to him."

"Well, I have. I'm the only one he trusts to work on his mini-fleet of '67 Ford Mustangs. He's got six of them sittin' in that old barn of his."

"Does he ever drive them? I've never seen him out and about."

"Yeah, he does, but at odd hours, like between two am and six am. In fact, everything he does is odd. But, he made a whole bucket load of money back in the day."

"Why is this good news for me? I mean, I won't be doing much driving between two and six in the morning."

"Well, you know how it is with collectors. They're never satisfied with what they got. In that respect, I guess maybe we're all the same. He won't be content until he's got every stall in that ole barn filled with a '67 Ford Mustang. He needs someone for a couple weeks to scour the countryside and come up with three more of his favorite cars. I sorta figured you being out of work and all could stand to make a little money, so I recommended you for the job. The old guy—Joey V is his name, but no one, including me knows what the *V* stands for—well, he don't trust many people. But he does trust me on account of I take care of his precious Mustangs. So, if you want the job, you just go ahead and hustle your ass up there and talk out the details with Joey V. He needs the three more Mustangs and you need some cash."

"Thanks, Bill. I'll run right up there. But shouldn't I call first?"

"Naw, Joey V doesn't take phone calls from much of anybody. If a new phone number shows up on his screen, he just ignores it. I told him that you might be comin' up to see him this afternoon and he said to just drive right up. The gate will be open."

The next day, I paid Bill in cash—all in twenties and tens because people still look at you funny if you give them fifty and hundred dollar bills. I guess they might suspect you of dealing drugs or something. Still, people still gossiped about the weird recluse Joey V. Some thought he had made his money in the Mob; others rumored that he must have won the lottery or something. A few speculated that he was an engineer and a brilliant one at that, who had made a fortune in the NASA program and then retired early. Still, others maintained that he had never worked a day in his life but had inherited a fortune from some unknown relative. As for me, I just hoped that he hadn't made his money in the Mob. From movies and television shows, I had blindly accepted the notions that mobsters paid people well in one of two ways: with money and lots of it if you were successful or, if you failed, with bullets and lots of them. But I reminded myself that I was probably being melodramatic about the whole affair. Maybe Joey V was just an old man who liked the iconic '67 Ford Mustang.

It didn't take me long to reach his mansion. I had assumed that it would have been a crumbling structure held together by vines. Instead, the mansion was just a fairly standard ranch style house with neatly manicured lawns and a flower garden in front and a vegetable garden in the back. The scene would have been postcard perfect in the spring, summer, and early fall. But now it was the last week in November and all I could see were blurred into variations of brown and grey. The man who greeted me sat on his small front porch, in an antique rocking chair. "Bill told me you would probably come. Nothing like being out of work that makes you want to work. I'm Joey and you must be Joe the out-of-work accountant. Nice to meet you. Let's go around to the back and I'll show you my six Mustangs. And fill you in on what I want you to do."

If Joey V was a mobster, he didn't look like one. At least, he didn't look like the ones depicted in films and television shows. Instead, he sported neatly trimmed, white hair, slightly thinning on top, just long enough to be neatly combed to the side. His sideburns descended precisely to mid-ear. His face was so clean-shaven that it must have been razor cut. His nose—well, it was nondescript, neither bulbous nor aquiline, just a nose. His blue eyes sparkled a bit when he spoke. His chin, well, it was as plain and ordinary as his nose. It was a chin. For a supposed recluse, his complexion was remarkably tan. He looked fit and trim. His white polo shirt revealed a forearm that rippled with fine muscles .His tan pants sported a razor thin crease that stretched down to his light brown deck shoes. Neither recluse nor mobster stood before me. Joey V gave every impression of being a successful, retired professional, a retired CEO of some established firm.

"I suppose you've heard lots of stories about me," Joey V quipped. "None of them, I suspect, are true with one exception." Here he paused for effect. "It is true that I have a passion for '67 Ford Mustangs. I regard them as the thoroughbreds of the automotive industry. And they are. But the automotive industry is crowded with fine thoroughbreds. For personal reasons, I just happen to have taken a fancy to the vintage Mustangs. Let's go over to my barn and I'll show you around."

As we walked over to the barn at a leisurely pace, Joey V continued. "We share one contact—Bill. He has vetted you. I think that 's the term used nowadays. He says you're between jobs, in need of money, pay on time, and have a family. His word is good enough for me. I'll fill you in on the details of your mission should you agree to accept it. First, however, let me show you my stable of thoroughbreds."

I wasn't quite sure what to expect. From the outside, the barn looked nothing like a showroom. Instead, it resembled an aging, abandoned structure with wooden planks missing in a few places and those old planks that remained didn't impress, warped and grey-brown, slowly rotting with age and exposure.

"I see that you, like everyone else, take a dim view of my barn. I want people to gaze at the exterior and take away a totally wrong impression.

Let me show you the inside. As we entered the structure through a creaky door on rusted hinges, we took in a completely different view. Once he flipped the light switch, we entered a new domain. Instantly, whiteness engulfed me. Blinking my eyes to regain focus, I found myself transported to a new, futuristic, mechanical marvel. The creaky old barn with warped and rotting wooden planks was swept away by stainless steel and chrome. I thought we were walking into an enormous safe. In a way, I suppose we were. Joey V entered his code and the solid steel door opened noiselessly. Five stalls lined each side of the enormous barn /safe. "Six of the stalls house my current collection of '67 Mustangs. I want three more stalls to be filled. That will be your job, my friend. The tenth stall I'll reserve for repairs. Bill has designed that tenth stall, transforming it into a bay for him to work on the cars. You won't find any hay here, just bare concrete." Joey V could have added that the concrete lacked any telltale signs of housing fifty-year-old cars: no oil stains, no traces of rust. "I keep my stable at a constant temperature of 67 degrees. As we slowly made our way to the rear, we passed Joey's six Mustangs, all glistening, just waiting to be driven. I couldn't keep my eyes off one of them, white with black racing stripes. When we reached the back, Joey entered another code and a huge door lifted, leading to one of the old-fashioned bubblehead gas pumps. "I pump my own gas, specially formulated for vintage automobiles. As we strode out into the open air, the gargantuan rear door closed and we returned to the moldy, rotting grey of the old warped timbers. "So, what do you think of my ruse?"

"I guess most people would glance at it from a distance and assume it housed maybe six hundred rats instead of six vintage Mustangs."

"Exactly what I want people to think. Of course, you won't advertise my barn's real occupants," Joey V. added, shooting me a look that didn't allow for any hesitance or denial. "Of course, Bill knows, and now you do. One day more people will come to know what my old barn preserves, but not now. Understand."

"I won't tell anyone, I swear."

"It's not necessary to swear. In fact I prefer that you do not. Just keep your word." Once again Joey's eyes bored right through me.

"All right, no swearing. I'll keep my word or lose any pay for whatever it is you want me to do."

"You may lose more than that," Joey retorted. In the back of my mind, I wondered if those rumors about Joey V's being a mobster had more than a kernel of truth to them.

"So, what is my first assignment?"

"You are to travel to Hell, Michigan, pick up a white '67 Mustang and drive it home."

"So, you're telling me to go to Hell?" I responded quizzically.

"It's an actual place, just a little to the east of Ann Arbor. I've also booked a hotel in Hell for you. You'll take the bus there and drive the Mustang back to me. All of the particulars are in this envelope. The drive home would take you about eight hours over the interstates, but I don't want you driving any faster than fifty, so you'll take the back roads. It may take y0u as long as twelve hours. All of the particulars are detailed in this packet."

"What if I refuse?"

"Here's a thousand dollars down and another thousand when you return. If you leave tomorrow morning on the bus by four am, you should be able to meet the seller in the Hell hotel and drive back the next day. If you do a satisfactory job, you'll make two more trips to pick up other cars. On those two other trips, Bill may join you. I'll want him to check out the cars thoroughly before I wire any money to potential sellers. Agreed?"

"Agreed," I answered and extended my right hand for a handshake. Joey looked down at my hand, paused, and then extended his hand to deliver a near bone- crunching handshake.

I had only one question: What would I tell Amanda?

JOURNEY TO HELL

If I told Amanda that I was earning a thousand dollars for two day's worth of work, she'd assume that, in my desperation, I was selling drugs or otherwise trafficking in illegal and / or immoral activities. On the other hand, if I handed over too little money, she'd wonder why did I bother. So, I took the purgatorial way out. I'd hand over two hundred and fifty dollars to her and then when I returned, another two hundred and fifty. That way I could hold the balance in reserve in case some emergency cropped up. Like probably another car repair. Still, I wondered if I weren't the object of some sadistic joke. Why would Joey V have me pick up the car in Hell, Michigan? It's not that far away from Ann Arbor, and he'd save the bus fare from Ann Arbor to Hell. Maybe old Joey was paving my way to some spiritual hell as well as the geographic one. Still, there's nothing illegal or immoral about picking up a car and then driving it from seller to buyer. It happens all the time. Still I was earning a hefty paycheck for two day's work. Joey V was offering me a choice I couldn't refuse. So, I didn't.

As I opened the door to my house, Amanda joked. "I didn't hear the old car clunking and clanking its way into the driveway. So, it's all fixed?"

"Yep, and for less than we feared. Bill gave us a deal. The whole bill amounted to less than four hundred"

"How much less?" Amanda asked a bit skeptically.

"Ten dollars."

"Well, ten dollars is still ten dollars. Thankfully, it wasn't six hundred."

"There's more." I teased playfully.

"More of what, Joe?"

Here's two hundred and fifty dollars more. Bill gave me a lead on a part-time job, driving a car from some place just east of Ann Arbor, Michigan, back here. I'll take the bus up there and drive the car back.

"Are you doing this for Bill?"

"No, for that eccentric old guy with the decrepit barn. He gave me an advance of two hundred and fifty and I'll get two hundred and fifty more when I deliver the car to him."

"Joe, is this all on the up and up? We can't afford legal bills in addition to what we're already dealing with. Five hundred dollars is a helluva lot of cash for just driving a car back from Michigan. They've got trucks that will haul half a dozen cars to Michigan and back for less than five hundred dollars."

"It's not just any car. It's a '67 Mustang. And Joey V. doesn't want it to go over fifty miles an hour, so I'll have to take the back roads for as much of the trip as I can."

"For Joey V, huh? Do you have to do anything else for him? Maybe you'd better check out the car inside and out to make sure you aren't hauling anything illegal."

"Oh, I will." To tell the truth, I hadn't even thought of that scenario. So, I rationalized. "Do you know how much a vintage '67 Mustang goes for?"

"I haven't had time to check out the latest vintage car prices. We're busy enough just keeping our cars running."

"Well, the starting price is seventy thousand, and the price goes up from there. Genuine Shelby's can go for one hundred and eighty thousand."

"So, you're telling me that, if we can hang on to our old Ford for another fifty years, it will be worth a fortune?"

"No, only a few models have appreciated in value. Ours will eventually die and we'll have to sell the remains to Junk-my-Car or something like that."

"Well, we can use the money—that's for sure. Maybe it is worthwhile to have someone, like you, to drive it back safely from Michigan. Just promise me to inspect front to rear so that you're sure you're hauling nothing but the car."

"Will do," I shot back quickly, maybe too quickly.

Amanda eyed me suspiciously as if she knew I wasn't telling her the whole truth—and I wasn't—so she suppressed any suspicions but must have been storing them in her memory bank. She paused before asking, "So when do you leave?"

"Tomorrow morning. I need to be at the bus station by 3:45 am."

"And I guess you're wanting a ride there."

"Yes," I responded meekly. To tell the truth, I was so enthralled with the opportunity to make two thousand dollars that I hadn't worked out the details.

"Well, for two hundred and fifty dollars, I guess I can drive you to the bus depot—even at 3:30 in the morning."

"Now that's true love," I concluded.

At 3:30 darkness still prevailed, but with little traffic we made it to the bus depot in fifteen minutes. Only a few headlights and some garish signs broke the night's hold. So, Amanda and I drove on with few words and no interruptions. We kissed each other goodbye just before I hopped off the car and into the bus station.

But, if the world lay dark and still outside, inside the terminal people were bustling about. Since I already had my ticket, all I had to do was to locate the bus to Chicago for the first leg of my journey. As I quickened my pace, others matched me stride for stride in a rush to board one of the five buses that would soon depart. Travelers were bumping into each other as they scurried to find their buses. Only when I boarded the bus and took my seat did the pandemonium of the rush to board ended as someone yelled out, "Is this the bus to Chicago?"

The stoic driver, who must have heard the same question two dozen times, always answered with, "That's what the sign says, so I guess it is. Come on and board." Occasionally he'd have to pause to deal with someone who was hauling an oversized bag. "Hey, buddy, you'll have to store that bag below—either that or pay for two seats." But three minutes before departure, the bus had almost every seat filled. The seat next to me remained empty. For a moment, I felt slighted and wondered if I had forgotten to shower that morning; but, as I looked around, I soon realized that I was odd man out. Most of the passengers must have been either twenty years younger or older than I was. Many seemed to be college age, perhaps half of the bus. A few young mothers with toddlers in tow— at least as much as toddlers can be in tow—made up the next largest contingent. And then there were others of retirement age, perhaps going to visit grandchildren or just to travel. And then there about four people my age, businessmen and women perhaps going to Chicago to look for a job or to do one. Soon, the bus ride north eased into its own rhythm as the bus cruised along the interstate until we reached Springfield, Illinois, where some half dozen passengers disembarked and another half dozen boarded. The seat next to me remained empty.

We reached Chicago on time, but the bus to Ann Arbor was delayed because of an early, unpredicted heavy snow. So, I sat and waited in the bustling depot on hard benches or seats where other passengers vainly tried to sleep or sit riveted to whatever was going on in their phones. Many might be searching for other travel options. A few college students opened books for a while, but then, seemingly bored or otherwise unable to concentrate, joined those who were trying to sleep. Then, three hours later, the PA loudly proclaimed that the bus to Ann Arbor would leave. This time, almost all of the passengers seemed to be college students. They talked of final exams and of the Ohio State / Michigan game and of the parties before and after. Then it would be Christmas and New Years before the month –long round of parties would end. Once again, I was clearly odd man—and old man—out as the seat next to me lay vacant. It did give me time to find out a little bit about Hell, Michigan. According to local legend, Hell traces its history back to the late 1830's. It started as a gristmill and general store and supposedly owes its name to the fact that the proprietor of the gristmill paid the local farmers in whiskey. When asked where their errant husbands were, some wives reported that they "had gone to hell." Today Hell is an unincorporated area that has no bounds. Fittingly enough hell can be everywhere, I guessed. It does have one institution of lower learning, Damnation University, where for a small fee, one can obtain a "Dam U" diploma. So, this place capitalizes on its name. I wondered how many other universities did the same. We soon reached our destination but did so behind schedule—so behind that I missed the connecting local bus that went to Hell and back again. I had two choices: 1) I could wait it out until tomorrow morning after I rescheduled my appointment with the seller or 2) I could rent a car and hope that the road had been cleared to Hell. I did the latter.

The drive to Hell lulled me into complacency—until I had arrived almost at my destination. "Oh, damn, I almost missed the exit," I screamed to no one but myself. But my sudden jerk of the wheel had sent me careening off the road right into a snowbank, actually to an artificially made mound of snow where the plows had dumped the snow and ice of the road for miles all into one inglorious mass of white snow, grey ice, and a black detritus of dirt, oil, and muck. Ironically, the salt or whatever chemical concoction it was that the highway department used to melt the ice on the roads had the opposite effect when the frozen and partially frozen heaps piled on top of each other. The mountains froze and froze over and froze over again to produce a barrier more dense and solid than concrete. I straightened the wheel and threw the gear into reverse and pushed down on the gas. No go. I was in an infinite spin or at least one that would last as long as my gas tank hadn't dropped to empty. So, I exhaled deeply and then kept a slow but steady press. Still no luck-- this is it," I muttered under my breath in puffs of grey whiffs. "What next?"

After an eternity that lasted maybe three minutes, I heard a tapping on my window. "Hey, buddy, welcome to Hell. You here for the Jock Sniffers' Convention?"

"The what?" I replied.

"You know the Jock Sniffers' shindig, the big meeting where the aged, busted and broke ex-pro players try to make it in the real world."

"No, I'm just here to buy a car," I spit out, a bit annoyed. "I'm getting paid to pick up a car for an eccentric millionaire."

The tow truck driver looked at me quizzically. And then he experienced an "AH-ha" moment. "I'll bet you're out of work and doin' this to pick up a little money."

I nodded and wondered if everyone knew I was out of work as soon as they saw me.

" Ok, I'll pull you out for free."

The tow truck driver backed about three feet from the rear end of my car and attached a massive metal hook, big enough to catch a whale, I thought. "Now when I tell you, make sure the wheels are straight. I don't think that you're that bad off, but sometimes you never know. Some guys bust their radiators when they smack into ice. But I don't see no radiator fluid leaking out, so I guess you're OK. With a slow, steady pull, I could feel that I had been eased out of the jaws of a wintry trap. "Thanks," I yelled out.

13

"No problem, buddy. Welcome to Hell. Go ahead and make a U-Turn back to the exit. There's nobody dumb enough to be out here in this weather other than you and me."

My anonymous guardian angel had stated it perfectly: nobody else had ventured out onto the snowy roads. Not even a truck was in sight. I did as instructed and slowly spun, swerved, and slipped over the next two miles to my destination, a motel. I needed to get some sleep before the morning meeting to pick up Joey V's new Mustang and drive home. I wondered if the roads would be cleared.

These thoughts at least kept my mind off the cold and treacherous streets. Before I knew it, I had arrived at my destination, an old 1950's style family run motel whose billboard proudly proclaimed all in caps, "FROM CLEATS TO WINGTIPS." As I turned left into the driveway, I kept gliding as I had hit an icy spot, heading right towards the rusty iron beam that kept the billboard aloft into the grey darkness above. "Hell," I mumbled through grated teeth before being able to right myself and steer away from the sign—another close call. Not wishing any more near crashes, I eased my way over to the most distant parking space, turned off the ignition, took a deep breath, and thought to myself," So this is what people meant when they said as 'cold as hell.' They weren't referring to the theological hell. They meant this place."

The motel clerk eyed me suspiciously and then began his spiel. "You got a reservation?" You're shit out of luck if you don't. Hell is booked solid, been so for about three weeks. I tell you this convention is the best thing that ever happened to this town. We'll be making money hand over fist, and it ain't just the ex-jocks. It's the jock sniffers that've got the dough. Man, I never heard so much BS about those high school glory days. From the looks of you I guess that maybe you played some high school ball, but not much since then."

I grumbled out loud, "Reservation for Joe Allmen." I was a bit put out about the motel clerk. Yeah, I had played some high school soccer and ran track and, yeah, I hadn't done much since then and, yeah, I was a bit paunchy around the midsection and, yeah, my ego was a bit bruised by his comments. At least he didn't directly call me a jock sniffer.

"Let's see, yeah, here it is, Joe Allmen."

The clerk changed his mood "Huh, prepaid and all." His gut was overflowing his belt, and he had some greasy food stains on his shirt. Still reeling from his assessment of me, I took a petty pleasure in taking him down a notch or two if only in my thoughts. I could be as small-minded as the worst of them.

"Here's your room card and number. I'm giving you two cards. Lose one and you'll owe me another fifty bucks. Checkout time is eleven o'clock. I see you're staying for one night only. The bar just off to the left. The rooms ain't much to speak of, but then most guys spend most of their time at the bar and get too blottoed to do much else. This time of year about the only thing you can do here is drink. Your first drink is on the house. The rest is up to you."

"Do I get a ticket or something for the bar?"

"Naw, I'm the bartender as well as the proprietor of this here establishment. I won't forget ya in the two minutes it'll take for you to order a drink. As I said, there's not much else to do around here this time of year. You know it's good business. Most get the first drink, and then they got to have another and another and another. Pretty soon and I'm swimming in booze money, you know what I mean?"

"Yeah, I see what you mean," I retorted as I took the bait and headed towards the bar, a hazy, murky, greasy corner of the motel just off the registration area. I guess the bar served food, or at least what would pass for the edible after a customer had downed a few drinks, for the pungent aroma of stale grease floated in the air and added weight to the miasma of smoke. The reservation clerk had bustled his way over to the bar, his bloated gut swaying this way and that. "No limits on smoking here, ya see, as I got a guy pays off the local cops to look the other way." As I later learned, in a strange twist of local politics, the bar area rested just outside the city limits in a no-man's land where jurisdictions were muddled.

"Hah, I knew you'd come," boasted the owner-operator. "Just call me Luke, but that ain't my real name. So, whatta you have, beer or brandy? This ain't no place for any froo-froo drinks, just the basics."

"Beer, do you have Budweiser?"

"Hell, no, we got our own local brew. Great stuff, some guys get to like it so well, they buy a whole case to take home with them." Then turning to pull a draft, he said n a low voice. "Besides, you might even get lucky." He

15

shot his eyes over to the far corner where three bar hags huddled over their drinks—brandy apparently, cigarettes dangling precipitously from their lower lips. From their hair styles—a shoulder length bob of bleached blond waves—I guessed that they might have been in their thirties although they looked much older. Even from a distance, one could detect the furrows of wrinkles, the result of far too many late-night escapades. Dressed in dark, probably black leather coats, they stay huddled together until one caught sight of me gawking at them and started to slip off her coat, revealing a red halter top that barely covered the mounds of flesh wrinkling underneath.

"See anything you like?" Luke whispered in a low voice.

"No, Luke, I can barely keep my eyes open. Thanks for the beer."

"Ain't ya gonna order another one?" he cried in a high pitched whine.

"No, thanks, Luke, as I said, I can barely keep my eyes open. It's been a rough night."

"Well, then how about a six pack for later on?"

"No, I've got to turn in."

"Well, all right." He picked up my half-full glass. "You could of at least finished your drink."

"No, really, I'm wiped out. It's good stuff," I lied and headed towards my room. In the back of my mind I thought that piss water would have been better, but I guess after three or four drinks of the stuff, no one knows the difference. Then I realized that I hadn't quite lied to Luke. All I wanted to do was shower and go to bed and then see what tomorrow would bring.

NEGOTIATING NEW
PERSPECTIVES

The seller agreed to meet me at seven the next morning. "We've both got a lot to do," he explained. Joey V. had led me to believe that the paperwork would take only a few minutes, a perfunctory matter. It wasn't.

At 6: 45 am, I arrived downstairs in the dining area of the bar—if you want to call it that. It was more a place to feed rather than dine, but it would serve our purposes well enough. Glancing over the breakfast menu, I noted that it consisted of variations on a theme. Hungry feeders could feast on one of three options: 1) mild chili with fried eggs, 2) moderately mild chili with eggs, and 3) the Devil's Delight—red-hot chili with fried eggs. I chose the latter, sensing that I'd never get to (or want to) experience this morning delight ever again. "You might want to order a side of hash browns just to take the sting away," the waitress advised. She looked like one of last night's bar hags only in a devil outfit. She had reddish-brown hair—possibly tinted—a bulbous nose, and a stomach that swelled over everything else. I wondered if she feasted on the Devil's Delight every morning.

In five minutes, a portly gentleman sporting a full, forked beard, speckled grey and white in color, sauntered in. He took off a heavy winter coat. At one time this coat may have been white, but now it was streaked with brown and black sludge from the recent snowfall. He came over and stood before me. "You the guy who's buyin' the '67 Mustang?"

"Not exactly, I'm working for the prospective buyer." I answered as I rose and extended my hand. For whatever reason, the seller ignored my gesture. "Well, I'm glad to see you're early. I've got a lot of work to do, so let's get down to it. You order one of the specials?" I nodded in agreement. Calling over to the waitress, the seller barked out, "Hey, Gladys, the usual."

"I figured that, '' she responded. "In fact, I already ordered it for you."

"Yeah, well, that's the way I like it," he grumbled in response. Then, turning towards me he shoved some papers in front of me. "Here, look this over. I want this done before I finish my breakfast."

I read over the first three pages and it all looked like a fairly standard contract. But then I ran across an item that I hadn't expected. "What's this?" I almost bellowed.

"It's a three hundred dollar transfer fee. It's standard here in Michigan for all transactions involving the transfer of a car from Michigan to a buyer from another state. You're acting as the buyer, right?"

"No, I'm just the hauler. Joey V. didn't tell me anything about this. Besides, if there's a transfer fee, then the state's Division of Motor Vehicles should be collecting the fee."

"No, three hundred bucks, no sale." He shot back, trying to convince me with his version of a death stare. His eyes were fixed all right, but he kept blinking them nervously.

"I'll call Joey V."

"Joe, tell that SOB I've got a lawyer on retainer to handle these shenanigans.

He's licensed in Missouri and Michigan and half a dozen other states. The contract is valid. All you have to do is to sign that you are temporarily taking possession of the vehicle to transport it for me. That's it."

I had set my phone on speaker, so the seller would hear every word that Joey V. had pronounced. He did. He didn't respond, just shoved the car keys in front of me and mumbled that the car was out front. "Hey, Gladys, I'll take my breakfast to go."

"He's a real schmuck," Gladys said as she set my Devil's Delight in front of me. I hated to admit it, but the red-hot chili and eggs fit the occasion—but I was glad that I had taken Gladys' advice and ordered the hash browns on the side. "Got to give the devil his due," I told myself, "But you've also got to balance it all." I reflected as I took a forkful of the chili and eggs followed by some coffee and hash browns. I wasn't sure how much of a delight the breakfast turned out to be, but, like potato chips and other and any salty snack, the more I ate, the more I wanted—to a point. I wolfed it all down in a few minutes.

" You want to top it off with a donut, Honey?" I think I had heard Gladys call almost everyone *Honey*. Still, chewing the last remnants of my Devil's Delight, I just shook my head. Gladys scrawled out the total on a check, handed it to me and waited for her tip. I handed her a ten and a one, leaving her a little over a two-dollar tip. She took that as a cue to continue. "Not everybody around here is like that schmuck who tried to shake you down for a quick three hundred. He tries that scam every once in a while when some poor soul from out-of-state comes in to buy a car. He even gets away with it sometimes. But it's all a big bluff. All you have to do is call the bluff and he'll fold and melt away as fast as an early snowfall."

Gladys was right. The snow had started to thaw into a liquid stew of fallen leaves, motor oil, dirt, bits and pieces of bark, and all littered with the detritus of modern society: plastic bags and fast food boxes, plus discarded beer and soda cans and plastic water bottles.

After I took my leave of Hell, Michigan, I checked the forecast: no more snow but the temperature wouldn't climb above freezing until the afternoon. While the interstates seemed to have been cleared of snow and ice—I could tell when I looked up at the cars speeding by on the overpass above me, the side roads weren't. So, it was slow going from Hell to Ann Arbor. I'd start to skid and then ease the wheel over to the direction of the skid until I regained traction. I repeated that maneuver seven times, but at least the drive itself kept me distracted from what was going on inside of me.

If I were more of a philosopher, I suppose I'd reflect on the vicissitudes of life and the necessity of steering into the direction of the skid-misfortune before easing my way out. But, I was no philosopher and nor professional driver unless you count being paid to drive as the only criterion for being a professional driver. I went slow, so slow that a few of the cars behind me blasted their horns in protest at me. I'm sure they were all far more adept than I was at navigating the snow, at least all but one of them was. One fellow who had blared his horn and probably given me the finger as he passed me spun out on an icy stretch at the bottom of a hill, doing a 450 degree turn smack into a snowdrift. I waved as I passed me, but he was too occupied with clearing the snow from his front end to notice my petty gesture. I can be just as mean-spirited as the next guy, and I had no one to blame, not even the devil for that fault.

Around Ann Arbor even the side roads had been cleared, so I could make up for lost time but speeding up to fifty miles an hour before I had to slow down and halt at the stoplights that seemed to be paced at every three or four miles. At this rate, I'd never make it to St. Louis before dark. To compound my distress, the Devil's Delight had just begun to do its dirty work on my gastro-intestinal system. Flatulence and bloat attacked me internally, as I had to give the devil his due. Thankfully, I was traveling alone, so no one else had to suffer through my distress. "Well, at least, I won't feel like stopping for food for a while. By now my fuel tank still registered enough gas to get almost past the Chicago area. But my route skirted the southeastern perimeter of Lake Michigan, I feared that I was about to experience the dreaded Lake Effect snowfall. And I was right. My knuckles turned whiter than the abundant snow that lay all about me. But the road remained remarkably clear. Back home, a three inch snowfall would tie up the back roads for hours, sometimes even days. But not here. Here my only enemy was my own gluttony. Orange juice, coffee, and toast would have suited me just fine, but no, I had to yield to fiery temptation and gluttonously wolf down a Devil's Delight. The Mustang's Select Shift Cruise-o-Matic transmission allowed me to drive with manual transmission when the going got a little rough and automatic transmission when the road lay flat and straight, free of snow and ice. No wonder Joey V. prized this modern engineering marvel--the Mustang.

As I skirted past the outskirts of Ann Arbor, I wondered what all those college students who had shared the bus ride up with me were doing. It almost pained me to think that a year from now, Amy would be joining them. Even though she would live at home for a year, perhaps even four, to save money, she would still have reached a certain rite of passage. In many respects, she would be an adult. Our relationship would shift even if Amanda and I still retained some elements of parental control. At times, the financial bonds would exert more pressure than the emotional ones. Maybe that's what adulthood means—acquiring enough money to be independent as an adult. In that case, right now I had more in common with an eighteen year old—still in transition, hustling in a few part-time gigs until I would be settled into a full-time job. Still, though, that parental control has tentacles or loving hands that could extend their force even from the grave. My own father and mother still shape me, now perhaps more than ever. In the frenzied rush to adulthood, we all sometimes rush past our own parents in the illusion of being independent. I realize that now. Once Amy and Tom were born, Amanda and I needed some help from our parents. Amanda still confided in her mother. Her father had died shortly after my own mother and father had passed on. I wish I could talk to them now and apologize for all those times when I had neglected them, wondering if Amy would distance herself from me as I-- deluded with bravado of youth-- had distanced myself from my own parents. Then a blast from the horn of a car passing me on the two-lane stretch of the highway resounded in my ears. "I'm drifting off, lost in thought." Perhaps the supposed lack of danger had lulled me into complacency.

So, the Mustang and I cruised along. Vainly, I tried to keep my attention riveted to the road, but in the distance I saw the skeletal remains of an old oak tree. Bereft of leaves, it stood out from the acres of plowed brown and black dirt that surrounded it. Its bare limbs stood out, skeletal remains twisted and gnarled into fantastic shapes. Another reminder of the long winter to come. Recalling the lines from a poem I had read in high school—"If winter come / Can spring be far behind"—my Mustang and I swept past the tree.

Far from the outskirts of Chicago, but still in Michigan, I stopped to fill the fuel tank and empty my bladder. The outside air was crisp and autumnal; the temperature hovered a little over the freezing point so the roads would be clear. More than one person stopped to gaze at my Mustang—at least it was mine until I reached home. All seemed crisp and cheery until I entered the market and restaurant of the pit stop. There the whole atmosphere reeked of deep-fried grease. The fried chicken swam in lakes of grease in the overflowing trays that lay just beyond the plastic windows. So did sausage patties and even the leftover scrambled eggs. I picked up a bottle of Pepto-Bismol and wanted to down the entire contents. But I slipped into the restroom, where I encountered not the fetid odor of leftover grease but the somewhat acrid sting of some cleaner, maybe Pine Sol, maybe something else. But one odor did not overwhelm the other. Instead, the two existed simultaneously, like a Cold War standoff. I downed the prescribed dosage of Pepto and left as soon as I could. I made a mental note to never stop here again or at least not to go into the fast food hall of horrors.

"Nice car," someone remarked. "And not a speck of rust. I saw you pullin' in, and that beauty just purred like a kitten. Must be nice."

It was. For an instant, I felt that rush of pride. But the car wasn't mine. I was just making some money, that's all. Still, it looked and performed better than my own car that was forty-five or so years newer. What was that about age—something like not getting older just getting better? I reflected on my own physical condition—definitely older but better? Naw, just older, no sleek lines, or anything remotely sleek and svelte. Just an ordinary guy in any ordinary middle-aged body, soon to become an aging body stiff and fitful as it lumbered on. But I digress. I still had a mission to fulfill and another thousand dollars to earn.

About forty miles north of Springfield, Illinois, I made my second and final stop. I didn't need to hand over the car with a full tank of gas. Joey V. had written that he preferred it to run on his own blend. Still, I didn't want to run it empty. Two to three hours of road still lay before us. So, I skipped the fuel pumps and parked right in front of the diner as it was getting dark. In late autumn, the red sun seemed to descend more slowly on the western horizon as if it were succumbing to the ever-darkening reality of night. I got out of the car and gazed at the sinking sun. Oddly enough, the sun's rays seemed more intense in the short days of winter and night. So, I felt a chill wrap around me. Then, I headed into the restaurant, apparently a family business. I hadn't heard any syndicated franchise with the name of Mel and Melba's Diner on it. The first door opened into a small cubbyhole with hangers for coats and a place to deposit muddy or manure stained boots. A sign about seven feet high above the floor beamed out the warning. "Just like at home, don't bring your filthy clothes in here." I did see two pairs of rubber boots lying there. Most of the locals must have known the rules. I wondered if they had brought a spare pair of shoes to change into. Two men in blue overalls and tan moccasins confirmed my suspicions. They were ready to dine, not just eat. They both were hoisting up huge forkfuls of cherry pie to their gaping mouths. They looked as if they worked and played and ate hard. Then a family of two adults and four children occupied the other table and were enjoying a platter of fried chicken. "You want some pie first, Mister? It's the best pie you'll ever eat.

It's all good. We got cherry pie from Michigan cherries, apple pie from Illinois apples, and lemon meringue from wherever that stuff comes from."

I knew the routine: pie first to give the cooks time to prepare the entrees that occupied a narrow range from hamburgers to fried chicken. The aroma of the chicken had made its way over to my table, so the choice was easy. "I'll take the cherry pie and the fried chicken special, also some coffee." The waitress, who proudly wore the *Melba* nameplate on her pink blouse, replied. "You know, Honey, that's exactly what I would have ordered. Are just stopping her or are you moving on?"

"Moving on. I'm driving a car to St. Louis."

"You mean that classic Mustang with the temporary tags sitting out there in the lot?" I nodded. "That must have cost you a pretty penny. You know that '67 Ford was my dream car."

"It's sort of my dream car as well. I don't own it. I'm just driving it to St. Louis to give it to its new owner."

"Well, there are far worse jobs than that."

Melba must have suspected that there was more than a faint tinge of self-pity in my words. So, I stumbled my way into a response. "You're right on that point, and I've worked some of them."

"Haven't we all, Honey. Haven't we all."

NEGOTIATING NEW PERSPECTIVES ON THE HOMEFRONT

I dropped the car off to Joey V. about 8:30 that night. He thanked me, handed over the thousand dollars and said he'd have another job for me next week. He seemed to be in a rush to take the keys from me and drive it around himself. "Good, you took your time and didn't put any strain on the old engine. Runs like a thoroughbred. She'll run even better on my specially formulated gas. Wait for my call next Monday. Same as before—half the money before the job, the other half upon completion." I nodded and we shook hands. Just as he had turned away and headed towards his new Mustang, he paused, looked back at me and added. "By the way, Joe, did you keep your gas receipts?"

"Yes," I replied, not revealing that I had just haphazardly stuffed them down in my pants pocket.

"Good, hand them over and I'll reimburse you for those. As for your food, well, that's on you."

"Fair enough." If Joey V were a mobster, he certainly had a strong sense of fair play. I reached down into my pocket, pulled out the rumpled slips of paper, smoothed them out, and handed them over.

"For an accountant, you can be a bit sloppy at times," Joey V. joked, shifting his eyes from the crumpled receipt to stare at me.

I didn't know if he was sizing me up or playing some joke, whose meaning eluded me. So, I just exhaled slowly. "You're right. I'll be more careful on the next trip.' I had bungled a few matters, a minor one about the gas receipts and a more important one—my less than honest explanation of my part-time gig to my wife.

I rethought my policy of not telling Amanda just how much I was being paid. I got home on time, hadn't been arrested, and had another road gig lined up. The thousand dollars cash would go a long way to dealing with the bills that had pressed down their heavy weight on us. The short trip allowed me two days to escape that worry.

But new worries confronted me as soon as I opened the door to my home. "Good, you're home. Tom has been nagging me every chance he gets about the new soccer cleats he swears he must have before the tournament over the Christmas break, Amy needs money for three college applications and to retake the ACT. At least her request is an investment of sorts. If she can raise her score by two points, she'll qualify for more scholarship money. And I put off paying the electric bill until you got home and got paid. We really can't keep on putting off our bills. We're starting to rack up late fees and falling further behind."

"Well, this should help," I said as I handed her a thousand dollars in cash. For once, I could play the role of the big shot. Momentarily, I envisioned myself flippantly thumbing through the bills—all twenties— before her anxious eyes, but then quickly dismissed the thought as being altogether too over-the-top, too much of a B grade movie, too gangster esque.

Amanda shot me first a sigh of relief and then one of alarm. "Joe, are you sure all you came back with was the Mustang and nothing else?"

"Only some gas receipts, but I handed them over to Joey V and he'll reimburse us. My next trip starts next Monday."

"So, more money will be coming in?"

"Right, and all in cash."

"How many more of these trips will you do?"

"Two, one next week and the other one, I hope, the following week. I think that Bill might join me on that trip."

Amanda surveyed me intently, straining to detect any sign of lies, deceit, or other chicanery. "Well, we do need the money and if all of this is on the up and up, I guess that's all we can ask for."

Wanting to end this conversation as quickly as possible, I just nodded and hugged her. At least I had had the good sense to hand over all of my money this time. Otherwise, Amanda would have known that I had kept something back and suspected me of far worse behavior. I rationalized that I needed to keep some of the advance payment for expenses along the way, like gas and food. And, once Joey V had reimbursed me for the gas, I'd hand that over as well for family use.

The next morning, I fixed French toast and garnished it with fresh raspberries. As good as it looked, I couldn't take a bite of it. I was still feeling the aftereffects of that Devil's Delight breakfast I had had in Hell. Even Amy paused long enough for a few bites. "Thanks, Dad, I've got to go. Did Mom tell you about those application fees and the ACT?"

"Yes, I'll send the checks as soon as I deposit some money in the bank."

"Dad, just what are you doing over at Joey V's? Some of the kids spotted your rust bucket of a car parked at his place overnight. And kids talk, you know what I mean."

"Oh, I know. So far, Joey V. doesn't strike me as any type of gangster as least as far as the ones shown in movies and on TV. He's hired me to round up vintage cars, '67 Mustangs to be exact."

"So, you get paid to drive cool cars? I mean, they're old and all but still cool."

"I'm glad to hear that you think they're cool. Anyway, Joey V collects the Mustangs. In fact, he's got a whole stable of them"

"In that old, rundown barn?"

"That's the place." For now, at least I'd keep the secret of Joey V's more futuristic garage to myself.

"That's weird. I saw something on the internet about people finding antique cars worth a lot of money. It seems they all were left in old barns. Well, got to go. Love you, Dad." She waved as she left.

Tom stumbled his way down to the kitchen, still wearing his pajamas. His classes didn't start until later. One of the great educational innovations of the modern era was a later starting time for middle school students, whose biorhythms operated better later in the day, so they said. From a purely unscientific perspective, I had all along assumed that the kids were sleepy at school because they stayed up super late scrolling the internet and Snapchat and Facebook and all other forms of social media. But what did I know?

"Dad, did Mom tell you about those shoes?"

"Yes, it seems that's all you talk about. Did you finish your homework?"

"Mostly, I can finish the rest during study hall."

"It's not homework, if you do it at school, right?"

"Ha,ha, Dad, very funny. Homework just stresses you out. The teachers know that. Besides, we can sometimes get help doing it in study hall."

"Do you ever ask for help?"

"Dad, do you think I'm some kind of dork?"

"Well, if you don't need help doing your homework and won't ask for help, what's the point of study hall?"

"Dad, you're just too old. Anyway, it's called Independent Work, not Homework. You should really pay attention during those Parent Orientations at the beginning of the school year. Anyway, thanks for the French toast. Gotta go. Don't forget those new Adidas I have to have."

"Don't forget all those people who don't have a place to stay or a meal to eat," I retorted—but as much for my benefit as for his. Lately, we had cut down on our charitable giving a lot. I knew if I didn't send a check to the St. Patrick's Center for the Homeless, I'd forget about it completely. I did, but that one check didn't make up for all those weeks I had missed. Still, like my son, I had been preoccupied with my own troubles, wants, and needs. Amanda was still sleeping. She had been taking on extra shifts while I was out of work, and in the process had worn herself out. So, she should sleep in a bit whenever she could. My little part-time gig didn't match her full-time position in stress, strain, or other tolls on the body and spirit. So, figuring that she probably wouldn't be still sleeping, I made two cups of coffee, one for myself and one for her. If she didn't want it, then I'd help myself to it. "Can't waste anything," I cautioned myself.

Amanda was awake and reading the news. Still, I tiptoed in and set her coffee down on the nightstand as quietly as I could. "Thanks, Joe. I'll bet you fixed some French toast, didn't you?"

"Of course, I'm not gainfully employed today, so all you have to do is refresh it in the microwave."

"Aren't you going to have any?"

"I'm still dealing with the Devil's Delight, so, no thank you."

"Just what is a Devil's Delight?" Amanda asked brusquely as if she had suppressed a slight tinge of jealousy.

"It's a hellish concoction of red-hot chili and eggs. And then to top it off, I had really tasty, but really greasy, fried chicken on the way home. I won't be mixing those two again. But they tasted so good going down."

"Well, sometimes you have to give the devil his due."

"I think I overpaid him."

"When do you work again?"

"Next Monday, but I don't know exactly where I'm headed."

"Same pay?"

"Same pay, plus the reimbursement for gas. The food costs are on us. I think I'll pack a few sandwiches and forgo any devilish delights."

Amanda didn't respond. Instead, she seemed preoccupied, just staring off into a void. In a few seconds, she turned to look at me, and spoke slowly deliberately. "Joe, I lost a patient while you were gone. He was only two years older than you. The cancer had spread to his liver. We really couldn't do much. He and his wife had two kids, about three years older than our Amy and Tom. The three of them just cried and cried, and there was nothing we could do."

And all I could complain of was a bellyache.

CALLING IN FOR REINFORCEMENTS

On Monday morning, promptly at eight o'clock, Joey V. called me and told me to come over as soon as I could. He didn't have to ask twice. I was already dressed and had comforted my healing stomach with some breakfast yogurt and bananas. By eight –ten, I was out the door.

Joey V. was waiting for me outside of his barn. "Your next assignment will be a bit more challenging and it may end in no outcome. I want you to go to a little place about forty-five minutes from Santa Fe, New Mexico. You'll have to take Bill with you so he can look over the car and determine if it's worthwhile, either to fix on the spot and drive back or to tow it back. I've already talked to Bill. You'll be driving his Silverado there so that, if you have to tow, you'll have plenty of power to do so. Bill also has a trailer he'll pull. We're not quite sure what to expect but want to be prepared for any and all possible outcomes. Your job will be to negotiate the price based upon the condition of the car. But, I'm not so desperate that I'll take the car no matter what. In these papers, you'll see what I would anticipate to pay based upon the condition of the car. If the vehicle is unrepairable, then the two of you will at least enjoy a little road trip. Bill can have ample time to assess the Mustang's condition. With two drivers, you should be able to reach there by Tuesday night, but too late to do any assessment. Wednesday morning, Bill will start his evaluation. Then all you have to do is to stand and look somber with the best poker face you can muster. I would like to own the car if it checks out, but only if it checks out. I'm especially interested in the condition of the transmission. The Select Shift

31

Cruise-O-Matic should be in pristine condition. Of course, that's what the seller claims. But talk is cheap, especially when someone is trying to get top dollar for a very used car. I'm willing to put in a new engine if Bill advises so; but, of course, I would prefer not to. Do anything you can to talk him down. Drive over to Bill's place on your way home and the two of you should sort out the details. You should leave before four am on Tuesday. Check out the car thoroughly on Wednesday and then drive home Thursday; or, if absolutely necessary, Friday. Here's the first half of your pay. Don't forget to check with Bill before you go home. Oh, and by the way, here's the expense money for the gas on your last trip."

"Will do." With cash I had leftover from the last trip supplemented with the gas money from it, I thought I'd hand over the entire first installment, all one thousand dollars, to Amanda. That would take the sting out of being gone perhaps the rest of the week.

When I stopped by Bill's, he was in high spirits. "A road trip, just you, me, the open road, and the Silverado, oh, and the car trailer. This is gonna be a blast. I don't get out much any more, so this is almost like a vacation. And I'm gettin' paid top dollar for it to boot. What do you say we leave at three am tomorrow morning? The weather looks good, at least as good as it's gonna get in early December. You on?"

"I'm on, Bill. Meet you here at three am."

"Better make it two-fifty, so we can get the road ready and be on the highway by three am."

"OK, two-fifty." Bill's eyes sparkled like a six- year-old's on Christmas Eve.

We were on. Amanda balked a bit when I told her that I'd be gone until possibly Friday, but the thousand dollar payout provided ample consolation. "Well, I suppose we're OK now. We paid off our electric bill, you sent off the checks for the ACT test and the three college applications. We've got groceries, so I guess we're all right. What about the soccer shoes, those Adidas ones Tom wants so much?"

"I think he needs to put in some of his own money. He has saved a little bit from gas cutting jobs last summer, right?"

"Yeah, he had to. I kept it for him."

"All right, what if we supply enough funds for the base Adidas, the least expensive one of the lot. If he wants those particular shoes, his own funds can supply the rest or he can be satisfied with the least expensive ones."

"That's fine. It's not as if we were swimming in money now. While we might not go under, we're just keeping our heads above water as it is." Amanda paused and looked at me as I was taking out an old cooler, cleaning it from last summer's picnics, and making a list of what to include in it. "What are you doing?"

"Joey V will pay for our gas but not our food. Sometimes the road food can sort of get to you"

"You mean like the Devil's Delight." I nodded and held my belly tight.

"Who is driving? You said Bill would likely be joining you."

"I don't know which of us will drive first, but we're taking Bill's Silverado and his trailer. We'll take turns driving, so we can go straight through."

"Good, that will keep the mileage off our old car."

"Bill is really looking forward to this road trip. He said he doesn't get out much."

"Well, the two of you can chaperone each other."

I pulled into Bill's place about 2:45 the next morning. The temperature hovered just around the freezing point, but Bill was standing outside his truck all ready to go. "Hey, Joe, what ya got in that big ole cooler you're haulin'? In the old days, it would have been packed full of beer."

"Those old days have long since passed me by. I do have two beers, along with salami sandwiches, apples, grapes, and some yogurt. I've also brought along some licorice and chips for snacks along the way."

"That's good. For a minute there, I thought I was gonna have to listen to some health food fanatic, lecturin' me about my unhealthy eatin' habits. I gotta confess, though, I brought along only four beers. In the ole days, when I said I had only a coupla beers, I meant only a coupla twelve packs. Now a coupla means two. So, I got two for tonight and two for tomorrow night, and that's it. If I would down anymore than those two, I'd be up all night, peein' me a river. Say, how about you drive first while I chow down on some deer jerky I got left over from last year. I also got some hot biscuits. You can have one of the biscuits. Say thank you, Bill, for thinkin' of me."

"Thanks, Bill."

"Say, you think we can make it to Oklahoma City before eleven o'clock?"

"We should be able to."

"Thanks be to god. I look forward to stoppin' thereabouts and havin' me some some of them breakfast burritos. You can eat all that yogurt and fruit stuff you want, but me, I'm havin' me four big, greasy breakfast burritos, and all the hot sauce I can drown those puppies in. Some hash browns, too. I haven't had any of that good stuff since last year. Now that's what road trips are for."

I didn't add that road trips were made for heartburn, too. I could almost see Bill tearing into those burritos like some adolescent boy. I wouldn't mind driving all the way to Oklahoma City. It would be dark almost half of the way and traffic would be light. It had been a long time since I had driven a truck with a trailer, decades even. The only time I could remember doing that was when Amanda and I were first married and moving to our apartment with a trailer full of furniture. I'd like to think that I managed that trip masterfully, but I didn't. It took me five trials before I could finally back the trailer in—and not sideswipe the parked cars nearby. It was late August then, hot, in the nineties. But I was sweating more out of embarrassment than from the heat. I wanted to make a good impression on Amanda, but didn't. At least, she just laughed off my ineptitude. "I don't think you'll ever make it as a truck driver," she called out.

But, for now, Bill and I were off. For the first twenty minutes Bill talked excitedly about eating burritos and seeing the desert Southwest. "It's sort of funny. You'd think that the desert would be boring, just rock and some low shrub growth, but it isn't. It's sort of pretty in a strange way. It makes you look real close at things and focus on in individual rocks, and vistas. It sort of expands your mind if you know what I mean. Say, this place we're goin' to pick up the Mustang. It's not far from Chimayo. Man, people from all over come to the Sanctuary Of Chimayo for healin'. They say that a bunch of guys who survived the Bataan Death March started marching there on pilgrimage right after World War II. Those guys were tough, too. Now we cruise along the interstate, snug as bugs in the safety of our cars and trucks. But not those guys, they'd march to hell and back if they had to. And folks get healed there, too, so they say. All of us need healin' in one way or another. Say, while I'm checkin' out the Mustang, you ought to take a little side trip to the Shrine. It might be the only chance you'll ever get. And, if I learned one thing after all these years, I've learned that you don't skip out on opportunities when the chance comes. You ought to go, Joe. Besides, I don't want ya lookin' over my shoulder the whole time. Makes me nervous as if you were some foreman ready to can my ass, which I know you aren't. But I'd feel that way anyway."

"You've got me convinced, Bill. If I looked over your shoulder, I wouldn't know what exactly you were doing anyway."

"Maybe I couldda made the trip on my own. Years ago I couldda. But not now. I'm getting' a little tired. So, if you don't mind, I'll take a little siesta while you're speedin' down I-44. Just remember that we got to make it to Oklahoma City before eleven o'clock so's I can feast on them breakfast burritos."

While Bill dozed off, I wondered why Joey V had sent both of us. Bill could have done the job by himself. Maybe it would have taken him two days to drive there, but it still would have been cheaper to have just sent Bill on the job. But Bill probably wouldn't have had the heart to tell the seller that his prized Mustang wasn't worth near the money he might want for it. I was the accountant. Did that mean I didn't have a heart? Maybe at times I did focus on dollars and cents more than I should. I was beginning to wonder if Amanda's and mine relationship had just degenerated into a quasi-comfortable financial arrangement. We lacked the passion we had, that intense embrace of life and with all its mysteries. We—or at least I—had been so consumed with money woes that I had overlooked other dimensions in life. Maybe Bill was right. I should go to the Sanctuary of Chimayo for healing of a different type. I wouldn't throw away my spreadsheets and ledger, though. Maybe I could add to them an accounting of a different type.

We made it to Oklahoma City well before eleven o'clock. Bill had woken up when we reached Tulsa and followed the map along the way. "Hey, Joe, you know what's different about travelin' through Oklahoma?" He didn't wait for an answer. "Well, most of the time people look for cities, small towns, you know. When you go through Oklahoma, you don't look so much for the mall towns and such. You look more at the signs that say Cherokee Nation or Choctaw Nation or Chickasaw Nation.

It sort of makes you wonder about how things were before the settlers and boomers came in. And then there's this burrito thing. I mean, it's a real mix of cultures—Native American, Spanish, Mexican, white. Sort of makes things interesting, right. Say, you'll see the burrito place I've been goin' on about in a little while. It's right off the interstate, so stoppin' off there won't derail us too much. Besides, we've got to fill our gas tank and empty our bladders and stretch our legs some. It'll be comin' up in less than forty-five minutes. Say, you got some of that licorice you had in easy reach." I nodded. "Thanks, give me something to chew on and keep me from talkin' my fool head off."

So, we cruised along. The landscape here didn't roll out; in fact, there wasn't much of anything rolling out, not even tumbleweed. But the winds blew through mile after mile of flat landscape without even many trees to block it. Even the trees that did grow had long since lost their leaves so the bare branches just bore the force of the wind. In about forty minutes, Bill advised me to look for an exit. "We'll be headin' for Myrtle's soon enough?" Bill proclaimed.

"Myrtle's? I thought you said it was a burrito parlor."

"Oh, it is, and a lot more than that. See that sign over yonder, 'Myrtle's Truck Stop and Diner, The Best Brats, Burgers, Burritos, and Steaks You'll ever sink your teeth Into.' You don't usually associate the name *Myrtle* with burritos, I guess. And maybe some folks would say that her burritos aren't authentic Mexican burritos, more like Tex/Mex food, although don't say Tex/Mex around Myrtle. She'll almost rip your head off. You got to say Oklahoma/ Mex. Myrtle sometimes feels that Texas gets all the credit, but Oklahoma has got some great food, too. As for me, I like their burritos and steaks. They were good twenty years ago and I'll bet they're still good now. I checked up on the internet to see if Myrtle's was still open. Boy, was I glad to see that ole Myrtle was still dishin' out the goods."

We filled our tank, went to the restroom, washed up and entered the main dining area. Bill wanted to sit at the counter, so we took our place. "Hey, Bill, it's been a long time," a plump woman with grey-blond hair greeted us.

"You still remember me after all these years?"

"How could I forget the one man who could down eight of my overstuffed burritos in one sitting?"

"Well, I've aged a bit, so I'll only order four. My buddy here—Joe's his name—he'll start with two, but I bet he won't end there."

I caught myself before I could voice any objection. Bill was just having too much fun to interrupt. The yogurt and fruit could wait until tomorrow morning. She poured us both a cup of hot, steaming coffee. "This will keep you up from those long hours on the highway," she boasted. I guessed she was right; it was certainly high octane stuff.

In a few minutes, Myrtle brought out Bill's four burritos with lots of extra hot sauce and salsa on the side and then the two for me. "You boys want some eggs over easy to help wash down those burritos? They're on the house since you ordered so many."

Bill just looked up. His mouth was too occupied with chewing to allow him a response, so he just nodded. So did I. Then the serious eating began. In short time, Bill had wolfed down his four burritos drowning in hot sauce and salsa even before I had finished mine. "Say, Myrtle, could I order four more as take out, you know, for the road?"

"You can order as many as you want, Bill."

When we pulled our bellies from the counter, Bill whispered to me. "You know that's what I like about Myrtle's: the best combination of Tex/Mex food, German brats, American burgers and steaks, and all garnished with southern hospitality. It's my kind of place. And you know what?"

"What?"

"It'll give you ballast for what's comin'."

I didn't know what Bill meant. He took the keys and we were off to Amarillo. In half an hour, I knew exactly what Bill had been talking about. The north wind was so strong that I feared it would send the trailer off to the south side. Bill was white knuckling it as the wind just threatened to blow us off the road. "Is it always like this?" I asked Bill

"Generally, but sometimes it's worse in the winter, and winter's comin' in early and fast." On cue, snowdrops started pelting us, or maybe those hard balls combined sleet and snow. Neither one of us needed Myrtle's high octane coffee to stay awake. The wind and snow did their job. We made our way past Amarillo and headed towards the New Mexico border.

Here the landscape and the weather shifted to an almost eerie silence. The wind gradually eased and the landscape featured multicolored hills of stone, all in different hues of reds, browns, and even whites. Instead of flat straight lines, the roads ran snake-like, meandering through one fascinating rock formations after another. Bill kept his eyes riveted to the road.

When the roads straightened out, we passed gambling casino after gambling casino, but saw few cars. "I've never seen so many" I remarked.

"Yeah, out here, the casinos are just about the only way many of the Nations can make any money. Some do well and some don't. That's the way it is."

We stopped at a small gas station just off the road. "After all that wind and the winding road, I'm due for a break," Bill said. A tall man held the door for us. He must have been at least six feet six. He had swarthy complexion and wore a black wool coat over a red plaid shirt and denims. He wore spit-shined combat boots. "Welcome to my store. Look around. You don't look like tourists, and it's way past tourist season. Still, you might see something to take home. I picked up a few items and turned them over. "Made in China," the label read and I grinned.

The tall owner grinned back. "All of the authentic Native American works have been shipped off to Santa Fe and Albuquerque. We can hardly keep up with the demand for our work. And besides, people who stop here can't afford those prices they pay in Santa Fe. Have you two dropped something off or picking something up? I can see your trailer out there."

"We just might be pickin' up a '67 Mustang if the price is right," Bill replied.

"So, you're headed to Chimayo, I suppose."

"How do you know that?" an astounded Bill asked.

"Word travels like the wind," he replied.

We drove the rest of the way to the outskirts of Santa Fe. Joey V. had us staying in a nondescript, cheap motel, about twenty miles from Chimayo. I think we were both still puzzling over how the owner of the gas station / tourist shop knew where we were headed—probably there weren't all that many '67 Mustangs hanging around and he just happened to know where one was. Probably.

GAINING NEW INSIGHTS: CHIMAYO

When we pulled into the motel, Bill was exhausted. He had expertly backed up the truck and trailer so that they weren't blocking anybody and we could head out easily the next day. "I don't know about you, Joe. But I'm headed for a hot shower and a cold brew, maybe two."

"Go ahead. You drove the toughest part of the trip. I think I'll just read about Chimayo and the Sanctuary. We're meeting the owner at eight o'clock tomorrow morning, right?"

"Right!"

I took out my laptop and did some digging of my own. Chimayo lies on the high road to Taos. While I've never been to Taos, I've always envisioned it as a place for multi-millionaires to idle their time away skiing or otherwise engaging in adult playing. But, as usual, my assumptions contained only half or maybe just quarter truths. Taos also features one of the oldest adobe pueblos in the Southwest, has a thriving art community, and an often photographed church. People could spend the entire day just walking about and admiring the art, culture, and history of the place. Still, Bill had advised me to focus my attention on Chimayo partially because the area was located close to where we'd pick up the Mustang and partially because of other reasons, which I didn't fully understand. The native Tewa Indians regarded Chimayo as a sacred place. The term *Chimayo* traces its origin to the Tewa phrase, *Tsi Mayo* for the hill lying close by to the San Juan River. Long ago hot springs had provided them comfort. When the springs dried up, the earth of the springs was supposed to retain some healing powers. In the Christian era, this sacred dirt is still supposed to retain its healing powers.

When the Spanish came, they established the village of El Potrero. My Spanish isn't all that good, limited by only a few years of schooling and a lack of practice. So, I did a quick search only to learn that *El Potrero* is Spanish for *Paddock*. Then I humbly had to confess that my English might be only slightly better than my Spanish, so I had to look up that word. *Paddock* refers to an enclosed area, (probably fenced) where animals such as horses or cattle are handled. Apparently, the term is used somewhat commonly, or used to be, in racing circles. In any event. The small village might have remained obscure were it not for miracles associated with it. In 1810, on Good Friday night, Don Bernardo Abeyta saw a brightly beaming light. He dug with his hands at the source of the light and found a crucifix according to some legends. As usual, multiple legends abound. The crucifix itself became associated with Our Lord of Esquipulas. Don Bernardo gave the crucifix to the local parish priest, who carried it to his church, but that night the crucifix mysteriously returned to its original burial ground. This seemingly miraculous event occurred for three successive days. In 1813, Don Bernardo Abeyta petitioned to build a chapel at the miraculous site. Later, in 1856, Chimayo also became home to the Shrine of Santa Nino de Atocha. In the fusion of Native American and Spanish traditions, Chimayo had retained its historic value as a place of healing for body and soul.

After World War II, survivors of the Bataan Death March initiated a Holy Week pilgrimage to Chimayo and the tradition continued at least until Covid intervened. According to many reports and photographs, pilgrims have left their canes, their crutches, and wheelchairs there after they have experienced the healing powers of the sacred dirt.

"So, Joe, did you learn anything?"

"Yes, I guess I was so wrapped up in the legends of Chimayo that I didn't notice that you had finished your shower, and were sitting on your bed, beer in hand."

"Yeah, years ago, no, decades ago, some of my buddies told me about it. One of them had made the Holy Week long march to Chimayo. He didn't need any curin' at least not physically. Well, that was a long time ago. Anyway, I went there, too, and found a little peace."

"Well, I don't know about you, Bill, but I'm bushed. I'll join you in a beer, then head for the showers, and then plop down in bed. Do you know where we're headed?"

"Yeah, it's up an old dirt road. It's gonna be a tight fit to get the truck and trailer up that winding hill, but we'll make it. Just to be sure, we ought to leave about seven-fifteen tomorrow morning, you know, in case we've got any problems."

"Problems?" I asked quizzically. "What problems would there be?"

"Well, Joe, as I said, it's gonna be a tight fit if I recall those hills right. We might have to do all sorts of maneuvering this way and that, and there just ain't much room for error. The street—if you want to call it that—is just one lane and barely that wide. We'll be able to tell if we're trespassin' on someone's land when the dogs start barkin' and the chickens start squawkin.'"

The next morning confirmed Bill's worst fears. The first one hundred yards or so seemed easy enough, just enough to lull one into a sense of complacency. Then there was a sharp turn to the left and the trailer got stuck in a stick fence and the chickens started squawking. A tall, swarthy man emerged out of an adobe hut and just started laughing. He had the broadest grin I've ever seen. "This happens every time one of you guys come up here with too much horsepower and too little sense. Come on, I'll move the fence for you. He swung a twelve foot section of stick fence out of the way, shooed the chickens off and directed Bill. Soon we were back to climbing that hill. He called out, "You two will have two more sharp turns. Just honk three times and someone will come to move a section of fence away so you can get by." We did as directed.

About seven-fifty, we approached a large adobe structure at the top of the hill. Adjacent to it was a barn or at least some kind of large wooden structure that could have been a barn. "I'll bet this is it? I'll try that three honk routine again and see what happens."

A slender old man with a shock of white hair crowning a bronzed face that had withstood decades of sun and wind approached. He wore an old pair of flip-flops and jeans but no shirt. His chest was as bronzed as his face. "So, you guys here to look over the Mustang?"

"We are. I'm Joe and this is Bill."

"And I'm Henry Ford the Tenth," he grinned. "Naw, don't worry. I've got a title and all. It even has my real name on it, the one on my baptismal certificate but not the one I'm known by around here. I'm Miguel, the archangel of archangels. I got that name because I live so high up here some people claim I'm just an arm's length from heaven."

"Come on, let me show you the car." He headed over to his garage and pulled away several stacks of straw. There it sat in all its glory: a forest-green '67 Mustang. "I started it up last week when I heard you guys were coming. In the old days I loved that car and cruised all over Santa Fe in it, but now my cruisin' days are over. The guy you're takin' the car to, is he a good guy?"

"He's been more than fair with us," I replied.

"Well, if he's fair to me, I guess we'll be all right."

"Do you mind if I start her up?" Bill asked.

"You've got your job to do. Do it." Miguel shot back. "As for me, I've got some work to do in my garden."

When Miguel left, Bill motioned me over. "Say, Joe, I'm gonna start 'er up and listen to the engine for a while." A small puff of black smoke drew a scowl on Bill's face, but it eased its way into a smile when after that initial warning sign, the engine hummed along without a trace of that dark cloud. "All right, Joe, I'm not sayin' I don't trust ya or anything, but haulin' that trailer around on these steep, winding curves ain't no picnic. I'll unhook the trailer for ya. While I'm workin' on the car, you go right on ahead and go to Chimayo, to the sanctuary, that is. Come on back in about two hours. By then I ought to have some idea of what this ole Mustang can do. Your job will be to figure out what we ought to pay the guy. Joey V. will wire him the money and then he'll sign over the title to us and have the whole transaction notarized and all. When you reach the bottom of the hill, ya might recall that there's a fork in the road. We turned up the west fork to get here. All ya got to do is turn up the opposite fork and head east a little ways and that will get ya to the road to the Shrine. Just remember what I said. It ought to take you no more than fifteen minutes to get there. And with fifteen minutes for the return trip, that'll give you an hour and a half just to browse around me. When ya get back, we'll do the business end of the deal." Agreed?"

"Agreed."

"All right, I'll go and unhook the trailer."

Bill had advised me well. I pulled into the parking lot of El Santuario de Chimayo in fifteen minutes or so, parking not far from the Santa Cruz River. For someone accustomed to the mighty Mississippi and the muddy Missouri, the Santa Cruz didn't seem like much more than a creek. But the rounded stones and sparkling, dancing waters flowing by captured my eyes and held them hostage. Then gazing upwards, I took in the surrounding hills dotted by green bushes no bigger than the small backpacks that many of the pilgrims carried. Still, my eyes traced upward along the weather beaten small ravines in the hillside to the blue sky overhead. Only a few stray fluffy cumulus clouds floated by. All seemed so serene.

Still, the stark simplicity of the place stuck deep into my inner being. I wandered over to the chapel, a brown adobe like building with twin towers and a small courtyard. In front of the heavy wooden doors to the chapel, a wooden cross projected from a rectangular base, no elaboration, no adornment other than a string of red flowers, so simple yet so moving. Even a gaggle of middle school children who passed me by remained reverently silent. Maybe they intuited the soul of the place far better than I. It occurred to me that all four elements converged in this place: the fire of the New Mexico sun, the water of the Santa Cruz, the earth of the sparse, arid landscape, and the clear air. The night before I had learned that the Tewa Indians regarded the place as sacred ground even before the arrival of the Spaniards.

Just then a blond woman probably in her mid-thirties approached us. She was about Amanda's height and sported leather sandals, jean shorts cut low, and a red tank top. Then it struck me that the two of us were the only Anglos around. All the others—including the middle schoolers I had seen but not heard—were Mestizos or Native Americans. Then she boomed out a little too loudly as she was apparently addressing only me. "I'm an atheist, of course, but the place does exude a certain quaint charm. It's on the National Register and makes all of the lists for attractions in New Mexico."

I guess she was checking off another to-do item on her tourist list. I had no idea how to respond. So, awkwardly, I stood mute. After a few seconds, she broke the silence with a polite but unenthusiastic, "Yes, Chimayo intrigues all types of people."

Still waiting for some response—but not getting one-- the blond woman said, "Well, I'm off to buy some holy dirt. It's a must have if you come here."

According to some, the holy dirt from Chimayo has healing powers and row upon row of crutches line one wall as testaments to miracles claimed. The Catholic Church has never endorsed the veracity of these claims, but many pilgrims have attested to the healing powers of the Lourdes of America. I took notice of one man who was pushing a wheelchair bound woman—probably his mother—into the left side of the chapel, where the holy dirt is found. She emerged, still wheelchair bound, but the two seemed at peace. Not all cures are physical. Even physical cures can stem from psychological dispositions. The rational side of me argued that the cures reflected a matter of will, a kind of self-fulfilling prophecy. Perhaps so, I wasn't so sure any more. From the vast numbers of crutches and canes left along the fence and from many of the pilgrims present and fervent, an impartial onlooker might acknowledge that, Indeed, this was a holy place. When the chapel bell struck nine times, to signal the hour, I found myself praying. And at nine o'clock every morning I still repeat that prayer.

I strolled over to the outdoor chapel. No mass would be said there this morning, but still it felt comforting just to sit and reflect in the peaceful atmosphere. Then I strolled over to a side building where I gazed upon a mural of the Last Supper. All of the personages there depicted Native Americans. Many of these Tewas had made the religion sometimes forced upon them their own. Sometimes, religion and culture become inextricably interwoven, and it's hard to detect the eternally sacred from the most transitory profane. In the case of that mural, though, the religion and culture interacted to make a powerful statement. The visual image spoke out that here, at least, religion and culture had found common ground.

With a little time remaining, I could still visit the chapel. So, off I went past large wooden doors and a small drop that I almost stumbled over. As is usual in many Hispanic churches, it was cool and dark, but the crucifix in the center of the altar riveted my attention. It was done in the Spanish colonial style, elegant in its simplicity with a trace of red blood streaming down from Jesus's side. I knelt and prayed a decade of the rosary, something I hadn't done in a decade or more. Then I reluctantly stood, genuflected and took my leave.

When the chapel bell struck ten times, I knew it was time for me to head back from my short pilgrimage and enter once again into the world of commerce.

In a short ten minutes, it was back to the world of dollars and cents. "So, Bill, what do you think?"

"Well, I'm glad we brought the trailer. I don't think we couldda made it back to St. Louis driving that ole Mustang. But you know what, it's still got some life left in it. The body's in great shape, as you can see. It's a little sluggish in the equivalent of fifth gear, so goin' seventy for long questions might do her in. But, if all Joey V.is gonna do is drive around town and just a little ways on the highway, it'll do fine. The ole Cruise-O-Matic transmission runs smooth even now. With regular maintenance and a little tender, lovin'care, that Mustang will last a while. I can do a complete overhaul when we get her back to my shop, but I don't look for any major problems."

"So sixty-nine thousand dollars wouldn't be out of line?"

"Well, if I were you, but I'm not, but I'll tell you anyways, I wouldn't start there. Why don't you ask Miguel what he wants for the car?"

"Just what I was thinking." I wandered over to the small garden that Miguel was hoeing. Even in December, he still had a few peppers and some green tomatoes growing. "Miguel, Bill looked over the Mustang, and we're interested in making an offer. How much do you want for it?"

"Well, it's been with me for so many years that it feels like family. My father drove it and even now I still take it to church and to the market. But times are hard and now we need the money. I understand that such vintage cars are worth a lot of money."

"Yes, some are; others are just old."

"Like me, huh!"

"Like both of us, Miguel."

"Would you pay fifty-five thousand dollars?"

"No, Miguel, it's worth more than that. I'll pay you sixty-five thousand dollars and have my employer wire you the money this afternoon."

"Your boss, he won't be mad at you for overpaying?"

"No, he'll just be glad we got the car." Joey V. would be glad he got the car, and he probably expected to pay a little over seventy thousand for it. I did have an obligation to Joey V to get him a good price, but I also had an obligation to set a fair price for Miguel, a man I had just met. But, then again, what did I know about Joey V. and how he got his money?"

"So, it's a deal, Miguel?" I asked as I extended my hand. We shook hands and I texted Joey V. to wire the money to Miguel's bank, where we would sign the papers.

"You didn't cheat Miguel, did you?" Bill asked. I shook my head. "Well, I'm glad for that. He's a guy who looks as if he's worked hard all his life. How much did you get it for?"

"Sixty-five thousand."

"Fair enough, all things considered. Let's go get the ole Mustang on the trailer."

FACING NEW PROBLEMS

The drive home was tiring, that's all. Bill and I both wanted to get home in one day, so we just drive straight from Miguel's bank, which was about fifteen miles from Chimayo, and decided to drive as far as we could get. Joey V. had allotted for another motel stay, but he hadn't booked one yet. "You guys just stay in a cheap place, all right, cheap but safe. If you think you could drive straight back, I'd appreciate it. Who knows what could happen on the parking lot of some seedy motel."

We did encounter a little snow, but it wasn't accumulating, just blowing in serpentine patterns across the turnpike in Oklahoma. When we stopped to get gas, someone always came up to admire the '67 Mustang on our trailer. "Where did you get that classic?" They'd always ask. We'd reply something to the effect that we just ran across it in New Mexico or our boss researched it and we just picked her up. "Can you still drive it?" Someone would ask, and Bill just nodded and gave a thumbs up. We pulled into Joey V' place about four am the next morning. He was outside waiting for us. "You saved me a motel bill and some possible damage to my new treasure, so I brought you guys some breakfast. You've got a choice: sausage biscuits or pancakes. We'll have a 'Mission Accomplished' toast with orange juice and then you two ought to head home and get some sleep."

I was feeling on top of the world, especially when Joey V. handed over the cash. The money troubles had vanished like the morning dew. "What could go wrong?" I congratulated myself. Bill and I shook hands and told each other we'd make one more trip and hoped it would be as good as this one.

But pride and false optimism go before the fall. When I got home, Amanda was still up. She was hunched over a cup of coffee and looked exhausted, eyes sunken and somber and red with loss of sleep. "I'm glad you're home, Joe. I've had a rough couple of days."

I sat down after pouring myself a cup of coffee, figuring that I had to brace myself for a long listening session.

"Joe, I think I told you that we just had a slew of new hires, right?" I nodded. "Well, they're new graduates with six months or less of experience. Anyway, I was assigned to mentor one of these novices. Anyway this Amber girl or woman graduated at the top of her class and thinks she knows everything. She's partially right. She's smart enough all right, and does her job—at least the way she sees her job—well. But, when I was sitting with an elderly woman who was nearing death---she died the next morning—my pupil rushed in, almost glared at the dying woman and rushed out even faster than she had rushed in. On break, my nurse-in-training, Amber scolded me. 'You shouldn't waste your time the way you did with that old woman.'

"Her name is Ruth, Amber. And why do you accuse me of wasting time?"

"Well, that woman was dying. We did what we could, but we couldn't save her. Our job is to help heal people. If we can't heal them, we're not doing our job. You need to spend time with the ones we can save, not with those we can't. Let her family come in and hold her hand. We have work to do."

"Amber, the poor woman doesn't have any family. Her children died years ago and so did her husband. She was an only child. As a mother she mourned her son killed by an IED in Afghanistan, her daughter lost the battle with breast cancer, and her husband passed away from prostate cancer. I don't think listening to her for five minutes and giving her a comforting hand is a waste of time."

"She died, didn't she? So, holding her hand was of no therapeutic value."

"And, in that case, Amber, neither did pumping her full of morphine."

"Her screaming was bothering other patients and the staff."

"Amber, you're in the wrong profession if you don't have any empathy with the pain and loss people are feeling. Sometimes, as health care providers the best we can do is to extend a sympathetic hand and some emotional support. It's not all science; nursing also has an emotional side. Sometimes the emotional support results in more healing than does the so-called 'best practices.'"

"Now you sound like my mother, not my teacher. I'm going to apply for a new mentor. After this incident, I don't think I need you looking over my supposedly cold shoulder."

"That's your prerogative, Amber. Just remember that you are allowed only one switch. Perhaps you're better suited for a different specialty in medicine instead of bedside nursing."

"I'm going to Human Resources during my lunch break. As I said earlier, I need to have a mentor more compatible with my philosophy of nursing care."

"Well, Amber left in a huff. Before I finished my shift, I got called in to HR. The director asked me what I had done to alienate my mentee. I should have kept my mouth shut, but I didn't. I asked the HR director if he had asked Amber the same question—what had she done to alienate me. He said that with the critical shortage of nurses, we had to nurse them along. 'Amber graduated at the top of her class, Amanda. We don't want to lose her.' Well, I almost bit my tongue off just to avoid saying anything too damning. I reminded him that I had worked for over twenty years at this hospital and had a whole string of excellent reviews. I admitted that Amber was, as he had said, brilliant, but some skills are better learned from experience far more so than from classroom instruction. He concluded by saying simply, 'Just make sure you don't do this again.' I felt belittled and worried my job was on the line. Doesn't experience matter any more?"

"It's the same in my line of work. When our small firm was taken over, our experience with our clients didn't seem to matter. It didn't fit with the new corporate model, we were told. So, we were all out on our collective asses with only a few days' warning. I sometimes wonder if people are afraid of experience and aging and all. It reminds them that we're all mortal and will face the same fate. For all of our differences, in the end we all face the same outcome whether we're rich or poor or middle class, smart, average, below average, had Ph.D.'s or only a few years of grade school. It's all the same. As we age, some of us at least come to recognize our shared fate and gain some empathy along the way. Maybe Amber will come around."

" Maybe, but I'm not sure it'll be in my lifetime. Didn't you tell me you had time to stop at the shrine in Chimayo?"

"Yeah, I did. When things settle down here and we can have a little time off, we ought to take a drive out there. It would be good for Amy and Tom and the two of us. We can stop there and maybe spend some time in Santa Fe and even Taos."

"I'd like that; but, since we're dealing with two adolescents finding common time off is nearly impossible."

"We can make some time."

"Good luck with that, Joe. Amy is so strung out about the ACT test she'll take on Saturday that she asked me to ask you to drive her there. She's hell bent on improving her score by two points so that she'll qualify for the dean's scholarship. The way she's so worried she'll probably score worse. She's got to come down a bit from this stress-high or she'll blow it. And then there's Tom. He keeps bugging me about those soccer cleats. He thinks he'll be the new Ronaldo and win a soccer scholarship. His nagging is driving me nuts. You need to deal with him. I've had it."

"I guess I had a bit of vacation. Chimayo really made an impact, and the drive there and back with Bill came off without any problems. The man who sold us the Mustang lived in a simple adobe hut with just stick fences. He looked as if he had worked hard all his life, his face wrinkled and wizened by the sun. He kept that old Mustang in pristine condition. It was a legacy from his father, maybe his only material legacy. Still, he seemed happy enough."

"He probably didn't graduate at the top of his class."

"I don't know. He may have. In any event, he seemed to be living the good life, even if times were hard. I guessed he'd figured it was just time to let go of his prized Mustang. I don't think he had any children to pass it down to or maybe he just thought it was time to let it go. I guess sooner or later we all have to come to that conclusion."

"I've never heard you wax so philosophical. What did you offer him?"

"$64,000. We probably could have given him less, but it didn't seem right. Bill had some doubts about how long the old engine could last on a long highway drive."

"Anyway, we both look exhausted. Let's go to bed. Promise me you'll talk with Amy tonight about the ACT."

"Will do, Amanda."

"You won't have to worry about making time to talk with your son. As soon as he sees you, he'll start nagging you about those shoes."

It didn't take long for each of us to go to sleep. I got up after four hours to go to the bathroom—the wages of some heavy coffee drinking. Amanda, who frequently worked the night shift, slept all the way through. Still unaccustomed to working nights, I figured I'd be better off getting some work done around the house and going to bed at my usual time. If I slept another four hours, I wouldn't be able to go to sleep at night. I tinkered around doing all those small jobs I had missed while gone to Chimayo. I didn't have to wait long for the inundation of my son's nagging to disrupt what had been a relatively comfortable routine.

Tom burst through the door, "Dad, you're home. Guess what, my coach told me if I keep on improving, I'll be a cinch to win one of those soccer scholarships in my senior year of high school."

"How many other players did he tell that to?"

"Dad, how should I know? But, I am getting better."

"Tom, do you know how many high school soccer players get scholarships?"

"Dad, what is this, some kind of quiz show? All I know is that a good player needs good cleats."

"Tom, do you want to play soccer because you like playing or because you're banking on it for a scholarship and then later for a job? There just aren't many openings in professional soccer, and only a small percentage of high school players ever play in college, and only a few of them are on full scholarships."

"Dad, come on, with you everything is dollars and cents."

"Tom, it seems to me that you're seeing dollar signs. You should be just playing for fun."

"Dad, I do play for fun, but you can have fun and make money at the same time. Mom said you were having a vacation when you went to New Mexico to get that Mustang."

"True, but it's not always that way. I lucked out this time. Most of the time a job is just that –a job. You do it to make some money and keep from being bored. When you don't have a soccer game to look forward to, all you do is complain about being bored."

"Dad, you're right for once. That's why I need those new shoes."

"Mom says that you were on her constantly while I was gone to get that high-priced footwear."

"Yeah, well, I did bring it up a few times, but I wasn't nagging, just calmly making my point."

"Last summer you made over four hundred dollars cutting lawns, right?"

"Four hundred and eighty dollars to be precise."

"And this winter you'll probably make another hundred dollars or so shoveling off driveways, right."

"Well, I don't know about that, Dad. A lot of the kids think I was a dork for shoveling snow. It takes away from my image."

"But it adds to your bank account. You have to save half of what you earn for college or tech school after high school. The rest you can spend freely."

"Well, sort of."

"And by *sort of* you mean when you can't convince Mom and me to spend our money on what you want."

"Well, yeah, but what does that have to do with anything?"

"Here's the deal, Tom. You're right about needing new cleats. The old ones are worn down to little nubs and your ever-growing feet are cramped up in them. You've gotten your fair use out of them and you do need new ones." At this, Tom's lips swung wide in delight and anticipation. "But here's what we'll do. We will supply the money for the base pair, about sixty dollars. Everything after that will be on you. If those cleats mean so much to you, then you'll be willing to dip into your own funds."

Tom's lips soured into a pursed, whiney expression. "Dad, you really need to rethink this whole matter through. Think of those cleats as an investment in my future, my soccer future. You come to my games. Don't you want to be proud of me?"

"Tom, you're right. I want to be proud of you, not of your shoes. You'll outlast those shoes. No matter what you see on-line or in ads, the player makes the shoes; the shoes don't make the player."

"So that's it, huh."

"That's our final offer. Mom and I will give you until Saturday morning to make up your mind. We can pay for all of your shoe or you can pay whatever you think you can afford. I'll take you to Soccer House after I take Amy to the ACT. I should be home by eight-thirty, and the Soccer House opens at nine, right."

"So, that's it, huh."

"That's it."

"Sometimes you and Mom just can't think big."

I didn't respond—no need to prolong the inevitable. Tom's right. It shouldn't be all about money and it isn't. I don't think Miguel's children—if he has any—ever wore the most expensive shoes or sported the latest faddish outfits.

Amy came home around five-thirty. After her classes, she had gone to an ACT prep class.

"So, what did you learn at the ACT class?"

"Dad, I learned that I'm stupid."

"What do you mean by that?"

"I got exactly the same score that I got the last time I took the practice test I mean, the questions were different, but my score was the same. I'll never get that scholarship."

"So, what if you don't get the scholarship, what happens?"

"I guess, I'll just have to figure out something. I don't know, maybe loans or work / study or something. I don't know."

"So, you do your best and not worry. Worrying won't improve your scores any."

"Yeah, but—"

"And I'm the same way. We stumble along, try our best, and every once in a while our best doesn't seem to cut it. It's so easy to get down on yourself. When I lost my job, I didn't know what I had done was wrong. Eventually, things worked out."

"Now, Dad, you sound like our instructor at the ACT Prep class. She said that if you don't know the right answer you can improve your chances by crossing out the alternatives that are clearly wrong."

"There's four options to pick from, right?"

Amy shrugged her shoulders. I took that as "yes."

"So, if you eliminate one choice, you have only three options?"

Another shrug.

"If you can rule out two options, then you've got a fifty-fifty chance at getting the right answer."

You've also got a fifty-fifty chance of getting the wrong answer."

"Amy, come on, you've got to think positive. These college tests are like intellectual games. You've got to play them or they'll play you. You go ahead and answer the questions you know right away. Then you key on the ones you don't know. Take your time and rule out what's wrong. None of us are right all of the time. But, we can figure out what's clearly wrong most of the time. So, just relax and try to solve the puzzle. If you're really stuck, skip one particular question and move on. If time is about to end, then just give it your best guess."

"Yeah, Dad, but some people just breeze through the test and put their pencils down with ten minutes left."

"Is there any reward for finishing early?"

"No."

"So, just take all of the time you get. That's all any of us can do. I know that it's easy for me to say this. I'm not the one taking the test. But just remember that it's all a game. Play the game but don't hyperventilate over it because, after all, it's only a game. It measures certain skills and abilities, that's all. No matter what anyone may tell you, six or even fewer years than that and nobody will care what your ACT score was. Here's what we'll do Saturday morning. I'll drive you to the test so you won't have to worry about that. We can even stop and get breakfast if you like."

"No way, Dad, I'll be far too nervous for that. Anyway, I feel sharper when I'm a little hungry."

"Well, I can't offer you much, but I can offer you lunch afterwards. You name the place."

"Deal, at least I can look forward to some soup and salad at BreadCo."

I dropped Amy off and wished her well—a paternal kiss on the cheek had to be avoided, I knew, as one of her friends might catch a glimpse of it. Still my eyes followed her as entered the school to take her test. She had wanted to arrive ten minutes early. We got there fifteen minutes ahead of testing time. She seemed relaxed and ready to face her fate, and all of that sounds a bit melodramatic. But, in her mind, she was, indeed, facing her destiny. So much happens between seventeen and twenty-five. Young adults make decisions that don't determine absolutely what the rest of life has in store, decisions about schooling, about careers, about spouses, and about drinking. But there's no doubt that these decisions have an impact—sometimes a big one. I had to admit that Amy would soon be—if she hadn't already been—exposed to the drinking and recreational drug scene. Some of my best friends, both men and women, had almost ruined their lives in the drinking and partying scene. At least, Amanda had consoled me when I told her my fears. "Amy, will be going to nursing school and in all likelihood have early morning rounds to make. There's nothing like a five-thirty wake-up time to temper the partying." I hoped Amanda was right. She probably was.

So, I headed home to pick up Tom for our nine am journey to Soccer House. I got home earlier than expected. Tom was waiting at the front door. "Let's go, Dad. I can't wait to get those shoes." I asked him if he had brought some money, and he flashed a wad of dollar bills as if he were making the deal of a lifetime. Maybe he was. When we strolled into the store, he rushed over to the display of" elite" shoes. Of course, in this case, *elite* and *expensive* were synonymous, simply interchangeable terms, the only difference being that *elite* evoked more snob appeal. As good as Tom thought he was, he had a few more years to prove that he merited elite status. When he saw the shoes, his eyes lit up. They froze in awe when he looked at the price tag, two hundred dollars. "Dad, you said you would give me the money for the base model, right?"

"You're right," I replied as I wandered over to the bargain table.

"So, how much does the base model cost?"

"Fifty-nine dollars, plus tax."

"And the elite model costs almost four times as much, so there's also four times as much tax, right?"

"Right again."

Tom picked up the bargain shoe, walked over to the elite counter and picked up a sample in his other hand. He was weighing them, the lighter the better. "Well, the elite version is lighter, but not four times lighter. It also comes in a larger number of colors. Other than that, there's really not much difference." He replaced the elite model back on its counter and strolled back to the bargain counter. He paused, deep in thought, and then noticed a slight upgrade in the bargain version. "For ten dollars more, I can get the color I want—orange—in the bargain model. OK, Dad, is it OK if I get this model on the bargain model and add ten dollars of my own to cover the difference?"

"Fine with me. I'll even cover the additional tax."

"Ha, ha, really funny, Dad."

A bemused clerk, perhaps in his late teens or early twenties, grinned widely as he took in a scene that he had probably witnessed a dozen or more times. He walked over to us and asked, "So, you've decided on a model and a color?"

"Yes," Tom belted out.

"Let me make sure you get the right size. Also, I'd wear these to a practice first before you wear them in a game. They're a good, solid shoe and you'll like them but you need to get the feel of the shoe."

"Oh, I will."

We made our purchase and headed home. Tom opened the box and admired his new purchase (which, of course, was more his parents' purchase). "Dad, I think I made the right choice."

"So do I," suppressing my urge to ask, "Why in the world did you have to have bright orange?" I dropped Tom off to break in his new shoes and drove over to pick up Amy.

In fifteen minutes, a mass of students rushed out of the exit doors. Amy wasn't one of them. Five minutes after the initial stampede, she emerged, walking with her friend Bridget. In contrast to the subdued tone of the morning, both were laughing. When Amy spotted my old rust-bucket of a car, she broke from her friend, who also headed over to her ride home.

"How was it?" I asked, probably a little nervously.

"Not as bad as I thought, but I still don't know if I did any better. I probably did a little better, especially on the Science Reasoning section, but I don't know how much better. But it's done, and I've got a plan, don't I?"

"You do."

I didn't know if my conversations with son and daughter had much of an effect. I did know, though, that there would be tougher problems for them to face in the future—ones like Amanda had faced as she held the hand of a dying patient. For now, I faced only little problems that loomed large for the moment, but these moments pass.

HEADING SOUTH

By seven o'clock Sunday evening, I still hadn't heard from Joey V about a third trip. I hated to admit it, but I had come to rely on his more-than-generous stipend. "Amanda, do you think he'll call?"

"You're worried about not having another road trip with your buddy Bill?"

"Well, yes."

"Just looking for an excuse to have some high times on the road?"

Once again, I hated to own up to the fact that I did, indeed, enjoy the freedom of the road—at least for two or three days.

"Well, I think you said old Joey V. still had one stall to fill. I wouldn't worry about it. He'll call."

He did, thirty minutes later. "Joe, come over to my place tomorrow morning by four am. I already talked to Bill. He'll be taking the trailer. Be ready to leave immediately shortly after four."

"Where are we headed?"

"Sulphur, Louisiana, the pride of Southwest Louisiana, in fact."

I told Amanda when I'd be leaving. "When will you get back?" she asked.

"Wednesday or Thursday."

"Try to make it Wednesday. You're having way too much fun."

On Monday morning, when I woke up at 3:15, I didn't feel that I was having all that much fun. Somehow or other, I managed to get dressed and out the door although I have no idea how. I arrived at Joey V.'s at 3:50. As I expected, he was out there to greet me, dressed in a heavy white winter coat, a red stocking cap, gloves, and boots. "I just came in from a little morning drive with my latest toy, the one you brought in from Chimayo. On the deserted streets, it was just me and my Mustang. That's the way I like it."

Five minutes later, Bill pulled in with his trailer all hitched. "Good," Joey V. almost shouted. "Here's the information." He handed me a manila envelope stuffed with all of the particulars. "You should be able to get there in a little less than twelve hours. Spend the night in Sulphur, Louisiana, and then show up at Virgil and Beatrice's place a little south of Sulphur. You should be able to get there in fifteen minutes, maybe less. It's a lot more humid down there than it was in New Mexico, so scrutinize the body of the car carefully for rust or for painted over places. I don't expect the Mustang to be in as good a condition as the last one you brought in. I also don't expect to pay as much. And again, if Bill thinks I'd have to sink more than twenty grand into restoring it, just turn around and drive back."

I hopped into Bill's truck on the driver's side and we were off.

"Glad you decided to drive first, Joe. As for me, I'm bushed. That 'Early to bed and early to rise makin' ya healthy, wealthy, and wise' stuff' is maybe a little true. I guess it'll keep you out of trouble. Ole Joey V. gets up long before the roosters start crowin' and he's wealthy. I guess we're getting' a little dose of wealth when he pays us. As for me, I don't feel any wiser at all. And for sure I don't feel all that healthy, just tired. It's just all a big mystery to me. Nothin' ever works out perfect. For folks like you and me, it's just all a little unclear, not heaven or hell, but that purgatory place some folks believe in. Well, I don't know about you, Joe, but I wouldn't place any bets in getting' down there in less than twelve hours. I'll bet ole Joey got that twelve hour business the same place I did—off some internet search. The estimated time is always a little low, in my opinion. It don't take into account stuff like bad weather, road construction, heavy traffic, or the human necessity to pee as well as the fact that your vehicle's necessity to gas up. Those estimates are based upon everythin' goin' smooth and nothin' ever goes smooth. And it sure don't take into account an ole man's need to pee a lot. I drank just half a cup, just enough to keep me awake and to stop me from stoppin' to pee just an hour down the road. Anyways, it's about time for me to doze off."

We headed down south along I-55 smoothly at first. Only the headlights and taillights of tractor-trailer rigs and every once in a while a pickup or two pierced the early morning darkness. It wouldn't be daybreak for close to three hours. But two hours into our drive, sleet started pelting our windshield, a half-frozen spitball from the heavens. Visibility was close to zero. For a while, I glued my eyes to the red taillights of the truck in front of us. But after ten minutes even that approach failed.

I had to pull over. At least bright overhead lights illuminated the exit ramp leading to a truck stop. Off I went and decided that I might as well pump some gas. Daybreak wouldn't come for another half hour or more, but no hint of the new day peeked its way through the dense cloud cover. Even if the sleet didn't make the highway impassable, it might make it too slick to continue until the MODOT rucks started out and coated the roads with some kind of saline concoction that would keep the sleet from making an ice rink of the road.

"What ya stoppin' for? Gotta pee? And I thought only an old guy like me needed to make pit stops so soon into the trip." As Bill hurried to get out of the truck, he slipped on an icy patch and managed to stay erect only by clutching to the door. "Damn, so that's why ya stopped. I don't blame ya." We hung around the restaurant along with a dozen or more truckers who decided to wait out the storm. That's all any of us could do. In forty-five minutes, the sleet stopped and the sun even broke through the clouds. We pushed ourselves off our chairs and away from the warm coffee and headed out into the cold air. Bill said he figured it was his turn to drive, so he took over the wheel while I calculated how long it would be until we reached Sulphur. "Well, we're not going to make it in twelve hours. If we're lucky, we might arrive around five-thirty. By then I'll be dark again. Out of darkness and back into it."

But Bill had his mojo working. The sun didn't shine brightly, but it did manage to break through the thick cloud cover every now and then. More importantly the sleet ended, but only after transitioning to periodic rain. But the roads weren't slick, so Bill could drive the speed limit—and sometimes over it—for long spells. We reached I-10 in Louisiana only half an hour behind that ideal schedule. We'd make it before dark and, at this time of year, the twilight lingered. Even after the official sunset, there was still a slight reddish glow, like that of a glimmering charcoal in the skies.

We had reached Sulphur.

We were both bushed, so we headed to bed and slept until five the next morning. Eager to beat a predicted ice storm expected to hit southern Missouri in thirty-six hours, we wolfed down some apples and oranges we had brought and two cups of very black and very strong and very bitter coffee. At six o'clock, I checked my phone for any messages. "Bill, I just got a text from Joey V. He said we should go to the Johnson place to look over the Mustang at seven-thirty"

"Well, it's supposed to take only fifteen minutes to get there, but I bet we get lost on some of these back country roads. A lot of 'em ain't even got marked road signs. I say we leave at seven."

"Agreed. I want to go out and stretch my legs a little."

"You go right ahead and do just that. As for me, I'm sittin' pretty right where I am. Just make sure to come back before seven."

"Oh, I will," I replied as I headed out the door. The temperature outside hovered around fifty, so that would have been pleasant enough if it weren't for the humidity, that just kept pressing in on me and the few people out in the street. I walked down a block under a thick layer of low-lying grey clouds. At this time of year, all seem to be enshrouded in greys and browns and blacks. At the end of the block, an old, battered sign pointed the way to the Brimstone railroad, a throwback to the days when the city mined sulfur. Now, petro-chemicals supported the town's economy as new signs advertised the names of three or more oil and chemical companies. Some residents could walk to work, but the majority sped along the main roads to reach work. At least, I guessed that's where they were headed. I didn't know if nightshifts were running, but all scurried about headed in the same general direction. "The town would be pretty in the spring," I noted as large stone or clay or wooden planter boxes abounded. But, now in early December the bright colors of the spring, summer, and early fall had all faded. With little else left to do, I headed back to our motel room.

"It's early, Joe, but I'm itching to go." So off we drove.

Bill's qualms about back country roads soon found justification. We ended up in one dead-end and had to maneuver the truck and trailer through a tight U-turn. "Well, hell, I shoudda known we should have taken the left fork in the road, and you said to. But, bullheaded as I am, I chose the right. There's nothin' lef to do but head back and take that other fork." And that we did after six dozen turns of the steering wheel, about a dozen backups, and probably ten dozen *hell*'s and *damn*'s and other assorted curses. We drove up the left fork to road sign that said "Johnson Road." Bill hesitated a moment then shouted out, "I don't give a rat's ass what the GPS says, we're goin' up this Johnson Road. It's gotta lead us to the Johnson place." It did.

But Bill stopped again. Ahead of us lay a concrete slab and beyond that a one-lane gravel road that seemed to go uphill at about a twenty percent incline. Before we crossed the dry creek bed, we paused to contemplate the sign that cautioned all comers, "Creek Subject to Flash Floods."

"Well, Bill, it's dry now," I remarked.

"Yeah, let's just hope it'll be dry on the way back."

Bill's gut instinct proved correct as we approached a rusty mailbox sitting atop an even rustier tractor. A hand-painted sign proclaimed to all who came there, "The Johnson Place." We would arrive with ten minutes to spare.

The road lay straight for about one hundred yards. Three tall and broad bald cypress trees, spaced about thirty yards apart lined each side of the gravel road. The trees must have been ancient as they rose almost one hundred feet high and ever-spreading branches almost touched each other. Spanish moss lay thickly on each tree burdening the branches and hanging low. In early December, the grey, bleak sky lent an almost funereal mood as if the moss were lamenting the loss of spring and summer. Just past the line of six bald cypress trees stood one lone cypress. It rose majestically and, for some reason or other, lacked the burden of the Spanish moss. The road took two turns just past this lone tree. The left turn led to the house; the right to an old barn that at one time may have served to store and dry tobacco. Now the wooden planks just looked weathered and broken and slowly easing their way to decay and ruin.

A lanky balding man in a heavy brown leather coat, a bit tattered in the sleeves came out to greet us. "You boys must be the ones ole Joey V. sent." We nodded our heads in acknowledgement. "Well, I'm Virgil Johnson and that's my wife Beatrice comin' out of the house. Most people don't call her Beatrice 'cause that sounds just way too fancy for us. We call her 'Bee' cause it's shorter and she keeps bees and sells honey in town. Of course, in December the bee keepin' don't keep her too busy. Let's head over to the barn out back."

The barn lay at the top of seven terraced plots. "Each one of my kids had a plot to tend, seven terraces, seven kids. Of course, now they're all grown up and on their own. I couldn't give the Mustang to just one of my children without upsettin' the other six. So, I decided to sell it instead. Our oldest daughter Amy tended that first terrace. If you want to call what she did tendin'. She more or less just let the collards grow wild, never takin' to a hoe. She always felt she was just too good for farm work."

"Now, Virgil, you're just getting' grumpy," Bee interjected as she bustled her way up to the three of us. "Amy always had her nose in a book and studied law. Now She's a state representative although she can get a little uppity from time to time. Farmin' just wasn't in her blood."

Virgil ignored his wife's remarks and headed us past the second terrace. "This one belonged to Buzz. He's our first-born son if you want to call him that. I never could figure out what the hell he was raisin', but he spent his whole youth raisin' hell. Now he works in New Orleans. I'll bet he's some kind of cross-dresser."

Bee hastened to add a postscript. "Buzz is savin' money to buy the restaurant where he works at night. He just always had a hard time keeepin' up with his older sister, that's all."

"Yeah, he got sandwiched between two girls. His younger sister Melanie was somthin' else. She could start a fight at the drop of a hat. But she was a good fighter and could keep her ground with anyone, boy or girl. She was one hell of a worker, though. She raised hell and tomatoes on her little plot, enough tomatoes once we canned 'em for the whole year."

"Yes, Virgil, you didn't add that she's got her own spread now, raisin' cotton mainly. She still grows tomatoes and sells them, fresh or canned, every Saturday mornin' at the Farmers' Market."

"Yeah, she was just the opposite of her younger brother Jed. He moves slower than a 'possum. He raised all kinds of hot peppers, maybe so he could eat 'em and stay awake."

"Jed's got got himself a fancy state government job in Baton Rouge," Bee added quickly.

"Yeah, them government jobs just suited him fine."

"Now his younger sister Stephanie. She's a real go-getter, makin' a bundle in hedge funds or somethin' else her ma and pa don't understand. She moved away from here to New York and swore she'd never lift a hoe handle again. She liked cash crops and grew a little cotton, not much 'cause there was never enough room for much. Still, she made a little spendin' money as a kid. She's back East now makin' money off other people's money hand over fist."

"She comes back to see us every Christmas and brings everyone expensive gifts. She bought me a brand new I-Mac, but I haven't figured out how to use it much other than to send e-mails to her. She says she likes e-mails more than letters. 'Just stick to the facts, Mom,' she always says, 'and keep it short.' I do. I swear I can type two hundred mistakes a minute."

"Now, that's not true, Bee. You keep a spreadsheet on all your bee business." Virgil added.

She blushed in pride. "Well, that is true."

Coming to the next terrace, Virgil hesitated. "Whew, it's getting' tougher and tougher every year to reach that ole barn. Here's where Beauregard, we call him just Beau, as it grew tiresome pronouncin' his full name. Anyways, he's 'somethin' of a gourmand I think they call it. He spent three years in Cajun country learning' how to cook Cajun, and he's' good at it. He likes his own food so much, he eats it all the time, mornin', noon, and night. Right now I'll bet he weighs over three hundred pounds."

Bee provided more details "He's got his own restaurant in Baton Rouge. All the bigwig politicians go there. Amy sees to that."

"Well, we reached the last one. Joey just raised corn. He works hard at the local chemical plant but just can't seem to get ahead. He spends most of his time wishin' he were just like one or other of his older brothers and sisters. He kinda resents their success."

"Yes, but he just got a promotion to foreman. I'll wager he's on his way to the top." Bee corrected.

"Yeah, well, we'll see about that. He does come over and tend his corn crop. He says it's better than inhalin' all them chemical fumes. I suspect he's right about that."

"Well, gentlemen, this is it. We've reached the top. The Mustang sits there in the barn. Right now it's not doin' more than rustin' away. Time to get rid of it finally, but Bee and I had some grand times in that ole car. Go ahead. Look her over. As for me, I've got some work to do. Here are the keys."

Bill muttered something about being tired with the Johnson family history. He was ready to get to work. He handed me a three- page diagram of the car. I was to note down any rust spots, one drawing displayed the left side, another the right and a third one the rear. "As for me, I'll get to work under the hood. My best guess is that it hasn't been driven too much lately. We'll fire her up and see."

Most of the rust was under the driver's side rear fender. Here the rust had eaten away about an inch of the body with lesser amounts above that—ones that could be buffed out. I'm no expert in bodywork, but it might be necessary to replace that whole section with one free of rust. I put down that observation in the report. The passenger side had rust, too, but relatively minor damage that wouldn't require total replacement. The rear part had major damage just above the bumper. The front looked good. I took a second trip to the rear of the car, where black smoke from the tailpipe was choking me."

"I guess I don't need to tell you that the engine is shot, so is the radiator. I don't think I can salvage any of the mechanical parts except the transmission. At least that looks good. It's hard to tell, though, until we get the other parts replaced and runnin'. Did you notice that the tires are almost brand new? I can't figure out why someone would put new tires on a car that couldn't go anywhere's. Beats me.

Anyways, if we're lucky and can salvage the transmission, put a new engine and radiator in—maybe we can find that at salvage yard, maybe not, we might have to put somewhere from seven thousand to ten thousand dollars just to get 'er up and runnin'. And then there's some nasty rust we got to deal with on the body. That old, yellow car was startin' to look like a banana goin' rotten. Let me take a look at your notes"

I handed him over the three sheets, and Bill just shook his head. "Man, this looks like anywhere from five thousand to eight thousand to clean 'er up."

"So, we're talking about putting in at least fifteen to twenty thousand on repairs, probably a whole lot closer to twenty thousand."

"Yeah, I'd stick to twenty thousand and throw in another three or four thousand for unexpected ones. You just never know with these old cars. Just when you think you've got 'em all fixed, something else goes wrong."

"All right, I'll say twenty-five thousand for repairs. If we subtract that from the sixty-seven thousand for a '67 in good condition, that comes to forty-two. I'll start by offering Virgil thirty-eight thousand."

"Yeah, that seems to be a good startin' point, I sure wouldn't pay more than forty-two thousand for her. What'll we do next?"

"I'm texting Joey V. now and giving him the Reader's Digest version of our appraisal. I'll ask him what' he's willing to offer, what's his top dollar offer?"

"I don't know. I'm tempted to start at thirty-six thousand. I'd like to keep it under forty grand."

"I'm sure that's the way Joey V. feels. Well, I'll stay here and putter around while you deal with Joey V. and ole Virgil. I think he and Bee are out back behind their house, harvestin' the last of the tomatoes, at least green ones, some collards, and some pumpkins, and who knows what else."

It didn't take more than ten minutes for Joey to respond. "Given this report, I wouldn't pay more than forty grand for this heap. I don't like the prospect of putting in more than ten thousand dollars to restore a car. But Bill thinks he can take care of the mechanical parts, and the bodywork seems doable. Forty grand is my top offer."

"All right, Joey, I'll try to keep it under forty grand."

"That's my boy."

I walked behind the house, and there I saw Virgil and Bee working away. "Say, Virgil, can we talk?"

Bee hollered out, "Virgil, it's time we got down to business."

"She's a beauty, right" Virgil puffed out his chest in pride.

"Well, Virgil, she could be a beauty with a lot of work. The engine and radiator are shot through with rust, so is the driver side rear quarter panel. There's twenty-five to thirty grand worth of work there just to get her up and running."

"So, how much will you offer? It's got brand new tires and all."

"That old car isn't going anywhere, new tires or not. Thirty-six grand is all we're going to offer."

Virgil scowled and blurted out, "Can't ya make it more? I mean that car means a lot to me and my whole family."

Bee turned away and mumbled loud enough for Virgil and me to hear. "I told you it was a dumb-ass idea to put new tires on, like lipstick on a pig."

To save Virgil some face and still keep my boss pleased, I said, "My final offer is thirty-eight thousand. Take it or leave it. I can't go any higher."

Bee responded quickly to cut off anything Virgil might say. "We'll take it. The man's right, Virgil. That car needs a whole lot of work and work we can't do. There's nobody around here who would off us thirty-eight thousand dollars. These fellas came all down from St. Louis. They might not want to come back empty-handed, but I know they don't want to get hoodwinked in the process. Thirty-eight thousand is a fair price. As the man says, there's a whole lot of work to be done. I say we take the offer."

Virgil put his right hand on his forehead and rubbed it hard as if he were trying to erase whatever visions of worldly riches he had imagined he would get from selling his one prized possession. Finally, he looked me in the eye and said, "All right it's a deal. We'll take the thirty-eight thousand."

There remained just one problem: how would we get a car that wouldn't budge an inch on Bill's trailer?

Bee had an answer. "We got two heavy duty gas powered winches and some steel cable and hooks we can let you use to get that car on your trailer. No, come to think of it, Virgil can get them set up. He and that other fella—Bill, right—they can attend to that. And you—Joe, right?—you and me are gonna go into town and start up a rumor mill. We're gonna strut into the bank, hand in hand, and attend to signing over the title. The car's in my name. We're going to let people in town think I'm some kind of what-do-ya-call it? Oh, yeah, a coyote. They'll be talkin' up a storm about how I dumped ole Virgil for a younger man. It'll be better than watchin' a TV Soap Opera. People always like to think the worst. Virgil's got his faults just like any man or woman does, but he's a hard worker and always tried to do right by his family. You can't really ask more than that, can ya?"

I nodded a yes and all the while wondered if this is what Amanda would say about me.

The two of us drove into town in Bill's truck, Bee snuggled in next to me. She was enjoying the joke, and to tell the truth so was I. We stuck to Bee's plan. I gallantly opened the passenger side door and extended my hand to help Bee get out. Then we strolled into her bank, hand in hand, and tried our best to keep from laughing. We did let the notary public in on the joke after Bee swore him to secrecy. Out we strolled, smiling broadly. Then Bee led me over to her lawyer's office. We walked in and Bee explained to the receptionist that she just wanted to get out of the cold for a while but not before introducing me. "This is Mr. Joseph Allmen. He's come all the way from St. Louis just to see me." The receptionist wrinkled her forehead and brusquely replied, "Oh, I see. Will you be staying long Mr. Allmen?"

"Just as long as it takes to take care of things."

"I see."

Bee had figured that she had done enough to jumps start the rumor mill and we laughed all the way back to her place.

Bill said that after a lot of cussin', moanin', and groanin' the two had gotten the car up on the trailer. "All we got to do now is to make sure that car don't come off the trailer before we want her to." We secured the car with chains and locks. When Bill left a mud mark on one of the brand new tires, you could see Virgil almost cringe in horror.

Then we were off, headed to Joey V's. We hoped to make it home by midnight. Neither one of us wanted to risk getting caught in an ice storm and staying in some cheap motel. We took our leave of Sulphur.

"I'll let you know how the rumor Mill turned out, Joe."

"Bee, what kind of game have ya got goin' on? Are ya up to your tricks again?"

"Of course, Virgil, it keeps me young at heart."

BALANCING ALL THE LEDGERS

Bill wanted to drive first. "Ya know as I get older, I have a hard time deali' with those oncoming headlights blastin' their ways through my eyes at night. We got about four and half hours of daylight ahead of us, so I'd appreciate it if you let me drive first. Then you take over shortly after nightfall. For sure we'll have to stop then and get some gas and grub at a puke an' go."

"Maybe we can forego the puke an' go and stop at a Subway or even a McDonald's or something like that. We ate up all our sandwiches on the way down here, so, Bill, it's your truck and your call."

"I appreciate that, thanks." Bill didn't say a word until we exited onto Highway Ten. Then he became chatty. "Joe, it took me a while to piece things together, but now I think I got at least all four corners and some of the small pieces of the puzzle that makes up Joey V. Well, for one thing, he's no gangster and never was one. The *V* he lets stands for his last name. It's really just the first word of a long name that I can't remember nor can most folks. It's *Voorheigen* or somethin' like that and it goes on and on for about ten more letters. I guess Joey figured it would just be easier for people to call him the easier short version of *V.* Or maybe he grew tired of everybody mispronouncin' or trying to pronounce his last name. And I ain't never heard no gangster called *Vorheigen-somethin'* or other. No, he was an engineer and a really good one at that. He worked at Ford for almost fifty years and saved up his money. He never spent a dime too much for anythin' until he decided to retire some years back. That's when he got this obsession thing about fillin' up his barn with '67 Mustangs and not carin' how much it cost. I know that 'cause that's when I started takin' up jobs for him. I tell ya somethin' else. I think I know why he never married.

Well, one day a coupla weeks ago, I wandered into Joe's house. He wasn't answerin' his phone and I had a question about the carburetor he needed for one of his cars. Nowadays hardly any cars that I know of have carburetors but back then they were big deals. Anyways, I called him—no answer. I knocked on his door—no response. So, I stuck my head in the room and I saw him in this dining room that he had converted into a study. On one side were photos and yellowing newspaper clipping about his career at Ford. Then on the other side were all kinds of photos of him and a young woman. They both looked to be in their early to mid-twenties. The woman looked like a mirror image of Joey only with longer and straighter hair that fell straight down to her shoulders. Back then men grew their hair pretty long, too, at least some of them did. Joey's curly hair grew out all crazy like over his head. Well, I thought the pictures were of his family and the pretty one with that long, straight, auburn hair was his sister. Except for the fact that Joey had curly hair and the woman had long, straight hair, there didn't seem to be any other speck of difference about their facial features. So, I asked him, 'Is that a picture of your sister?' And he said 'No, my former fiancée.' The way he said it sorta struck me as if it pained him to say it. He quickly turned the subject back to a neutral topic like that carburetor. Then, when I saw that Johnson couple and saw how different Virgil and Bee were I got to thinkin'. Say, Joe, what all did you and Bee do in town while Virgil and I got that old rust heap up on the trailer?"

I told him that Bee had concocted an elaborate joke. She was going to get the old rumor mills and gossip parlors humming with the idea that she had dumped old Virgil and turned into a coyote to run off with a northern carpetbagger she had met. I told him about how we strolled into the bank like a young couple in love. She wanted to hoodwink the whole town. She didn't fool everybody but just enough to get the gossip chattering away. She said if we pulled it off right there would be two or three widows in the area that would shower old Virgil with gifts of homemade pies and casseroles and stuff like that. She just wanted to see their expressions when they saw her and Virgil still together.

"Do you think the two of you pulled it off?"

"Maybe, she said she'd text me in a week or so and let me know. In any event, our little play-acting made the routine trip into town to sign over the title a lot more interesting."

"You know what, Joe, that difference between Virgil and Bee got me to thinkn'. You know that old sayin' about how opposites attract?"

"Yes."

"Well, maybe and I say just say maybe Joey V and his former fiancée never married because they were too much alike. I don't know. Either she did leave him for another guy or died mysteriously or entered a convent or somethin' like that, but anyways he never got over it. As for me, my money is on the idea that his former fiancée left him for another guy, someone that didn't resemble him in any way shape or form. As I said, I don't have all the puzzle pieces fitted exactly together. And ya know somethin' else? When you and Bee sealed the deal in town and I texted ole Joey about it, he called me right back. He almost sighed and said, "She would be pleased, really pleased about that." My guess is that he was referrin' to his famous, former fiancée. I'll bet he's spent his whole life tryin' to please someone he never could. It's all sorta sad. Now I could be wrong, but that's the way I see it."

"I think you're onto something, Bill."

"I'll never know for sure, but then there's lots of things we'll never know for sure. Maybe we shouldn't."

After that, Bill didn't say much about much of anything for the rest of his shift. But, as long streaks of twilight light descended upon us, and the sun sank into the western horizon like some grand pumpkin fading away, Bill became talkative again. He had his way. We pulled into a puke an' go, where the smell of the grease overwhelmed even that of the gas fumes out in the bays. Bill went in and picked up some of the greasiest fried chicken I had ever laid eyes on. The brown paper bag was saturated with a thick, slimy coat of grease and not just at the very bottom. "I picked me up some chicken and two bags of boiled peanuts, Cajun style. Whenever I head south, I do love to get those boiled peanuts, and the chicken is the best there ever is. Anyways I left out one important detail about ole Joey V. Back in the day when the '67 Mustangs were bein' developed. Joey worked as the junior engineer on that Select Shift Cruise-O-Matic that helped to make the '67 the classic that it remains today. Now, again I'm speculatin' a little bit, but I'll bet he did most of the work on that development stage and the senior engineer took most of the credit. That's the way it goes most of the time. There's just no justice in this world. I've never had to do a lick of work on the transmission. Joey attends to that and to that exclusively. I bet he still remembers the day he took that former fiancée out for a spin in a brand new '67. Maybe that's why he's so obsessed with them."

"I bet you're right, Bill. I think you've done a fine job of putting the pieces together. Anyway, it's my turn to drive. I didn't have to worry about falling asleep at the wheel or any of that white line hypnosis thing. As soon as Bill finished off the chicken and both bags of boiled peanuts, he fell fast asleep and started snoring so loud that he'd wake the dead.

As for me, I was looking forward to getting home. My traveling days would be over next week as I settled into a new job: about the same salary-wise as my old one but a lot better as far as benefits go. It seems odd, but Amanda's health insurance at the hospital where she worked really wasn't very good—high deductibles and high premiums to boot. Anyway, in six months we could switch over to my company's plan. Sometimes I felt guilty during the weeks when I wasn't working. Even these trips for Joey V. seemed a little like a vacation while Amanda toiled on at home. Maybe she wouldn't feel quite as stressed out when she didn't have to view herself as the sole breadwinner in the household. I hope so. She's been under a lot of pressure lately while I went frolicking off to Michigan, New Mexico, and Louisiana. She stayed home when she wasn't working and had to deal with all the issues affecting adolescents, and there's always a lot of those.

After I got home, (around one am the next morning,) Amy was still awake sitting downstairs with a light on and pretending to watch some TV show that really didn't interest her. "Dad, I'm glad you're home. I paid a little extra to get advance notice of my ACT score. I raised it a little—one point—but not enough to get the Dean's scholarship. I'm so disappointed."

"But you did raise it, and from what I understand that one point increase will get you some scholarship money, right?"

"Yes, it's called the honors scholarship. It's worth about half of what the Dean's scholarship is."

"Look, Amy, your mom and I are really proud of how hard you worked. You did your best and that's all that matters. You'll do fine. Besides, we got the money thing straightened out. You'll have to take a little loan, not a big one. Your mom and I will pitch in some money, and you've got some savings. You're set for next year and for the remaining three years. After that all that matters is how you perform on the job. In a few years after you graduate, no one will care what your ACT score was." I knew I was offering up platitudes, but sometimes that's all we can do. Amy was disappointed, and nothing I could do or say mattered. But I had a role to play, and I think Amy realized that.

"Thanks, Dad. I think I'll head up to bed and try to get some sleep. Or maybe I ought to study. I've got to ace my courses and keep my GPA up. I've got three tests next week to prepare for."

"But they're next week. For now just get some rest."

"My plan exactly, I guess."

When Amy stepped upstairs, she didn't exactly do so with resounding certainty. Maybe I had been just a little encouraging, maybe not. In any event, that's the best I could do.

I might have had better luck with Tom—just maybe. On Saturday, after his soccer game, he raced down the stairs and yelled out to anyone who would listen. Since I was the only one there, I listened." My new shoes worked out great. Three of the guys on my team were suckered into buying those pricey elite models. They played the way they always did—sucky. During the pre-game warm-ups, they were flashing everyone with their new cleats. Me, I just played my usual game with my cheap end shoes. They did the job and so did I. I scored two goals and almost had a hat trick. I boomed one off the crossbar, just inches away from a third goal. I was great."

"Glad to hear that you had a good game, but don't gloat too much. You've got more games to play. Enjoy the success but don't bash your teammates with terms like 'sucky.' You could have a bad game, too."

"Yeah, right, Dad."

Tom returned to the sanctuary of his room, probably still gloating. He might have learned a lesson, or he might just have celebrated himself. "Well, he did save himself some money,"" I reminded myself.

But I've gotten ahead of myself. We still had to deliver the last '67 Mustang to Joey V. Bill and I pulled in around one am. Joey was outside in the cold night air, anticipating our arrival. He said nothing until we managed to push the car into the ninth stall. Then all he said was, "She'd be very proud of me." That's all. Bill and I exchanged both knowing and puzzling looks. We both figured that the *she* referred to his former fiancée, but why she would have been pleased by this full stable of '67 Mustangs remained an enigma and would probably remain so.

The following Monday I started my new job. Joey V's generous payments had cushioned the blow of unemployment, so for now our money problems seemed at bay. It would be a year and a half before I had enough vacation time to plan a family trip to Chimayo. I think we needed time to reflect. It wasn't all about the money—but that's easy to say when you have enough money to pay your bills and put a little bit aside for emergencies and a retirement in the distant future. But it was time to plan for the future, both the near and distant futures. The ledgers weren't completely balanced just yet.

THE ORACLE OF HERE

A FOREWORD & A FOREWARNING

All characters in this book are fictitious; accordingly, anyone looking for resemblances to living or deceased persons will be disappointed. Fiction allows us an escape from reality and a retreat from the mundane even as it teases us, if only momentarily, that this world of letters is real. However, if the characters and situations remain as flights of imagination, perhaps the stories themselves may provide some element of truth.

LUKE

―――――――――――――――⌒――――――――――――――――

"Luke, don't even think about it. There's no way you could pull this one off. There's that deep ravine about seventy-five yards off and then beyond that there's dense woods. You might get a split second to react. And even if you managed to react then, how would you make it across that ravine?" Tom spoke in a low whisper, barely audible. I didn't turn my right ear towards my friend, but kept focused on a slight gap between the trees about 150 yards ahead of me. Besides, if I spoke, the frigid air would only transmute my breath into a revealing fog. It had turned cold. Winter had come a little early. A fringe of snow blanketed the ground and painted the pine trees with a glowing luster that the sun, which still lay low, highlighted. I tried to blend in with the dense oak trees that grew to the edge of the ravine. Then, the pine trees dominated beyond. "Tom's probably right," I thought to myself. I gave my friend a nod as if agreeing with him, but then quickly fixed my eyes on a narrow space between two towering pines. I didn't know what force was driving me, but that small break in the woods soon locked me into a frozen focus. Somehow I sensed that that blank opening had a meaning I couldn't fathom. But then I dismissed all such thoughts. "Who the hell am I kidding? Tom's right. It's probably time to move on." But I didn't. I slowly eased myself down on the cushion of light snow and of fallen oak leaves, first kneeling and then gradually extending my legs out so that I hugged the ground in a prone position. Tom shot me a glance that spoke to me, "What is Luke thinking? He must have gone crazy." Maybe I had.

But seconds later, that blank space between the pines filled with an enormous presence. Then two eyes bulging from that presence peered into me. I shook my head as if I were tottering off into insanity. Then in my mind's ear, I thought I heard a single word bellowing out at me. "Here!" the voice sounded. That's all, just that one word "Here." I've never forgotten it. It haunts me still. Then mechanically my right eye zeroed in on the crosshairs and I heard a loud blast. Then it was over.

"That's one hell of a shot, Luke," Tom remarked as he slapped me on the back. "Hell, that's not just a ten point buck you got. Even from this distance, I can see he's gotta be a twelve pointer. Now all you have to do is to figure out how to get him back over here. I can go back and get the four-wheeler, but that ravine's jagged tangle of rocks would be too much for it. You'll have to walk down and up through that jungle of limestone to get to your buck. Good luck. I'll go fetch the four-wheeler. How you manage to thread your shot through all that maze of trees is beyond me. Anyways, one hell of a shot."

Mechanically, I thanked Tom for the compliment and then stood up, shook off the snow, and started a slow walk. Getting to the ravine was no problem, or so I thought at the time. Getting through it presented another difficulty altogether. The tree line stopped twenty or so yards before the ravine, but there was no end to the piles upon piles of oak leaves that crushed under the weight of my boots. These remnants of autumn also covered small ditches, probably created by spring floods. I soon found myself stumbling and cursing my way through knee high ditch after ditch after ditch. At least Tom wasn't around to laugh at my stumbling and falling. An onlooker would have thought I was drunk, but I was stone-cold sober. After my third fall, which sent me sprawling into a prone position, I stared at the frozen leaves that rose to my nose. "Why in the hell did I take that shot?" Tom had been right. I wasn't drunk, just stupid for letting some force take over and pull the trigger. But there was no choice now. I forced myself up, doing an awkward version of a combined pushup and burpeee. For the moment, I congratulated myself for reaching the edge of the ravine. For an instant, I assumed that I had found an easier path. Because of the downward slope of the ravine, I'd have to go north to eventually head south. After about twenty paces, I studied what appeared to be the easiest route. A mass of limestone seemed to rise up and even lent me a false promise of easy going. "Looks as if I can just stride over from this spot. It would be a walk in the park." Of course, it wasn't. A thin blanket of snow over the mound of leaves created the illusion of a bridge. In turn, the leaves and snow concealed the irregular mass of quarter-sized limestone, flint, and chert that formed not a bridge but a gravelly quicksand. My boots broke the frozen bond that flimsily and fleetingly existed. My first step sounded the alarm: first a crunch and then the rustle of small rocks giving way. Soon I was on my ass. "Damn, that hurt," I screamed to no one in particular. But, I had gone this far and had to go on. I once again pushed myself up and crawled over a few yards before I felt safe enough to stand. Wrong again. Within two tiny steps I was floundering again in a sea of loose stones and half-frozen leaves. Back to crawling on my belly. I reached up to grab a root that projected out into the far side of the ravine and pulled myself up. "At least, I didn't lose my rifle," I congratulated myself on a minor victory. Tom had taken all of our equipment with him when he had left to get the four- wheeler, about half a mile away. I had made it to the other side of the ravine.

The buck lay dead but with eyes wide open, staring and poring into me. In the past I had dragged a fallen deer half a mile or more, but the ravine prevented me from doing that. "No," I whispered to myself, "I'll have to carry him on my shoulders." I didn't feel proud, just duty bound to bring my prey home. Although I had field dressed many a deer, I never looked forward to the butchery. In this case, I sensed an uneasiness, almost a sacrilege. The buck lay not defeated but almost enthroned. "He must weigh as much or more than I do." I gently eased him up on one shoulder and then slung his other side over, so that he hugged my shoulder and neck as the morning sun illuminated the scene. Nature is cruel and death is never pleasant, just an inevitable means to some unknown end. I braced myself for a slow, tortuous return trip. Oddly, enough, my steps grew stronger and more stable with every stride. Stopping by the edge of the ravine, I told myself that I'd have to take sideway steps to make it down and then up again. The rocks were too loose. I'd fall again and again. But I didn't. I walked across feeling my burden but never slipping or sliding. Somehow I felt stronger as I reached the other side. Then I uttered words that still haunt me. "We made it." We, not I. What had made my *I* into a *we*?

What a riot of emotions whirled within me: regret, shame, pride, reverence, awe, emptiness and fulfillment—all at once.

"How in the hell did you make it back so fast? I thought you'd be flat on your back by now. Man, you were like some Hercules or something. Have you been working out?"

"We made it together," I responded.

Tom shot me a look that told me he was thinking I had gone crazy or was on meth or something.

"Yeah, well, whatever. Anyway, I was right. He's a fourteen pointer by eastern count, a twelve by western. He must weigh more than you do. I still can't figure how you made it back as if it were a walk in the park. You take some pills or something? If you did, then give me some."

"No, Tom, maybe just an adrenaline rush probably. You know the kind where some guy can lift a car when someone's trapped underneath." I don't think that Tom was convinced. I wasn't even convincing myself.

"Yeah, just what you say, an adrenaline rush. Come on, let's get back to camp. What will the guys say when they see your trophy buck. You gonna have his head mounted?"

"No, that wouldn't be right," I replied almost as if some other voice had spoken through mine.

"You sure you aren't on something, Luke?" I didn't respond, just shot Tom a look that told him to go to hell. "Yeah, well, whatever you say. He's your buck. But at least let me take some pictures. Otherwise, nobody would believe me. " Tom shook his head. "I still don't see how you managed to thread your bullet through that maze of trees. It was like you had programmed it with some kind of supersonic guidance system. Anyways, eventually, you'll have to let us mere mortals in on the secret."

"No secrets, Tom, just something that came to me in a flash."

The road back to our encampment rattled me with all the bumps over rough terrain, but for some reason I was more concerned with the condition of my buck than I was for myself. Tom didn't say a word on the mile or more ride back. Maybe he was too intent on not turning us all over. Maybe he was still wondering what had gotten into me. I guess I should have been feeling good, but I wasn't. Finally after maybe fifteen or twenty minutes, we made it back to our destination, where six other hunters were assembled. Four of the six had already dressed their kills as blood drained from the carcasses held high. We had drawn lots to divide up the territory into four quadrants, two hunters per quadrants. Tom and I drew the west quarter; Matt and Seth the east; Mike and Gabe, the north; Mark and John, the south. We wanted to make sure that the hunters shot deer, not each other.

"Wait'll ya see this one, boys. Old Luke here just scored himself a buck of a lifetime. Gather round." Tom was waving his arms frantically as if he were the town caller, which in this case I guess he was.

There was no mad rush—after all, these were adults, not kids; and a certain skepticism and perhaps some jealousy reined in any enthusiasm. Mark stepped ahead just a stride or so ahead of the others, who were determined to show that they weren't eager. "What 've ya got there, Tom?" Whatever it is, it's as big as a prize bull. You guys shoot some wandering bull?"

"Come on, Mark. Take a closer look," Tom bellowed.

Mark went ahead and gazed down at the stricken deer. "Damn, well, will ya look at that, a fourteen pointer. Damn, shot right between the eyes. I've heard of that in some movies, but I've never seen it in real life/"

"That was Luke's miracle shot," Tom said as I shifted in my seat uneasily, and then stepped down. Tom rambled on. "You guys should've been there, nothing but oak trees on one side and a dense growth of pine on the other and then in between a deep limestone ravine, all slicked over with snow and fallen leaves. Luke here had only a split second when the buck turned to look us over. I don't know how old Luke did it; but, boy, he did it, threading that bullet right through all the trees and that was it. But that ain't all. Luke musta been on steroids. He just hoisted that buck over his shoulders and strode over that ravine as if he were struttin' in some parade. You guys shouldda been there."

Gabe broke in. "It's sorta hard to tell how much of this is BS and how much of it is true. The next thing you'll tell us is that old Luke boy was walkin' on water."

"From the way he crossed that deep ravine, I wouldn't doubt that he could." Tom stared Gabe straight in the eyes.

"Well, all right, if you say so. Anyway, there ain't no doubt the fact that Luke pulled off a great shot. How far away were you, Luke?"

"Maybe one hundred and fifty yards or so. There was a deep chasm separating us from the buck and there were a lot of trees. That's all I got to say." The rest of the guys, all seven of them, took my reply as the final statement.

After Matt, Mark, and John took my buck off the four-wheeler, Seth asked me if I were going to have the head mounted.

"Luke told me he wouldn't mount the head, something about not feelin' right about it. Right, Luke?"

"Right, Tom. The other reason is that Rachel would nag me about spending so much money to have that large head staring down at everyone, especially in the living room. 'It's morbid,' she'd say."

"Yeah, well, Luke, you're right there. Anyway, you and your family will have enough venison to get through most of the winter, so it's not all a waster. And we've got pictures to back up any charges of BS if someone questions our story."

We took prey to a butcher shop not far away, maybe fifteen miles, but we drove fast. It would take a while to process all that meat. All of us had scored at least one kill. Tom had taken his limit, two tags, on the late afternoon before I had, so there was a total of nine deer to be processed. We had checked our deer in at the Conservation Office just a couple of blocks away from the butcher shop. The town itself, Salem, was a pretty quiet place except during deer season. Other hunters were milling about before they headed out into the woods. Tom was quick to tell all of them about my hunt; some of them even believed him.

At the processing plant, the owner, a guy in probably his late fifties with a grizzled beard and thinning white hair, asked me if I were going to have the head mounted. Tom spoke for me. "No, sir, Luke just doesn't feel right about it."

"Whatever you say. It'll make it easier to process the deer if you don't and you'll have a little more meat. It'll be cheaper, too."

"Yeah, well, that's what Luke's wife would say. " Tom interrupted. "So, about when, should we come back to pick up our meat?"

"Three days. You guys are lucky. You're the first ones in, so we can get to work right away. Don't forget to bring good freezer coolers. You don't want any meat to spoil. We might finish the work sooner. If we do, I'll set all the venison in our deep freezer. Who should I call to let you guys know when to come back? As I said, we might be ready earlier."

Tom spoke for the group. "Call Luke here. He's the guy with the fourteen pointer. Did you see where he shot him?"

"Yeah, I did. And in all my years I've seldom come across a shot like that. —maybe once in a generation or so. What did the buck do, turn his head to you at close range?"

"Hell, no, Luke was some one hundred and fifty yards away and had to shoot through a tangle of trees. How he managed to pull that shot off I'll never know. And then he had to toss that buck on his shoulders and walk down and up a steep ravine."

"Well, Mister, I've heard a lot of stories in my many years of doin' this sort of work, and most of them are just BS, but for some reason, I guess you're tellin' the truth."

"Yeah, we are," Tom boasted.

We all paid our fees for the processing. I paid last after the others had already walked out to their cars and trucks. For some reason or other I quickly burst out. "Would you save the skull and antlers for me?"

"Sure, and there'll be no charge for doin' so. I'm part Cherokee for real. A lot of folks say they are nowadays, and some of these claims are true. It used to be that folks would hide the fact of Indian blood; now it's different. People who never met an Indian—they call 'em Native Americans now—get all dressed up in what they think is Indian garb and prance around a fire and bragging about their ancestry. Me, I just accept it. Anyway, my grandfather told me tales of how some Indians kept the skull as a sacred symbol or something. It's probably better than mounting the head and neck—which is a waste of good meat if you ask me. So, sure, I'll do that for ya, no problem."

When I left the processing plant (I just hated to think of it as a butcher shop), I called out to the other seven guys, "See you next year if not before."

On the drive home, I saw two deer dashing across the road and the remains of a raccoon—just fur smashed into the concrete. "It's such a waste," I thought. Then I looked back at the times I'd ride with someone who'd joke about the ever-present roadkill. It wasn't funny any more.

RACHEL

I had no idea of what to expect when I arrived home. That single word that rang out in my mind right before I pulled the trigger still rang through my mind. What did it mean and why had I so kept it seared in my mind's memory. Normally, I told my wife Rachel everything, but this time I didn't think she'd understand. I didn't understand, either. I found myself sitting in my driveway, the engine still running. How long had it been running I didn't know. Somehow time, measured in seconds, minutes, hours, days, months, years, decades had lost its significance. All had collapsed into that single word, "Here." I shook my mind free of the thought, just as my dog Amanda shook off the raindrops. I'd have to at least appear rational—even if my teenage daughter Cassandra (aka "Cassie") swore that her parents, even her mom, had stumbled into their dotage. Even twelve-year-old David took note of the fact that his once invincible father wasn't as fast nor as nimble as he once was. I composed myself enough to turn off the ignition and swing the door open, but I had to think through and plan even these mundane activities. So, I took a deep breath and forced myself to stride into my own house.

Our dog Amanda was the first to notice me as she heralded my arrival with loud barks and frenetic tail wagging. I could barely open the door as she crowded every space. When I finally got in, Amanda jumped up and licked my face. Somehow I sensed that she knew something big had happened to me. Her brown eyes bored into me.

Rachel greeted me with a kiss, a light tap on the cheek. "Well, Luke, don't just stand there gaping. What have you or will you bring home? I hope your little three-day vacation was productive. You should see the grocery prices. Ground beef—you know the basic hamburger—is up over nine percent. And chicken—would you believe that—is hard to come by. The store ran out of wings. About the only things on the shelves are chicken thighs. The freezer downstairs is almost empty."

"Well, it will soon be full." I replied as nonchalantly as I could.

Cassie, who had chosen to ignore my presence until now, burst out. "Does this mean we'll have venison burgers, venison meatballs, venison bacon, venison, steaks, venison pie? If you could pull it off, Dad, we'd have venison ice cream for dessert."

"I'll have to work on that venison ice cream thing. Who knows? It may become a Christmas favorite."

"You aren't thinking of a venison fruitcake, are you? Dad, I know how you love fruitcake."

"Well, the venison fruitcake might be easier to pull off than the venison ice cream. You know back in the day, people ate meat pies all of the time."

"Dad, you wouldn't—would you?"

"I make lousy pie crust, Cassie."

"Don't we know."

"You're always welcome to cook the dinners, Cassie. Mom and I are pretty worn out when we get home from work, so you and David could earn your keep by fixing dinner."

We both knew that I had called her bluff as she just turned away and went to her room, excusing herself with the comment, "I've got homework to do. Ciao."

Then David greeted me. "Dad, do you have pictures?"

"Are you doubting my word?"

"Aw, come on, Dad. Just back up that comment about filling our freezer with some evidence?"

"Are you still watching reruns of *Law and Order*, David?" I replied as I took out my phone and tapped on it nonchalantly. David just gave an eyeroll. "All right, David, here it is,"

"Aw, Dad, we're gonna have to buy a bigger freezer."

Rachel bent over to get a look. "Did you get a deer or a moose?"

"I'm not sure what I got. It's the biggest deer I've ever seen."

"I guess you more than paid for your three days off –this year at least. When do you pick up the meat?"

"Well, let's see, today is Tuesday, but it's a late Tuesday. Even the sun is down. I guess either Friday night after work or Saturday morning. I'll get a call."

"Can I go with you, Dad," David asked. "And when will you take me hunting?"

"Next year you'll be thirteen and old enough to go on a youth hunt. Your sister declined the offer."

"You mean that you asked her!" David seemed shocked. Then he tilted his head sideways and observed, "Well, I guess I'm not surprised. I mean she declines everything. She even calls her so-called friends, 'Lulu-lemon-heads.'"

"Well, David, none of us are perfect, not even you."

"Yeah, Dad, you've told me that a thousand times. I scored two goals in Monday's game, two, and they were both great shots."

"Great," I responded, but so far David had been playing in self-esteem leagues, where the squads were balanced and everyone got equal playing time. My mind wandered off to my concerns for my children, as the minds of parents often do. Soon he'd be in high school, where the competition would accelerate. He might get cut or spend most of the season on the bench. Even after twenty years I still felt a little stung by being cut in my sophomore year. At least, that disappointment spurred me on to work harder. Things were different my junior and senior years. A little humility didn't hurt anyone. Cassie criticizes everyone else because she's not sure of herself. She puts up a screen of sarcasm and cynicism because she doesn't know how to cope with no longer being a little kid and Daddy's little girl. I acted the same way when I was her age. In contrast Ruth seemed to have been born with an adult mind and an adult perspective. Even her parents, now deceased, had told me that. In any event, that mask of being tough and cynical and sarcastic is easy to put on. Maybe we all have false faces. It's a hell of a lot easier to criticize others instead of yourself. Most of the conversation between Rachel and me now centers on our concerns for our children. We used to delight in their every movement. Now things were different.

I had to catch up on the eighty e-mails from work for the two days I had missed. It didn't take long to deal with most of them. I worked in a small office, where two co-workers must spend ninety percent of their work-time sending pointless e-mails and giving advice to reluctant recipients. By now I had figured out which ones I could delete and which ones I'd have to pay attention to. After half an hour, Amanda came in to give me that hurt puppy look even though she was five years old, so in dog years she was close to my age. I knew what that meant, so off we went on a walk.

About half a block away from home, Amanda spied a squirrel. She froze and assumed an attack mode--eyes staring fixedly at her prey, her left forepaw lifted, her tail pointed straight back at a slight angle. She was ready to race. The squirrel paused for a second or two, assessed the danger, and then raced towards a tall oak nearby, maybe twenty feet away. Amanda had never caught a squirrel, but she always acted as if she were an experienced hunter. When she was a puppy, she'd strain against the leash. Now she abandoned her attack mode once she realized that her prey had escaped up to the safety of the tall oak. Amanda had caught a young rabbit once, and it wasn't a pretty sight. Death never is. No matter how many years her breed had been domesticated, they retained the predatory instinct. So, did I, I guess. It was nothing to brag about; it was just the way of Nature and Nature can be very cruel. And gentle. The air was brisk. The temperature hovered around forty even as the sun was sinking over the western horizon. The sky dazzled the eyes with a rosy hue. All was calm above.

Amanda looked up at me. Nothing unusual about that, especially when she wanted a treat. But this time her eyes weren't begging. Her stare fixed upon me as if she knew what I had been thinking. Maybe she did or maybe she didn't. I had no way of knowing, but now her look signaled neither approval nor disapproval, only empathy. I was no longer the master and she the mere pet—as if that situation were ever the case. We strolled together like two old buddies.

When we circled back home, Cassie greeted me with a pleasant surprise "Dad, guess what?"

"What?" I replied, expecting the worst. "I thought I'd let you and Mom off the hook for dinner. Guess what I made while you were off walking Amanda."

I was about to say cereal with milk, but I caught myself before I made a complete fool of myself. "Chili?"

"No, not that. Maybe I'll fix that the next time."

I shot my daughter a puzzled look. Just when I thought she had lost herself in sophomoric cynicism, she surprised us with childlike enthusiasm. "All right, you got me. What did you make?"

"Grilled ham and cheese sandwiches, salad, and soup. Well, all I did with the soup was open up a can and pour the soup into a pot, but the two other dishes I fixed myself while Mom was on the phone with one of her patients." Isn't that cool?"

"Yeah, great, thanks." Once again, I had to hold back some snarky comment like I hope the soup and sandwiches and soup aren't cold but hot. I guess I really was my daughter's father after all.

We enjoyed a simple but great dinner. Even David complimented his sister. "It was great, Cassie. You didn't even burn the grilled ham and cheese sandwiches."

"Thanks, David. Coming from you that was a real compliment."

Rachel and I just exchanged a look that silently said, "Maybe this is as good as it gets."

That night Rachel and I talked things over as we usually did before bed. "Luke, did you mean it when you said that you'd take David on a youth hunt. With all of these school shootings, I worry about him being around guns."

"How many of these school shooters took gun safety classes and hunting classes and had the family's firearms locked in a safe?"

"Probably none, Luke. Still I worry."

"So do I, but I think I'll worry more when we try to teach David how to drive. Do you remember how it was when you had to teach Cassie? I took her out once and my nerves were shot. You handled the instruction from there on and did a good job. Cassie hasn't had an accident or a ticket, at least not yet. Some of her friends haven't been as fortunate."

"You're right there, Luke. Cassie's friend, Erica, crashed into a tree and totaled her car. She hasn't been driving since Cassie told me. But Luke, you've changed the topic. We were talking about David hunting, not Cassie driving."

"True, but as the children grow up, they'll face more and more dangers. They need to learn to handle them. Learning to hunt means developing precision, prudence, and above all else respect for animals."

"How can you learn to respect animals if you kill them?"

"What did we have for dinner?"

"OK, Luke, I see where you're going with this."

"Meat from the grocery store has been sanitized. It comes in nice, neat packages with only a minimum of blood. You never make contact with the animals you eat. You become detached, so detached that I've seen some people laugh off a death when they see road kill. Some even kill a lonely opossum on purpose just for the hell of it and then speed off, maybe to buy some prepackaged, precooked beef patty. Nature can be cruel and kind, generous and stingy, loving and hateful. Hunting isn't the only way we can learn to respect the animals we depend on; but, if David shows an interest in hunting, he'll learn to do it the right way."

"All right, Luke, you can step down from your soapbox, and I'll reluctantly agree. But David is so young."

"But he's getting older. I won't push him into hunting. But, if he shows an interest, I'll make sure he does it right. You don't just go tramping off into the woods and start blasting away. The video game violence is worse than hunting. There a player can vicariously kill, utterly detached from the horrid reality of death and dying. Just as people can buy meat at the grocery store without ever coming close to the animals they feast upon. People don't know the cost of death. Even our wars are waged at a distance with rockets, missiles, and drone attacks. We're not around to witness the butchery we cause."

"Well, Luke, you're right about one thing. Death is never a pleasant sight and now we distance ourselves from it and pretend it doesn't exist. Just tonight I had to console a woman, about my age, who was dying of breast cancer. I detailed the therapy regimen, but I feared it was hopeless. The poor woman was dying and there was nothing I could do to prevent it. This summer Cassie will candy stripe at the hospital. She needs to see that life is not all about her and her wants. There are lots of needy people out there. She needs to expand her vision."

"Aren't you afraid she'll get sick and die going to the hospital five days a week? I mean she'll be around a lot of sick people."

"All right, Luke. I get your point. And I can see where Cassie gets all of her sarcasm. Good night for now. We'll talk this over again."

As for work, well, that's another thing altogether. Technically, on Wednesday I was still on vacation, but I had reports to finish, e-mails to address—at least the ones I didn't automatically delete--and calls to make. Basically, I worked from home. So, while I was at home while everyone else was off to school or to work, at least I'd be around to greet the furnace repair crew. But before and after the repairmen came, I wasn't home alone. Amanda lounged by my side except for the time when we took walks. We took a break and drove over to a park about three miles away. We walked winding trails that meandered through a heavily forested area encircling a good -sized lake. Amanda walked on, as dogs do, sniffing odors undetectable to me and relishing the brisk air. Around a bend, where a large birch tree had fallen into a pool of rainwater, a deer looked out at us. Amanda suddenly stopped and readied herself for a strike that she would probably never make. Most dogs by themselves are no match for the hooves of an angry, frightened deer. Upright on its hind legs, a deer can lash down and shred a dog to pieces. That's why dogs hunt in packs. One or two dogs distract the deer and keep him occupied while other dogs strike from behind. It's all a savage affair and not uncommon in places where feral dogs run wild. But Amanda was anything but feral. The deer continued to eye us suspiciously. The buck, probably a yearling, had learned quickly who was friend and who was foe and who was simply neither. Slowly the buck wandered off, all the while eyeing the two predator types who had intruded into his woods. I wondered if he knew what I had done only a day before. Satisfied that the deer had wandered off, Amanda resumed her stride after looking back at me, as if requesting permission to proceed. On we went, two intruders in the woods, predators without prey.

On Saturday morning early, around five am, I left to pick up my meat. Simon, the owner and chief meat processor, had called on Thursday and left me a message. On a wintry Saturday morning, few other cars were out, so the drive was a solo affair. I asked David if he'd like to come, but he opted to sleep in as did Rachel, Cassie, and even Amanda, who had curled up into a tight ball and opened her eyes just wide enough to let me know that she was fine where she was.

When I got to the processing plant, Simon stepped out onto the small porch that extended around the front of his shop. "I called you first because I wanted to give this to you in private. I don't think that the other guys would understand. He handed over a large pinewood box. I knew what was inside and opened it to confirm what I already knew. The skull and antlers were stripped of all flesh and lay entombed in that simple box. . Simon must have taken special care to make sure that the remains had been stripped of all that would decay. I thanked him and shook his hand. "There aren't many guys who request what you did. I'll bet that you don't even know why."

"No, I guess I don't. It just seemed to be the right thing to do."

"Yeah, I think it was. You come back next year and I'll bet you can tell me why then."

"I hope so."

"Don't fret none. You will."

I left, feeling puzzled both over my actions and what Simon had said.

LOU

On the Thursday and Friday in between my trips to Simon's Wild Game Processing plant, I found myself going to work, writing scripts for billboards, mail campaigns, radio and television commercials. Creativity Plus was a small firm with big ambitions. At least, that's what Lou, our boss and chief executive of our seven-worker firm, proclaimed to anyone who would listen. Lou stood at five feet ten inches, an average height, but he had towering ambitions. He had a receding hairline, a mouth that could either bark out commands or soothing compliments, a prominent chin, and an equally prominent waistline. His white shirts were never tucked in but always freed themselves and stuck out in random spaces. His pants at one time exhibited a fine crease, but that, too, had long-since gone the way of his once trim waistline. His moods varied from those of a benevolent dictator to those of a crazed megalomaniac, issuing conflicting orders to his cowed staff. His outbursts of rage, however, ended with longer periods of calm benevolence as if he had purged himself of some demon. We all learned to tolerate his outbursts, realizing that the storm would pass. And we all worked for him for the same reason: the basic pay remained relatively low, but Lou distributed lavish bonuses to those who produced. In short, he was both cruel and kind, tyrannical and conciliatory. In that respect, he and Nature shared the same ambivalent nature. When in his benevolent, paternalistic phase, he liked to speak of his firm as a family. If so, he acted like an overwhelmed single father figure who couldn't handle the stress. Unlike Nature, he had little maternal about him.

Two of the seven employees seemed content with enduring Lou's bipolar moods. They never cowered when Lou bellowed. But they also never received the praise—and the bonuses—from their employer. Cameron and Karen both smirked away in apparent contentment, satisfied with their lot. The duo functioned as the company's gossip columnists and devoted all of their energy to writing lengthy four and five page e-mails that no one ever read. While I was away on my mini-vacation three day hunting trip they searched the internet for stories about hunters who had died in accidents or seriously injured themselves—often because of their own carelessness. They recounted one tale of a hunter high up in a tree stand who had fallen down and broken an arm and a leg. I checked out the story. Cameron and Karen omitted the fact that the injured hunter had drunk "only a coupla beers" according to his account. However, he had also littered the tree stand with two dozen beer cans. Apparently his definition of "A coupla" referred to two twelve packs. With the worst of winter yet to come, they also lectured us on safe winter driving protocol. And then there were the endless e-mails about Covid precautions. The two had already spent six months "working" from home and so had the rest of us until we tired of zoom meetings. If we had to, we'd meet outside and sometimes we did. We all realized that we might have to quarantine ourselves again, but didn't need the constant barrage of advice. Miguel, our firm's techie, had more than once responded to one of Cameron's e-mails that we could read the news ourselves and 'thanks but no thanks" for the constant e-mails. After that, he simply joined the rest of us in instantaneously deleting any e-mail from the two of them. Why Lou kept them on the payroll was anyone's guess. Despite his bluster, maybe he couldn't bring himself to fire the two. Later we learned that the two were his wife's relatives, close cousins. Maybe Lou ruled at work but at home his wife reigned as empress.

The three other co-workers did their job and did those jobs well (Four of us if you include me in that category, but I'll let you judge). Miguel excelled at anything technical. He could help any of us when we were spinning in some infinite loop of computer reality. He could also set up the cameras and recordings for TV spots or for zoom sessions or anything else technical. Outside of work, he devoted himself to family and to soccer. As he said, "Day to day, family mattered most, but at certain times soccer dominated his mind. He coached his two children's teams and on weekends set aside some time to watch professional games on television. Sometimes, so he told us, he'd have to record the games and then watch them later. The cruelest joke someone could play on him was to tell him the score of a game he had recorded but hadn't watched yet. As a result, during our lunchroom conversation, we'd be careful not to mention the scores of any games until we were assured that he had watched the game.

The four of us sat at our desks when we were in the office and engaged in small talk, at least when we weren't out on location filming a commercial or attending to other matters. Cameron and Karen always left the office for lunch but, as far as the four of us could tell, they "dined" at different fast food emporiums. We could tell by the oversized Styrofoam drink cups they brought back to the office.

Lexie specialized in coaching many of our clients in stage presence. As I mentioned, ours was a small firm, so we did a lot of Mom and Pop commercials for roofing companies, for car dealerships, for flooring companies, for HVAC repair firms, and other local businesses. Often the owners of the companies—and the sources of our income—wanted to feature themselves and their families in the TV spots. While these amateur actors and actresses were sincere in their beliefs about the companies they had invested so much money and energy into, sometimes they needed some instruction and practice in stage presence. However good they were at their craft--and I think they were not only competent but masterful in what they did—sometimes they lacked stage presence. Some would talk in a monotone voice, standing rigidly, almost in a rigid military pose. Others would overreact with exaggerated movements and hyped up voices. Lexie's constant advice was to talk and act as if you were with friends and family, be natural, be yourself. You want to make friends with your audience. She showed admirable restraint, patience, and consideration when she coached our clients.

The last member of our lunchroom quartet was Tony. I'm excluding myself from any further description as readers have already drawn their own conclusions about me. Tony organized special events like tent shows. Many of the local automobile dealerships sponsored massive tent shows, so in good weather Tony would attend to all of the details and work in collaboration with the rest of us in promoting the events. When winter came and tent shows wouldn't attract people, Tony would arrange for shows in motels, auditoriums, and other indoor venues. He faced a crisis when Covid hit and many people avoided crowded indoor arenas. He had hosted several indoor / outdoor events where he would use heated large tents and limit the number of attendees, so he'd schedule slots about an hour apart. When one crowd left, then another would enter. People could sign up for a specific time slot or, if they wished, show up anytime with the risk of being turned away. Tony's plan worked. Because many potential customers feared that they would lose out on the special deals that these fairs offered and the time slots limited the number of attendees, the slots always filled. When word got out that the slots filled quickly, even more people wanted one. So, Tony kept himself busy, in fact busier than ever even in the midst of a pandemic.

My job consisted of writing scripts for the radio and TV spots and the text of e-mail and snail mail campaigns. In the words of Indeed, the job search company, "Copywriters, or Marketing Writers, are responsible for producing engaging, clear text for different advertising channels such as websites, print ads and catalogs. Their duties include researching keywords, producing interesting written content and proofreading their work for accuracy and quality." I did all that and worked in close cooperation with my three colleagues.

All went along routinely until Friday after lunch when Lou made his grand announcement. Miguel was preparing to set up the sound system at a Saturday outdoor / indoor event that Tony was organizing. Lexie was coaching the owner and family on how to deliver the script I had written for a TV spot that would air on a local channel. All the usual stuff.

At 1:30 Lou burst out of the private office where he had sequestered himself for the last two days, perhaps longer. "Gather round, girls and boys. I've got some news."

Tony, our specialist in special events, whispered to me, "I'm getting the ax. I know it. Receipts from shows are off over fifteen percent from last year."

"You've made the best of a bad situation, Tony. You're OK. I'm sure of it." I wasn't so sure myself. Maybe I'd be getting the ax. Hell, maybe all of us would be. Creativity Plus brings in peanuts compared to the big agencies in town. The only consoling thought was that I couldn't remember a time when Lou had ever fired anybody—not even his wife's cousins who did little more than collect a paycheck, a paltry one but a paycheck with benefits no less. I shot Cameron and Karen a glance. Both sported a smug grin, their lips spread just wide enough to produce a slight dimple in their cheeks.

"Boys and girls," Lou belted out, his right hand running through the scant hairs still left on his head. "Little old Creativity is going INTERNATIONAL."

Miguel whispered a sardonic response, "I guess he means we're all being deported or exiled."

Lou was so enthralled with the grandness of his announcement that he either didn't hear or even seek the approval of his team. "Right here in this miniscule office space, we're going to make international history. We start with an advertising blitz on Kyrgyzstan Kuties."

"Oh, Lou, "Karen queried, "Just where is Kyrgyzstan?"

"I'm glad you asked that, Karen. It borders Kazakhstan."

We could all tell that Karen was about to ask, "So, where is Kazakhstan?" but she checked herself and responded, "Thanks, Lou. That clarifies matters."

"Now, Lou, when you talk about *Kuties*, do you mean those little orangey things?" Cameron asked.

"No, Cameron, I'm talking about the very foundation of advertising: SEX. You all may have seen some of those e-mail solicitations for beautiful Russian women who yearn for American men. Well, Kyrgyz women represent the best of the East and the West. In fact that little saying will be the foundation of our e-mail and snail mail blitz. We may even try a few radio spots. Then, maybe, we can expand to TV, maybe a fifteen or thirty second blurb on late night TV after the kids have supposedly gone to bed."

I don't know what impelled to stand up and object with a rhetorical question, but I did. "So, you're talking about Buy-a-Bride?"

"Look, Luke, if some lonely, sex starved guy meets a lovely lady from an impoverished country and rescues her and gives her a good life, who am I to judge?"

Lou either didn't sense the cynical tone or had decided to let it fly by him. He was still gloating over the half- a -million dollar contract he had won from a London firm named Exotic Adventures to promote Kyrgyzstan Kuties. "If we can pull this campaign off, we stand to land a contract to advertise for the main export of Kyrgyzstan: GOLD. You heard me folks: GOLD. With all of the inflation and the dollar going to hell, gold may be the key to future wealth. And the main export of Kyrgyzstan is gold, lots of gold, over a billion dollars worth. So, Luke, start writing some copy and don't forget to make 'The best of the East and the West' the main message. I like that little phrase. It's got a ring to it and is easy to remember. First we sell sex, then onto gold. Nothing beats lust and greed for good copy. I don't want to be bothered. I've got to prepare for an eight pm teleconference with Ermet, Omar, and Zamir—our contact people in Bishkek. It'll be eight am, Saturday morning their time. I want to show them some results. Come up with something good and get it to me pronto."

I did rush over to work—editing my resume. I wanted no part in this Buy-a-Bride scheme. I couldn't quixotically storm out and quit. I needed the work but I also didn't want to view myself as a pimp. Most marketing and advertising firms weren't hiring, biding their time until the economy settled into a pattern of steady improvement. Either Lou was so desperate that he'd risk his company's reputation as a family –friendly firm or he'd spent too much time scrolling the internet looking for love in all the wrong places. In any event, I'd have to hustle or at least pretend to.

By six o'clock Friday night, I had written the rough copy for an e-mail blitz and a letter campaign. Miguel had researched to identify our target audience, men in the thirty plus age bracket. He had even found out how many hits there were advertising Lovely Russian women or exotic Oriental women. Not always, but occasionally he could even identify who had sought what. He grinned sardonically when he told me that Lou's e-mail had received scores of hits. "All in the interest of gathering data for our campaign, of course," he concluded.

At five, forty-five, Miguel and I submitted our work to Lou, who was tapping away furiously on his computer keyboard. "Lou, here are rough drafts and outlines of our mail and e-mail campaigns, just as you desired, 'The Best of the East and the West.'"

"Sure, sure, guys, just drop it on my desk and I'll review it later."

When I got home around seven, I found a note Rachel had left on the kitchen table, "Gone shopping. Be back around eight. Cassie's gone to a basketball game. She drove David there, too, with the promise that he wouldn't hang with her once they arrived. See you later. Love, Rachel."

All alone, I stepped down into the basement at a funereal pace and opened the wooden box and gazed into the empty eye sockets of my buck. "What am I doing?" I said out loud but heard no answer. I closed the box and headed upstairs. I knew what Rachel would tell me when she got back. "Polish your resume, send it out, but don't expect anything." I didn't. Amanda came over to me with pleading eyes. "I know, you need a walk. Well, it'll do us both good."

PHIL

That Friday night, I fell asleep in the family room, lounging comfortably in a recliner—or at least as comfortably as any middle-aged father whose sixteen-year-old daughter was driving home at night. When I heard the garage door open, I roused myself from my fitful sleep and tried to appear as sharp as I could be. I still sported the clothes I had worn to work although by now they lay on me crumpled and perhaps a bit musty. As I age, I'm finding myself a bit crumpled and musty all of the time, so perhaps Cassie wouldn't notice anything unusual in my appearance. Glancing at the clock, I saw that it was 10:45. "Good, right on time."

"We stopped for Taco Bell, Dad. You want some?" Cassie asked, fully aware that I'd decline the offer. "They don't have any venison tacos, but there are two bean burritos left."

David's eyes focused on the Taco Bell bag. He lusted after those burritos, ready to snatch the bag from his sister's hand the minute I declined the offer, which really wasn't much of an offer in the first place. "No, thanks for asking me, though."

"OK, little brother and I are headed off to our rooms to conduct a little networking with our friends. Ciao."

Cassie and David headed upstairs with the latter chowing down on the two remaining burritos. I guessed that Cassie was trying to try her adult voice. It was all so much easier when the two of them were young. I pulled myself upstairs, taking each step one at a time. I'd try not to wake Rachel, but I failed in that attempt, too. When Rachel looked at me, she felt relieved that the two had arrived home safe and sound without incident.

"Luke, while you dozed off downstairs, I checked the weather forecast for tomorrow. It looks as if we're getting a break in the winter weather. The temperature is supposed to climb up to the high fifties, maybe even low sixties. We can pack a picnic lunch just as we did when the two were young. What do you think?"

"It's a great idea, but I don't know how our two mini-adults will feel about it."

"If they grouse and whine, we'll limit our stay to two hours and then have lunch in the park. It's either that or cleaning their rooms and the basement."

The next morning when we roused our offspring from their sleep, the nine am sun shone brightly. Rachel and I had correctly guessed that our two adolescents would object. "We're not little kids anymore, Dad," Cassie complained.

"No, you're not, but then your mother and I aren't either. We'll limit our stay to two hours. Then around noontime, we'll have a picnic lunch in the park."

"But, Dad, I've got a two o'clock soccer game," David whined.

"I know, and I also know that we'll be home in plenty of time for you to get ready for the game."

"You and Mom aren't going to post any pictures on Facebook, are you? I'd die if my friends saw me in some post looking like a little kid."

Here Rachel took over. "OK, no Facebook posts. It will just be between parents and children"

"I don't regard myself as a child any more, Mom."

"OK, how about offspring instead of children? Does that work for you?"

"Mom, don't be ridiculous. Fine, we'll go, but we don't have to like it."

"So, you two will wage a pouting strike?" I asked.

"You're as ridiculous as Mom," Cassie replied as she turned away and shook her head in dismay.

We drove silently to the zoo. After I parked the car, Cassie made a point out of slamming the car door even before David had exited. But only ten minutes into our two-hour sojourn, David burst out, "Listen to that roar! I never heard that before." An adult male lion was unusually active and roared delight—maybe at the warmer weather. Most of the time when we passed the great cats enclosure, the lions were sleeping, perhaps to display their indifference to the crowds of people gawking at them. But not today. The lioness in the compound also stretched her lean, muscular body out and returned the roar with one of her own. David and Cassie stood there, fascinated. We then moved on, but the allure of Nature stayed with us. For some reason, I recalled the etymology of *fascination*, derived from Latin *fascinum* meaning *witchcraft*. And bewitched we were as other sights and sounds drew our attention. The lone polar bear was frolicking in the pool, his massive padded feet just barely touching the glass wall that separated animal from human. After we had spent time with the great cats and bears (at least with the one that wasn't sleeping in her den), we stopped to see the great apes. It had warmed up enough that the gorillas and orangutans relaxed in the outdoor setting. One red haired ape—presumably the mother-- was cradling a baby. "Dad, they look so human," Cassie observed. See how she's holding that baby so gently. And the baby, too."

"Yeah, Cassie, I've seen pictures of you when you were a baby. Looks just like you."

"David, do you have to be such a smart mouthed brat?" Cassie asked.

"Just sayin.'" Was his muted response.

When we finished our tour with the chimpanzees, gorillas, and orangutans, we stopped to pay our respects to Phil. A large, almost life-statue of Phil the gorilla guarded the entrance to the indoor display of the great apes. The top of the statue showed a little wear as day after day, visitors patted it. "Dad, why do we always stop here?" David asked. "Did you ever see Phil in action—I mean when he was alive?"

"No, I didn't. My father did, though, and told me he would retaliate against the boys who teased and tormented him by jumping up and down making phony monkey sounds—the same way that group of boys over to our left are doing."

"But apes aren't even monkeys," Cassie broke in. "We learned that in the zoology unit of Bio class. But," here she shot a blazing look of contempt at her younger brother. "That's just so middle school."

"I wasn't making stupid monkey sounds." David objected. "It was those other guys. Anyway, Dad, how did Phil retaliate? I mean he was in a cage, wasn't he?"

"There was a small pool of water at the edge of his enclosure. He would very slowly inch towards it, very nonchalantly. Then, in a flash, he'd wet down his tormentors. Then, just as nonchalantly, ease his way back to the far end of the cage, far from the maddening crowd. He was a real character. They say he and his keeper shared a Budweiser at the end of the day when all of the visitors had left."

"Just one of the guys, huh, Dad. Is that statue for real, Dad?" I nodded. "But look at those massive arms and that huge chest. I bet he couldda crushed some guys if he wanted to. How much did he weight, I mean when he was alive and all?"

"Well over six hundred pounds, that's for sure. They say he died of a hunger strike."

"You mean like political prisoners?" Cassie asked. "We read about that in World History class. "A long time ago, back in the 1970's some Irish prisoners went on a hunger strike in British prisons."

I glanced back at the statue. "They're not so different from us, are they?" The bronze eyes, bored into me fixedly. Sculptures and paintings can freeze a moment in time and render it eternal. What were the images of Phil's eyes telling me? 'Here' they seemed to say but not with words. Then my mind wandered back to that same moment when the buck's eyes resonated with that same simple word. What did it all mean?

Rachel's words transported me back to the mundane present from my thoughts of eternity. "Well, we have enough time to eat our picnic lunch by the lake, right, Luke?"

"Yeah, sure, of course." I stumbled through the words. "Right, let's go." Rachel gave me a puzzled look.

"I was just thinking about what my own Dad told me about Phil, that's all."

"Sure, Luke, whatever you say."

Well, Mom, what's for lunch?" David asked.

"Don't tell me cold venison burgers," Cassie groaned.

"No, of course not," I retorted, shaking my mind loose from its labyrinthine rapture or delusion or whatever it was. "Cold burgers, venison or otherwise—beef, veggie, whatever—would be ridiculous. We're having bologna and cheese sandwiches, venison bologna, of course."

"Dad, you disgust me. You're joking us, right? I mean I've never heard of venison bologna. In any event, it sounds absolutely nauseating."

Rachel decided to play along with the gag. "Now, Cassie, that's no way to talk to your very own father. Have you seen the price of bologna nowadays? And I don't mean venison bologna, just the Oscar Meyer kind."

Both Cassie and David shot us an eyeful of exasperation and despair at their sorry lot. It was time to end the attempted joke. "No, we're having a choice of peanut and jelly or ham and cheese sandwiches, apples, carrots, and homemade brownies."

"Oh, the usual," Cassie lamented, yearning for something exotic as long as it didn't consist of venison.

We walked over to a picnic table lakeside. In low-lying areas, a thin veneer of ice remained. Ducks spraddled their way across, their webbed, wide feet allowing them to walk on the thin ice. Even if they sank, they could swim. The same couldn't be said of us humans. We'd be floundering around, thrashing in the cold water and cursing and blaming either our own stupidity or someone else's.

"Dad, why don't you go duck hunting?" David asked.

"I suppose Amanda could be trained to retrieve any fallen ducks, but I wouldn't know how to do it. Duck hunting demands some time, training, and the money for both, to say nothing of the additional licenses and fees you'd have to pay."

"At least those ducks won't be hunted," Cassie observed. "They look so cute, making their way across that ice."

"Say, Cassie, what kind of sandwich did you choose? Rachel asked.

"My favorite, ham and cheese. You know that. It's always been my favorite."

"Where does the ham come from?"

"Well, that's a stupid question, Mom. You go to the supermarket and buy a package of it."

"So, where does the supermarket get these packages of ham from?"

"Dunno. That's a stupid question, Mom."

"Not really, Cassie," I interjected. "For you, the ham is conveniently packaged. It's a commodity, like a jar of peanut butter. But that ham came from a living being."

"Yeah, Dad, but I didn't have to kill the pig to get the meat. Someone else did."

"In any event, a living being, a breathing, walking, snorting, eating fellow animal had to die, so you could have your ham and cheese sandwich. It's true that you didn't have to kill the pig to eat its meat, but someone did. Maybe if you had to butcher your own meat, you'd respect animals all the more."

"Dad, you sound as if you're arguing that we should all be vegetarians."

"No, we're omnivores. Perhaps we should eat less meat than we do, but meat is part of our diet. We should just respect the source of our food more. That's all I'm saying. Some of these commercial feedlots and slaughterhouses seem to regard animals as commodities, not as fellow beings. Chicken, pigs, cows, even sheep sit in cramped cages to fatten up before being beheaded and sliced into pieces, ready for grinding into sausage or other products. We share a lot with animals, sometimes more than we think we do."

"Yeah, Cassie, you're descended from that baboon we saw, the one with the big red butt." David's contribution to the discussion wasn't appreciated. He soon became the locus of thunderous eye rolls.

"All right, Dad, you might be making some sense. In World Cultures class, we learned that some Native Americans prayed to the souls of animals they had killed. Do animals have souls?"

"I don't know, Cassie." I replied. "But maybe they're not that different from us. I think Amanda has become a part of our family."

Trying to restore some of his lost credibility, David asked, "Do people eat dogs?"

"In some countries they do."

"I don't know, Dad. That'd be sortta like cannibalism."

Rachel determined, wisely, that it would be a good idea to switch topics. "We've got apples and brownies next, no meat."

On the drive home, my mind wandered to that one word I heard or imagined I had heard as I laid the buck low, "Here." It was an instance etched into my mind, just as real as that statue of Phil, immortalized in bronze.

But we had arrived back in temporal existence. "David, you'll be home in plenty of time to make it your two o'clock soccer game," Rachel said.

"Your Dad will take you. I've got to finish up some staff training online. Cassie, what are your plans?"

"I've got this bio report to do. It's due Monday?"

"What's it about? "I asked.

"Sortta what we were talking about?" Cassie reflected. "On evolution and our relationship with animals."

"So, what is that relationship?" David asked in a slightly sarcastic way. I shot my son a glance that essentially told him that sometimes silence is, indeed, golden.

"I guess we're more like distant cousins than anything else," Cassie responded.

BUCK

When we pulled into our driveway, David lost his devil-may-care sarcasm and started putting on his game face. He had watched one too many a pre-game procession of determined professional players silently parade onto the pitch, eyes fixed and rigid, focused on some future glory. In fairness, though, this game meant a great deal to David: bragging rights in the south county league. David's team would meet the current division leader, the Blue Devils, who hadn't lost a match in thirteen outings. David's team played either exceptionally well or exceptionally mediocre ball, depending upon the level of competition and the mood of the squad. They were as fickle as midwestern weather. People are fond of saying "If you don't like the weather, stick around it will change." Unfortunately, the converse also operated. If the weather were nice and pleasant, don't get too giddy. It will change. And changing it was. The excursion to the zoo took place under sunny skies, with a temperature in the mid to upper fifties. On the way home, the cloud cover rose just as the temperature was dropping. By two o'clock, the thermometer had dropped to the high forties with heavy cloud cover and a blustery north wind. By half time, the wind chill had dropped until it felt as if it were below freezing. David blocked a shot with his exposed left thigh, and grimaced slightly from the stinging impact, which left a red scar momentarily. Despite the cold, the teams played on. By halftime, the two squads remained tied. I couldn't hear what the coach was saying to his players, but they all looked ever the more determined as they left the huddle. When the whistle blew, both squads were energized and raced around the pitch if for no other reason than to keep warm.

David's team had three substitutes and the other squad four. Both coaches substituted freely, so there was no question about playing time. Besides, the players enjoyed a brief respite from the cold rain that was starting to fall down on them. A few minutes to dry off a bit and a sip of hot chocolate and each boy was eager to get back into the action. The referee asked each coach if they wanted to play on, and they both took a quick visual scan of their players' faces and shot back, "Play on." And so they did.

I found my mind wandering back to the zoo. We saw some spider monkeys chasing each other through the artificially created rain forest. Two of the chimpanzees played a similar game. They swung from branch to branch in what looked like a game of tag. Amanda and a neighbor dog would play a similar game only they kept on the ground as they would race around and chase each other until they had temporarily worn themselves out. Then they'd pause, perhaps take a drink of water, and then start the merry madcap mock battle all over again. Several times the two dogs would play a canine version of Capture the Flag, with one dog yanking the scarf off the other dog's neck and then parading around with it, daring the other dog to win it back. To add insult to the theft, the winner of the moment would even toss the captured scarf up in the air and catch it. This show of bravado only allowed the unscarfed one time to launch a counterattack, retrieve her property, and snatch away the other one's scarf. And so the game went on until both declared a ceasefire and rested before resuming the mock battle. I guess we all need to play, animal and human alike. As we age, we take ourselves too seriously to acknowledge that we play. Instead we have to justify our playtime by calling it "working out." But we're really still playing. A lot of people my age try to justify all the time and money they spend on hunting or fishing by claiming that they've brought home the bacon—the venison, the fish, or whatever. But in a lot of respects they're still playing. I doubt that many of us would survive in a hunting / fishing community. And, if we did, we'd experience far lower life expectancies. Still, there's a need for play in all of us, human and animal.

I wondered what type of game—if a game it was—my buck was playing with me. Was that word I heard or thought I heard, the "Here" that echoed in my memory, just a way of taunting or daring me? I didn't know. I still don't.

All that time, I was getting drenched by those penetrating bullets of ever frigid rain. The ref blew the whistle and once again talked to the two coaches. As I later learned, they didn't want to re-schedule; they didn't want to just call the match a draw; they both said that they would play the remaining twenty minutes and then settle the matter. I guess I would have made the same decision. The players were already soaked as it was. At least the constant running warmed them a little physically and that hope of winning warmed them emotionally. Even for the losing team there would be the consolation that they did their best. Even a tie would give them the glory of having made it through the pounding of an indifferent Nature. Many of the parents / spectators had retreated to the relative comfort of their cars. As for me, I just hunkered down as any animal would, headed tilted down slightly to deflect at least some of the cold rain, arms close by my side in a self-embracing pose, nose exhaling a wispy trail of smoke, eyes riveted on the match before me.

Then, in a moment of exaltation, I saw Number 10, my son David, dive through the air to head the ball into the far corner of the goal. The cross from Number 9 of his team, Joey, had been perfect. Pushing himself up from the muck, David shook his head, apparently not knowing if he had succeeded or failed. But there was no doubt about the outcome, when his teammates thronged about him and hugged him closely. A little over five minutes remained in the game. All David's team had to do was to defend as they had been doing and launch counterattacks when their opponents had pushed too far ahead. But, confident in victory, David's teammates relaxed just enough to allow one forward on the other squad to drift off to the left wing ever so slightly, completely unmarked. The opposing midfielder on the right wing delivered a pass perfectly, switching the field of play completely. The unmarked forward had been making parallel little runs and sometimes backpedaling enough to remain onside. He trapped the ball deftly, with his left foot and drove towards the goal, forcing the keeper to come out and try to block the shot. The Number 9 of the Blue Devils simply lofted the ball over the head of the goalkeeper and into the net. David's squad just watched in painful despair. Only seconds remained in the match, and both sides just seemed to be enduring the inevitable: a tie. The players shook hands—actually the motion was more like a slight touch to hands that slung low by their sides. Then the boys huddled by their coach for words that most of them barely heard. They were cold, they were wet, they were disappointed. All they wanted to do was wrap a dry towel around themselves and sit quietly for the ride home. Later on, though, they would relish and embellish the narrative of the game. But at that moment, they just wanted to go home and take a warm, relaxing shower.

When we pulled into the driveway, Rachel greeted us with a one word order that she barked from the doorway separating the kitchen from the garage. "I've got two towels, the big ones, for each of you. You heard me. Take off those filthy clothes in the garage and wrap yourself in a towel. David, you go first. Just look at you!" For the first time I took a long, objective survey of our son—at least as objective as I could be under the circumstances. Rachel was right. David had streaks of mud running down his face. And matters only worsened as you looked down. His jersey was splattered with mud, especially on the back, as his heels had kicked up droplets of Mother Earth. His socks before the game had been white; now they were a murky mix of rainwater, lots of mud, and specks of still unmarked white. David tiptoed his way to the shower. He deserved the first take. As for me, I wrapped the towel around my midsection and stood shivering in the kitchen. I still wonder what a looker would have thought if he or she had spied an almost naked man, still shivering, while a standing woman nearby eyed him carefully as if he were some poor specimen of humanity.

"Luke, you're a mess," Rachel finally confessed. "Here," I'll fix you a cup of hot chocolate." I stood by, still shivering, and just nodded my head. "So, how was the game?"

"It ended in a tie. David scored a goal, but then the Blue Devils countered with one of their own. David's goal was the best he's ever made."

"Well, that's good. David's been practicing endlessly. A couple of days ago when you hadn't got home from work yet, I had to scold him and a friend when they came in from the rain. They had been practicing diving headers in the rain."

"That's how he scored, a perfect head into the far corner. You should be proud of him."

"I am, but you're still a sorry sight."

I suppose that I was more than a sorry sight: naked except for the towel around my midsection, still shivering and chattering my teeth. Rachel took pity on me and belted out a command to David, who was luxuriating in the soothing balm of a hot shower. "David, hurry up. You're using up all the hot water."

When I finally managed to impose a little self control and stop my shivering and chattering, the cold still enshrouded me, but didn't present a pitiable sight—more one of horror. As Cassie strolled into the kitchen, she exclaimed, "Dad, put some clothes on," and then exited quickly.

Rachel called again, "David, get out of the shower." Then she turned to me as she sat down at the kitchen table. "Luke, I'm getting too tired to be constantly haranguing our two kids. In fact, I feel exhausted most of the time. I'd like to cut back on my hours at the hospital, but then there are those pesky monthly bills to pay." She blew out yet another exasperated call. "David, get out of the shower."

"Yeah, OK, Mom, I'm just about finished." David's response didn't elicit much hope. When David would be asked to wind up a twenty minute telephone conversation, he'd respond with "I was just about to hang up." When we would be ready to go to church or to an aunt's house (David had three of them, but no uncles), he'd yell back, "In just a minute." At last he emerged from the shower, as hungry as a bear just waking up from a long hibernation. He opened the food pantry door and snatched a tray of cookies and a bag of chips. Now he was in his element, munching and crunching away on junk food.

I walked over to the bathroom, slowly, a poor imitation of an abominable snowman. Upon opening the door, the warm, moist mist of David's lengthy shower lingered. For a moment, I joked that I was entering a sweathouse, in some mystical form of purification. The water ran hot for perhaps a minute, then cooled to lukewarm, and then to cold. David had consumed almost all of the hot water. I'd have to wait for at least an hour for our water heater to fill the void that David had left. "Still," I consoled myself, "that's the fate of many fathers."

After the far too brief shower, I dried off and went down to the basement, impelled by a force I didn't understand. I took out the pine box with the skull and antlers of the buck I had killed. In death, stripped of all flesh, the buck seemed even more imposing. The hollow eye sockets seemed to stare and bore into me. "Forgive me," I said. And then I recalled that many Native Americans would pray to the spirit of the animal they had killed, not for sport but for food. When they asked for forgiveness, they'd also ask to partake of the animal's spirit, for the strength, the power, and the energy of the slain deer or buffalo, maybe even of the seemingly lowly rabbit.

My reverie ended quickly, though, when Cassie called down the stairs. "You're in luck, Dad. Mom took over your turn of cooking and fixed a food you'd like."

"What's that?"

"Dad, you're impossible. You know what. Mom fixed venison steak for you, David, and her. As for me, I get all the Green Goddess salad I want. So, everybody's happy, at least for a little while."

"I'll be right up." Gingerly, almost reverently, I packed the skull and antlers back in the pine box. "I'll be back," I said to the voice that called out to me, "Here."

Usually, on a Saturday night, dinner is a catch-what-you-can affair: leftover pizza, grilled cheese sandwiches, in the winter some canned soup or chili. Then we'd go our separate ways. But tonight we all sat down and enjoyed a family feast. David was too tired to go out. Cassie said she didn't like to drive after dark in the rain. "Besides," she added. "the cold rain is supposed to change to snow. There might be a layer of ice under that snow." Just a few weeks ago, Rachel and I later learned, Cassie had spun around three times on an icy road and almost whirled herself and her brother into a creek. Cassie had sworn her brother to silence about the near accident, but he could keep a secret only so long. A week later he explained to us why Cassie didn't want to risk driving when the weather was iffy. "Just don't let Cassie know I told you," David begged. We didn't.

After dinner, all retreated into the family room—that is, after David and I had done the dishes. The TV was on, but I wasn't paying any attention to it, still knotted up in untying the meaning of me and my buck. Cassie was texting on her phone. Rachel was reading a book. Only David paid any attention to the basketball game that was streaming on the TV.

Then a few minutes later, the phone rang. Rachel handed me the phone and whispered, "It's Miguel from work. You'd better take this in the kitchen, away from all of the noise.

"So, Miguel, what's up?"

"How's your Russian?"

"Worse than my Spanish, and you know how poor my Spanish is. All I know, or think I know, is *Dah* and *Nyet*, and I'm not sure I'm right about those."

Well, you'd better brush up. Lou wants the two of us to go to Bishkek, Kyrgyzstan. The two languages there are Russian and Kyrgyz. I thought there might be an outside chance that you'd know a little Russian."

"I've seen Putin on TV."

"Very funny. No, Luke, I'm serious. Lou has bought us round trip airfare to Bishkek via Moscow. He even wants to know your shoe size so he can buy you some snow boots. He said he tried to call you, but I guess you missed his call."

"Yeah, I did get a call, but didn't pay any attention to it because I didn't recognize the number. I assumed it was just one of those annoying robocalls."

"He must have called you on his personal phone, not his work phone. Anyway, we're off to Bishkek two weeks from Sunday."

"Why the two of us?"

"He said we'd be there to connect with some guy named Zamir. That guy speaks English. We're supposed to develop ideas for the Kyrgyzstan Kuties campaign, do some interviews, and develop some feel for the local culture."

"And this is for real?"

"Check your work e-mail. Our itinerary is already there. Our hotel is booked, too, as is surface transportation from the airport. From what I hear, you'd better dress warm. Ciao."

I walked back to the family room in a death march. "What's wrong, Luke? You look as if you've died. What is it?" Rachel stood up and walked over to me. "Luke, has someone at work passed away?"

"No, Rachel, at least it's not that. Is my passport still in the safe?"

"Yes, that's where we always keep it. From your look it doesn't seem that you're going to some tropical paradise."

"No, Lou has Miguel and me headed to Bishkek in two weeks. We'll be gone for seven days, but I guess two of the seven will be spent traveling."

I had gotten David's attention. "Bishkek, Bishkek, that sounds like some weird soup."

"David, it's the capital city of Kyrgyzstan in central Asia. We learned a little about it in World History class when we were studying the break up of the old Soviet Empire."

"I don't know, Cassie. It still sounds like some kind of weird soup to me."

"Luke, what else do we need to know?"

"Dress warm."

ZAMIR

On Monday morning, Lou called us into his office. "I want you two guys to act as the point-men for our campaign. Luke, I know you have misgivings about this whole ad campaign, and I thought it over last night. You've got a point. We've got to walk a fine line between promoting a dating service and promoting prostitution. But right now our little agency is drowning in red ink. We can't make it through the next fiscal year without this contract. So, do what you have to do to keep this thing on the up and up, but don't screw this up for us. If you do, we'll all be pounding the pavement, looking for another job, capiche." Lou 's eyes bore into us. He wasn't just suggesting; he was ordering: do the job or get out. We both found ourselves nodding. Then he lowered his gaze and shuffled some papers in front of him. " It won't hurt if you can at least learn a little conversational Russian. It will help you get around in the capital city, but not so much in the countryside. Well, don't just stand there. Get out of here and start learning some Russian."

As we both left Lou's office, exhaling slowly, Miguel turned to me and asked, "So, Luke, what are you going to do?"

"I'll get enrolled in some program like Babbel or Rosetta Stone and start learning some Russian. But I don't know how much we can learn in less than two weeks. As for walking that thin line Lou talked about, I don't know. That fine line might turn out to be a slippery slope."

"My sentiments exactly. Maybe we ought to update our resumes, just in case."

"You're right on that score."

"Hey, you two guys look as if you're headed off to an execution," Lexie asked. "And here I thought that you two guys had scored an all-expense paid trip to some resort."

We both responded in chorus, "Have you ever been to Kyrgyzstan in the winter?"

"No, but at least you'll get away from the office."

"Don't worry, Lexie, we'll be here electronically if not physically. There's always e-mail, ZOOM meetings, Facetime calls, and a whole assortment of ways to have a rich office life. Covid quarantines taught us that."

"Yeah, well, good luck. Office gossip has it that we win a three-year contract or we win ourselves a place in the unemployment line. At least that's what Karen says. And she's in the know, you know, because of family connections."

"Yeah, we know," Miguel and I said in chorus.

Just a cursory glance at Russian language caused me to wince: thirty three-different letters and all in Cyrillic script. While the Moscow airport might have signs posted in English or at least some people who could speak my native tongue, the situation in Bishkek could be quite different. So, I opted for as much oral language as I could learn in a few weeks, but even then I wasn't sure of my pronunciation. I might be better off just claiming ignorance and trust that somewhere somehow an English speaker would be around. Miguel and I talked it over. We'd still try to learn as much as we could but our expectations remained pretty low. After all, we still had our regular work to do.

Around three-thirty, Miguel sidled over to me. "Cameron and Karen are still out on their midafternoon break after their hour and a half long lunch. I thought I'd look up to see if there were any documentaries on Kyrgyz culture. And one of them really stuck out. There's a film called *Ala Kachuu* that fits in with our project."

"What's it about?"

"Bride kidnapping."

"What!"

"Yeah, Luke it seems that girls get abducted all of the time, that is, if they're of marriageable age."

"What's considered marriageable age?"

"Fifteen and older."

"Yeah, well, we'd better be dealing with eighteen year olds and up and we'd better not be doing any kidnapping."

"Well, Luke, it seems that some of the kidnapping is a matter arranged secretly by all of the parties. I think I remember a musical that had a somewhat similar idea?"

"You mean one where the parents arrange for an 'abduction'?"

"Yeah, it came out a long time ago. One of the songs got to be real popular, 'Try to Remember That Kind of September.'"

"That was from *The Fantasticks,* Miguel."

"Yeah, that's it. Well, anyway the film I was talking about, *Ala Kachuu,* mainly talks about nonconsensual kidnappings of young girls and women by much older men, sometimes arranged by the parents of both the bride victim and the groom / kidnapper. Apparently, the custom runs strong in the countryside even though it's banned legally. This is sort of like what we'll be doing. You know convincing young women to 'date' American men, probably older American men or at least ones that would do on-line searches for lovely Asian ladies."

"You know what, Miguel. I think Lexie would be better suited for this job than I would be. As a woman, she would have more empathy with some of these lovely Asian women—and by that I mean they've got to be at least over eighteen—than I ever would. I think I'll talk it over with Lou."

"Good luck, Luke, but I doubt that Lou will bend on this one."

"Why do you think that?" I asked. I thought I had rationalized a perfectly good excuse for not going.

"You'll see."

So, I called Lou and told him I wanted to speak to him about the trip to Kyrgyzstan. He told me, "Sure, come on in," in a friendly, amiable sort of way. When I explained my reasons for not wanting to go, his buddy-boy smile transformed into a stern, patriarchal, tight lipped mouth that barked out, "I'm not about to pay for two hotel rooms, and I'm not going to have any gossip about my having Miguel and Lexie shack up for a week either. You're going and that's it."

"All right, boss. I'm going."

"Damn straight you're going. Get out of here while I still keep you on the payroll."

121

So, I exited. Miguel gracefully refrained from saying, "I told you so."

All the way home, I mulled my dilemma over. I thought of Cassie, "She's only seventeen. What if some old goat would have her kidnapped and 'marry' her? This was all too much. Rachel said she's been feeling tired lately and has talked about cutting her hours on the cancer ward. I don't see how she has been able to handle all the suffering, pain, and death for this long. Cassie will be going to college. And David will be starting high school. It's not exactly the best time to go job hunting."

When I pulled into the driveway, I knew I'd have to talk the matter over with Rachel. I did, and her response echoed my first thoughts. "Get your resume out, do some networking, make sure everything you do is legal with the Kyrgyz thing, and bide your time. If you just can't stomach the whole thing, resign. I can take on more hours at the hospital. They're desperate for help anyway."

"No, you really can't take on more hours. I'll figure something out." After dinner I went down stairs on the pretext of looking for a tool. I opened my pine box and stared at the hollow eye sockets: nothing. My oracle had nothing to say to me. Yet, as I ascended the stairs, I heard that one word echoing in my brain: "Here."

Thirteen days later I found myself sitting in the Moscow airport, waiting for our connecting flight to Bishkek. After Miguel and I spent an hour of walking around and gawking at the kiosks that probably offered overpriced souvenirs that we couldn't afford, Miguel got a text from Lou. "Hey, Luke, guess what? We finally have a contact person in Bishkek. Lou said that a guy named Zamir would meet us after we pick up our luggage. He's supposed to speak English as well as Russian and Kyrgyz. He'll be wearing a bright red stocking cap and a heavy coat trimmed with brown bear fur."

After unsuccessfully trying to sleep as we waited for our connecting flight to Bishkek, finally the screen lit up with the news that our flight was boarding. We stood up and stood in line of perhaps sixty people, most of whom seemed to be Russian businessmen. It didn't take them long to figure out that Miguel and I were Americans. One burly Russian who stood behind us eyed us suspiciously and then asked in clipped British English, "Are you two speculating in gold?"

I knew from my research in the last two weeks that gold was one of Kyrgyzstan's leading exports. When I told him that we worked in advertising and weren't dealing in gold, he looked relieved. "You Americans seem to rather enjoy getting in other people's business, so forgive me if I seemed too forward. The business in gold is getting more intense especially as the dollar declines."

I wasn't sure how to respond. Was this Russian trying to goad us into an argument?

Then, reading my body language, the Russian hastened to add. "Forgive me if I seemed too inquisitive, but the quest for gold seems to bring out the worst in us."

There was no way Miguel and I were going to explain our true mission. We both slunk back at that thought. Maybe we were feeling like pimps, I don't know. I lamely responded that we were going to advertise the beauty of the country.

"Then you should have come in late spring. The parks and city squares are very—what do you call it—green. But you're coming in the winter. You should come again and hike through the Tian Shan mountain range and the national park. The view of the glaciers is spectacular." His tone seemed more friendly now, or at least not hostile. I guess he figured that, since we wouldn't be competitors, he could be gracious.

"Oh, it's our turn to board now," I said, holding my official documents in hand.

Our Russian acquaintance extended a hand and said, *"Do svidaniya,* good by and good luck."

"And the same to you." I didn't know what to say as the officials shuffled through our papers and looked at us suspiciously. I guess we Americans would do the same to Russian nationals. The flight to Bishkek proved to be uneventful if a bit bumpy. We were served some excellent tea, though, as well as some kind of biscuit that was delicious but whose name I forgot. When we finally landed and picked up our luggage, which apparently had been searched and gone through several times—Miguel and I could tell when we reached our hotel and opened our baggage only to see the clothes we had carefully folded had been left in disarray—a bearded man sporting a red stocking cap and a heavy coat lined with brown fur approached us.

"Greetings and welcome to Bishkek, one of the greenest cities in the world. That is, in the springtime and summer. Now it wears a white blanket of snow. You two gentlemen must be Luke and Miguel. Mr. Lou told you I would meet you here, no."

"Glad to meet you, Zamir, right?" Miguel asked. Yes, you've got it right. I'm Miguel and this is Luke."

"I got you two all fixed up," Zamir said proudly. "Since you two are Americans I got you one night at the Ramada Inn. You Americans seem to want a home away from home as they say. But then your boss, Lou, he's very cheap. Then I take you to a very nice place, breakfast included. It's not as expensive as the Ramada Inn but it's very good. It's called Tour Asia. You two get a special price, thirty-one US dollars a night, each one gets their own bed. The thirty –one dollars, that's about 260 Soms per night. Not many Kyrgyz people can afford that. It's a good deal, and that's what you two are after, right?"

Right, Zamir," both Miguel and I responded.

"I will walk you two to my car." It's a Russian car, a hatchback Lada Granta. Maybe not so good by American standards, but it works, most of the time. I'll help you in." With our luggage, one bag each and the three of us, we appreciated Zamir's offer. He didn't say anything until we had secured ourselves inside.

Once inside, we became a captive audience to Zamir's monologue. "So, you came here in search of women. That we have, the most beautiful women in the world. But everyone from all countries in the world says that. Still it's true. And my wife would kill me if I said otherwise. You two, you have wives?" We nodded in response as we felt that Zamir was more comfortable holding the podium so to speak. He rambled on.

"I have contacts in the government, not high level ones, but the ones that matter, the ones with the secretaries who really handle the details. And it is, I think you say, all in the details. Anyway, the secretaries are cheaper to bribe. Everything here runs on bribery. How do you think you got your papers so quickly? No official fast track fees, no unofficial bribes. I bribe all in small amounts of god dust. It's harder to trace and the government secretaries deal with lots of matters. A little gold dust here, a little there. It mounts up. And the secretaries know it. Their pitiable salaries, I feel sorry for them. But what they make in bribes, now that's another matter. You know officially Ala Kachuu, bride kidnapping, is illegal. It goes on all the time. The big shots in the Secretariat think they ended the kidnapping with their big laws. Their big laws mean nothing, not a thing. Go out in the countryside and see with open eyes what goes on. Same as in your country, I believe. But that is the way of the world. Anyway, we are getting close to the Ramada. It is only a short walk to Ala-Too Square and the monument to Manas. You need to stretch your legs after the long journey? After that, I take you to restaurant. You get breakfast at Ramada but other meals on your own. We have excellent mutton dishes. If you want pork, you must go to Russian or Chinese places, but the local beef and mutton is the best there is. Ah, here we are."

We unloaded and checked in. One of the hotel clerks spoke English and took care of us. Our room resembled the ones in America. After quickly unloading—we'd have to switch hotels the next day—we took Zamir's advice and walked over to the Ala-Too Square. Even in the snow, it was an imposing place. Miguel and I both appreciated the warm new boots we wore, courtesy of Lou. We noticed, too, that the streets allowed for ample green space—at least green in the summer and spring. From the distance we snatched glances of the snow covered tops of what we guessed was the Tian Shan mountain range. But we also spotted a few high rise buildings –probably apartment complexes—that had all the grace of Soviet era functionality: rigid, straight lines, cement—grey workers' paradises. But there were no beggars on the streets.

The real work would begin tomorrow after we had moved to the Tour Asia hotel for the rest of our stay. But Miguel and I did appreciate the chance to unwind a bit at the Ramada. Our jet lag confused our dinner and breakfast times. In any event, we took Zamir's advice and feasted on a mutton dish that was as good as Zamir had promised. Then we readied ourselves for the next moves: a new hotel and interviews with some of the women Zamir had found and ---we hoped—not kidnapped. I hoped to be inspired bay what the women said; Miguel hoped to get some good photos.

LEILA

By 7:00 am local time, Miguel had already set up some camera equipment and his computer station. He would photograph each candidate after Zamir, accompanied by his two associates, Ermet and Omar, had obtained basic information from each woman: marital status, date of birth, residence, family, contact information about near relatives. Omar and Ermet spoke in Kyrgyz to four of the candidates. I gathered that they spoke about many topics. I suspected that the two were coaching the women about what to say when Zamir questioned them. If Ermet and Omar were "coaching," Zamir turned a deaf ear to it. However, Zamir did confess that his two associates had connections with many tribal leaders in the countryside. He also suggested that I provide a little bribe money to the two, who would in turn bribe the tribal elders.

Miguel scurried about to set up his photo shoot. He had decided on a backdrop of the lofty Tian Shan mountain range, lofty snow capped peaks and gigantic glaciers with a blue sky above. He had already privately made the decision not to coax the women into any of the standard "Cute babe" poses—the model clad in negligees her pursed lips heavily coated with flaming red lipstick, her eyes sparkling and directed directly at the onlooker and fixed with a come-hither look and lots and lots of cleavage showing. Instead, Miguel had them pose as they would for a professional interview. The four Russian women, two of whom spoke excellent English, knew exactly what Miguel was looking for. They sat relaxed with their hands clasped loosely in their laps. Instead of focusing on bursting bosoms, Miguel focused his lens on their faces. He teased them into a smile and had them wear their fur hats and coats. None of the Kyrgyz young women spoke English, so Miguel had to have Zamir explain what he wanted to Omar and Ermet, who, in turn, explained the directions to the nine young women. I wasn't sure how much was lost in translation, but Miguel wanted them as much as possible to wear their native costumes and look as if they were attending a festival. Three of the women declined the photo shoot on religious grounds, maintaining that Islam forbade any picture taking; the other six apparently found no problem with the photography either because they had grown up in a less strict religious background or they had rationalized that they had to make concessions to a culture that differed theirs. Like Christianity and Judaism and perhaps all religions, Islam embraced many different levels of interpretation as long as core beliefs remained intact. Of course, adherents differed on what exactly the core beliefs were. In any event, Miguel's decision set the tone. Several of the women exhaled in relief. They feared that they might be giving themselves to an international prostitution ring. Instead, they found themselves in a job interview.

Like Miguel, I had already determined my own course. If Lou didn't like it, well, I'd have to face him later. I decided to go with my gut instinct, and my gut instinct told me that I'd need two interviews: one in the morning and one after lunch with each of our candidates. In the first interview, I'd have to let them speak freely. I wanted to get to know them before I asked more pointed questions. Besides, my experience told me that the best source of ideas often came from clients. So, after noting down basic information—age, education, work experience, religious background, I let them respond freely to just one major question: why were they willing to participate in this program? Sophia, a twenty-four year old divorcee, shot back an answer that dazzled me in its frankness. Sophia leaned back in her chair as I struggled to record her responses. ""Yes, I would like to experience being a wife and mother, but I want to keep my professional life also. I am an engineer and am proud of what I have accomplished. I will not surrender my pride for some man's stupid lust. I understand that this is possible in America or other country. But I am not, what you say, desperate. I married two years ago. Bad experience. Husband all nice and polite before marriage. Then he became the czar of the house, or so he thought. He come home drunk and then want me drunk. Then he try to sodomize me. Disgusting. No, I want nothing to do with drunks. Too many of the men here in Bishkek spend the whole of winter drunk. And when they are drunk, they are mean. Maybe I around just group of bad men. Maybe not. I want to start all over again. Maybe it will work, maybe not. I am willing to try. But no 'Buy a Bride.' No. First we write, then we talk. Maybe if all goes well, the man comes here to see me. I do not wish to be any man's dish of caviar. If he comes here, we have dinner, we talk. Maybe more than that, maybe less. But you ask no money of me, so maybe, just maybe, all will be as you say on the up and up. Sort of strange saying, no?" I suppose I should have expected that kind of response from an educated mid-twenties woman. Still her frankness got me to thinking. Maybe there's a way out of Lou's Kyrgyz Kuties b.s."

However, what shocked me more than Sophia's candid response was to listen to many of the same thoughts reflected in the words of Leila, a strong-willed girl from the countryside. Leila's birth certificate or what passed as her birth certificate—I had no way of knowing—indicated she was nineteen, but she looked a few years younger than that, maybe about my daughter's Cassie's age. She did speak Russian as well as Kyrgyz, but, since I spoke neither, I had to rely on Zamir's translation. To his credit, I'm pretty sure he translated accurately. When I asked Leila why she wanted to participate in this program, she replied just as forthrightly as Sophia had. ""My life in the countryside has been at times harsh, but it taught me that I need to be strong. I do not want to be married off. You have heard of the custom of Ala Kachuu, bride kidnapping. I do not wish to be like a sheep, married off to a man who already has several other sheep in his fold. Some old lecher, who buys brides as if he were at a market. If this is what you propose, I want nothing of it. I can stay here, maybe move permanently to the capital, Bishkek, get a job, and pay my own way. I am not a sheep and never will be. You may ask me if I would like to be a wife and mother. My answer is yes, but only on my own terms. If I can meet men who would value someone like me, then I am open to your offer. If not, I will go my own way, like the snow leopard of the mountains."

Not all of the women I talked to resembled Sophia and Leila. A few clearly were willing to prostitute themselves and be married off to some wealthy American or German or anyone who would make their life easier. Others so feared being kidnapped that they would be willing to do anything to escape what some people used to call the 'fate worse than death." Still Sophia's and Leila's words resonated in my mind. As the morning round of interviews ended, I asked Miguel if he would be willing to take a second round of pictures with a pose and setting of the woman's choosing. He replied that he liked the idea. "Maybe we can come up with something good that we never expected," he replied. "Yes, a lot of the time a candid shot packs more punch than a staged, posed one." So, we had a second round of both photo shoots and interviews.

During lunch, I sipped the hot tea slowly as I mulled over nest steps. The Kyrgyz Kuties was out. What would be in took some reflecting on both my own values and those of women like Sophia and Leila. Finally, still sipping tea for over an hour and crossing out idea after idea, I thought of an alternative to the whole Buy-a-Bride business. We'd call it *PARTNER*: *P* for *Proud, A* for *Adventurous, R* for *Rooted, T* for in *Tradition, N* for *Noble, E* for *Enigmatic, R* for *Regal.*

Then I ventured into domains that weren't mine. The company, Exotic Adventures, who had hired us strictly for advertising purposes, was based in London until this time, the company dealt primarily with adventure vacations all over the world. Based upon some reason, probably spreadsheet data that showed the profit potential of expanding their scope to online dating services, Exotic Adventures was expanding its definition of adventures. I focused upon the general outline of a plan that would honor our contract with Exotic Adventures but at the same time keep me from regarding myself as a pimp. I remember what Sophia had said, "First we write, then we talk. Maybe if all goes well, the man comes here to see me." What if Exotic Adventures offered a contract for a basic package, which would provide the customer with the names and e-mail addresses of, say, five to ten Kyrgyz women who would entertain the idea of corresponding not just with American men but men all over the world. These contacts would have to be screened with background checks and other security measures. Then as Sophia said first they would write, then they could talk, perhaps over Facebook, and then Exotic adventures could offer a second package that would include a trip to Bishkek for the two parties to meet face-to-face. The package would include hiking trips through the Tian Shan mountain range, national parks, local museums, and dining at some of the better restaurants in town. For this proposal to work, Exotic

Adventures would have to work out the details, and, as they say, it's all in the details.

Five minutes before the afternoon round of more interviews and photos, I talked with Miguel about my idea. His response was what I had expected. "Lou will blow his top and lose whatever remaining hair he has left. He'd say something like, 'I hired you two assholes to conduct interviews, take some sexy pictures, and come up with an advertising campaign, nothing else. What did you do out there, get wasted on vodka all the time?'"

"Well, Miguel, you're probably right." But then I paused. "What if I e-mail both Lou and Exotic Adventures about my proposal?"

"You mean go over Lou's head?"

"I guess so."

"It's been nice knowing you. Luke, but if you go over Lou's head, you'll lose your head in the process. Keep me out of it."

Don't worry, Miguel, I'll keep you out of it. I don't know, but this is a risk I think I just have to take."

"Let me guess. You were thinking that your own daughter Cassie was just about the same age as that one Kyrgyz girl. I think her name was Leila."

"You know me too well, Miguel."

"I just hope you're right, Luke."

"So do I."

We finished up the afternoon round. We had two more days of interviews. The women—I think some would more appropriately be called girls—seemed to be getting younger day by day. I don't know what exactly Ermet and Omar told the relatives of some of the girls but I can guess it went something like, "We can get your daughter, niece, sister, whoever married off to a rich American, Englishman, German, or whoever." For all I know Zamir may have told them to say that. One of the last ones we interviewed was a young Kyrgyz girl from the countryside. While I balk at guessing any girl's or woman's age, this one couldn't have been any older than twelve whatever her so-called birth certificate indicated. Still, Zamir's ability to navigate the Byzantine labyrinths of under-the-table bribing of bureaucrats and local leaders made him invaluable.

We finished our interviews but had to spend another day attending to other matters: filling out government forms. A form is a form is a form. I have a tendency to enter information on the wrong line and have to start over again. We had interviewed three dozen women (as well as ten girls who were clearly underage and would not participate, another three or four women, who "walked the streets" we would register but not promote). We had to file all of the information we had gathered. Hereafter, the London-based firm, Exotic Adventures would handle all matters in Bishkek.

I hadn't received a response to my e-mail outlining my proposal. I didn't expect to get an immediate response from Exotic Adventures but Lou usually would shoot back an e-mail response right away. Lou went with his gut instinct, and both his gut and his instinct were marvels to behold. I asked Miguel why Lou hadn't replied. His response was ominous: "Lou may be waiting to see how Exotic Adventures reacts. Or, he may want to ream you out in front of all of our small staff, make an example of someone who violated chain of command by going over his boss's head and sending that pernicious e-mail to one of our clients without Lou's approval. Or he may be researching different sorts of Inquisition-like tortures—no blood but lots of pain. Or he might combine several of these options or employ all of them."

"Thanks for the words of consolation, Miguel."

"No problem. By the way, are our plane tickets already paid for?"

"Yep, paid for and nonrefundable. Why do you ask, Miguel?"

"There is another option. Lou could leave you here without your ticket home. But, since the tickets are already paid for and are nonrefundable, he won't use that option."

"Just then Zamir burst. "You guys work fast, got all paperwork finished in one day. Now you have time for fun, a hike through along mountain trail. I can book you a guide. You know sometimes foreigners get lost in snow and ice."

Miguel whispered to me, "Maybe Lou has arranged things with Zamir. We'll get 'lost' in the mountains and never return."

"Say, what you guys talking about?" Zamir asked.

"Just talking over options," I responded.

"Oh, you want to stay in town and 'date' sexy ladies? Well, I can arrange that, too."

"We'll go on the hike," I shot back.

"Good, good, I arrange everything and go along for the ride, no. I know an expert guide. He knows where you can see our famous snow leopards, very rare experience to see snow leopards in the wild. So, he has binoculars just in case we can't get close. All good?"

"I pick you two up early, before sunrise, six am or maybe a few minutes later. That way we can be on the trail for sunrise, beautiful sight. Sun's rays hit the glaciers and all is one big sparkle. Beautiful"

"All good," Miguel and I responded.

The next morning we got up in more than enough time to get ready for the day's adventures. "What time is it?" Miguel groggily asked, simultaneously yawning.

"It's four am local time."

"I can't sleep," Miguel sighed. "I guess I'll get up and get an early start. What time is Zamir going to pick us up?"

"Six or a little later. My guess is a little later. I'm going to write Rachel."

"Sort of like your last will and testament," Miguel quipped. "Maybe I'd better do the same and text Yolanda."

But I had underestimated Zamir. He rang for us promptly at six. He and the guide sat in the front seat, while Miguel and I awkwardly made our way to the back. Zamir steered us through the snow packed streets expertly. When we arrived, at our starting point about an hour later, it was still dark. A wooden cabin stood at the base of a huge mountain. Our guide led the way to a large wooden door. A fire heated and illuminated the inside of the one room cabin. "Eat, eat," commanded Zamir. "You will need lots of energy, burn calories on the ascent."

"We're not climbing to the top, are we?" Miguel asked. Even in the darkness of a pre-dawn faint light, we could tell that the mountain loomed up to the sky.

"No, no, we climb maybe a third of the way up and then walk a winding trail all around the mountain and come back here at maybe one o'clock. Then have lunch, then go back to hotel."

Any of our misgivings were dispelled by the first streaks of light that hit the icy glaciers at the upper ranges of the mountain. The white snow-packed trail led us around at first lofty pine trees and then shorter and shorter ones until towards the end of our ascent, all we could see were a few branches of scrub growth sticking out from the snow. After a two hours' hike, our guide motioned for us to sit low and peer across a ravine about a quarter of a mile away. He took out his binoculars and so did we. There, just across from us, we spotted a snow leopard stalking some unseen prey, paws placed gently and slowly on the snow. Then he turned and looked at us fixedly. When we finished the hike, Miguel said he thought the big cat was warning us to stay away, that this was his prey to stalk. As for me, I thought the cat's eyes were boring into my brain with the one-word message: *Here.*

Our guide rose slowly and turned our small party of four back on the trail. Soon we would be heading home.

CASSIE

We survived the hike and the tedious ride home. But there was nothing tedious when Rachel texted me while I waited at the Moscow airport. "Cassie's had an accident." It was 8:30 am Moscow time, so that means the accident must have occurred sometime around 10:30-11:30 the previous night. I felt so useless. I texted back, "Is Cassie OK?" and the response shook me even more. "I think so. She's being checked out right now in the emergency room. I'm hoping that she's more rattled than hurt." I hoped so, too. Our flight wouldn't take off for another four hours, so I all I could do was sit and wait and worry.

"What's wrong, Luke?" Miguel asked as he put his hand on my shoulder. "You look like a sitting statue of Death, all pale and eyes staring off into never land. Did Lou text you?"

"Cassie's had a car accident. I don't know much else right now, and there's not a thing I can do except sit here and wait and worry."

"Here, I'll get you some coffee." Miguel strode off to the coffee kiosk. I think he just wanted an excuse to let me deal with my grief. We all assume day-to-day that everything's under control. "I've got this," we say. But we don't. We deceive ourselves with frenetic activity. Still, a little self-deception now and then may be our only hope. But here I sat, thousands of miles distant, still in shock. In a few minutes, I'd shake myself free and pull myself out of that deep pit of self-pity. Then maybe I could come up with a plan of action although Rachel has probably covered over her worry, sorrow, and grief by handling all the details. She'd need some support later when she could do no more. Miguel brought back a cup of hot, steaming coffee. I thanked him and took small sips. He knew that anything he would say would be utterly meaningless, too weak to crash through that wall of worry and grief that had shut me in. Sometimes, it is better not to say anything, and right now this was one of those times.

Thirty minutes after take off, on the flight from Moscow to New York, Rachel texted me again. "Cassie has some really bad bruises and broken ribs from the impact of the air bag. Other than that—and that's bad enough— she's OK. She was coming home from a basketball game, the District championship game, when a drunk driver ran a stoplight and smashed into her. The whole driver's side of the car is smashed in. The paramedics had to get Cassie by going through the passenger side. The drunk driver must have been going incredibly fast as there's not much left of the car. Maybe it can be fixed or maybe it will be totaled. Cassie's resting now and will be released tomorrow. She was so scared she'd be crippled for life—and so was I. At least there's no question about whose fault the accident was. Apparently, the police hauled off the drunk, who had no idea of what he had done. Love, Rachel."

"Can I Facetime Cassie when we land in New York. I've got another layover there? If not, I'll text you."

"OK, what time will that be?"

"Around two in the afternoon."

"That'll work. Cassie should be released from the hospital around 11:000 am. They're just making sure she didn't have a concussion or any internal injuries. The SOB was going so fast that anything was possible."

"Will your daughter be all right?" Miguel asked. He had a daughter of his own, about David's age. Soon she would be driving.

"She should be OK. Looks like bruised and broken ribs. It must hurt like hell, though.

"You know, Luke, I have a daughter, too. Soon enough she'll be old enough to drive. And I've got to admit, that thought scares the hell out of me. But Cassie has no permanent damage, right?" I nodded. "Still, I bet she finds it hard to breathe with all the bruising and cracked ribs. That's plenty bad enough."

"Yeah, it is."

"How is your wife taking all this?"

"Right now, I think she's so wound up with taking care of Cassie that she doesn't have time to worry. That will come later. As for the car, I don't know."

When we landed in New York, I called Cassie Facetime. She was home now. "Dad, I never want to drive again. It hurts to breathe and my face is all puffy and purplish-blue. When will you be home?"

"I should be home around nine pm. Miguel said he'd give me a ride home, so Mom won't have to come and get me."

"Good, I just want all of us—Mom, you, even David, and me—I want us to be together. It hurts to breathe."

" Don't talk, Cassie. We will be together sooner than you think. Get some rest now. Love you."

"Love you, too."

After the shock had worn off—in the near future Cassie should be back to normal and not want to have anything to do with me or her younger brother—so for that I was thankful. Then my mind drifted back to Leila, the Kyrgyz girl about Cassie's age. What if she did come to America for a relationship with some guy she had just met? I don't think she could drive a car and we are such a car-dependent society. What would she do if her parents and uncles and aunts and cousins weren't around? I didn't and still don't know. Maybe she's got her reasons for wanting to leave her society. Maybe she's got the notion that all Americans are rich. A lot of people from other countries think that and to a certain extent we are relatively rich, but every day we're also skirting the cliff of disaster. The car accident could have had much worse outcomes. I might get canned and be out on the streets desperately trying to get another job and just when Cassie and David need the most financial help I could muster. Cassie will be going to college and David will be starting high school. Even if Cassie's car gets totaled, we won't get enough money to find her a comparable replacement—not with the cost of used cars. I thought that we're all just a slip away from falling off the cliff.

When I finally arrived at my hometown airport and picked up my luggage, I wasn't quite sure what to expect. Miguel still offered to give me a lift home, but Rachel texted me and said everyone wanted to come pick me up. My stomach was still churning although at a much slower rate. Time may heal broken bones or bruised bodies, but it doesn't necessarily heal matters of emotion and spirit. Still, I was overjoyed to see Rachel and David. "Where's Cassie?" I asked, a bit nervous that I hadn't heard all of the details about her injuries.

"She's still in the car, too embarrassed to expose her bruised face to public gawking. For now at least Amanda can keep her company. So, how does it feel to be back here with only your family, far, far away from all those Kyrgyz Kuties?"

"Great! You wouldn't believe all those forces that drive those women— some of them still girls—to leave their homes and go to America or some other distant land. Did I tell you I saw a snow leopard in the wild? On the last day we had some free time, so we hiked through the mountains with Zamir, our contact man in Bishkek, and a guide. It was amazing." I thought my best recourse lay in changing topics, keeping my work among the romantically (but mainly financially) starved Kyrgyz women to myself.

"Dad, did you get a shot off?" David asked.

"Nope, no guns. Snow leopards are protected at least legally. Besides, I don't know of any recipes for snow leopard."

"Dad, very funny," David replied. "So what did you eat, McDonald's?"

"If there were any McDonald's, I didn't see any. It's true that those fast food joints are almost all over the world, except perhaps for Antarctica, but, no, we ate mainly mutton."

"What's mutton?" David asked,

"It's sheep meat, David. We've had lamb before."

"Does it taste like a hamburger?" David wanted to know, as inquiring stomachs are prone to do.

"Not exactly, it can sometimes be a little tough. It all depends upon how it's cooked. Most of the people in Kyrgyzstan don't eat pork. They're Moslems."

"No bacon?" David asked, genuinely shocked.

"In the Russian and Chinese restaurants and shops, there's pork, even some bacon in the hotels that curry to foreigners, but that's all."

David was still trying to take in the idea of a world without bacon. "Well, David, if food prices keep going up, there won't be much bacon in our household either." Rachel told him rather matter-of-factly.

"Does that mean we'll be eating that mutton stuff?" David asked, still worried.

"No, right now at least around here, mutton costs even more than bacon," Rachel added.

"Oh, good, good" David said softly, relieved that for the moment at least, he wouldn't have to change his diet.

We soon made it to our car. Rachel had decided to use the short-term parking lot once Cassie had said that she wanted to stay in the car. She was snuggling with Amanda, who had sensed that Cassie, like a hurt puppy, needed some hugging. Amanda had placed her head in Cassie's lap with her forepaws extended out on either side. When I saw Cassie, I had to hold myself back from saying anything other than "I love you." Cassie's nose was still swollen, her eyes still encircled by purplish-blue bruises, even her lips remained puffy. It must have been hard for her to speak. She just nodded in response and mumbled, "Thanks, Daddie."

I knew she was hurting once she said "Daddie"; she hadn't called me that in years, content with the monosyllabic Dad."

Here Rachel broke in, probably because she didn't want Cassie to speak too much. "Cassie has been great through all this. She's a lot tougher than you might think. The hospital staff in the emergency room told me that. The drunk who hit Cassie was charged," Rachel, explained. "But he has no insurance, so I don't know what's going to happen next. We've got coverage for uninsured motorists, but I'm not sure how long it will take us to get any money. Apparently the other driver spends all his money on booze. He doesn't have any insurance and apparently any money to speak of. At least Cassie will be back to normal in a few days."

"Thank God for that," I concluded.

"Even David has been nice, taking special care of his sister. It's sweet to see them together, David fussing about and waiting on Cassie, who is at least enjoying some unexpected attention."

"They're great kids. We're lucky to have them," I commented.

"So, you're not going to leave me for some nineteen year old Kyrgyz Kutie?" Rachel asked pertly.

"Not a chance."

After we got home and got settled, I took Amanda out for a walk, explaining. "I need to stretch my legs after sitting all that time in airplanes and airport lobbies. I won't be gone long."

"Luke, leave your cell phone here," Rachel added.

"OK, why?"

"So, you won't be making any phone calls to one of your Kuties."

I took Amanda out into grey, overcast skies, that kind of late winter purgatorial day. I looked up into the skies and mumbled something about "A cold rain coming." Amanda must have sensed the coming weather, too, as she quickened her pace. She never did like rain and even the scent of coming rain upset her. "Well, it'll be a quick walk, no time for Kuties. I wish Rachel wouldn't feel any jealousy. But then I thought it over, using the walk-in-another- person's shoes technique. What if the tables were turned—to lapse into yet another cliché—and Rachel had to interview dozens of men for a Huge Hunks of Honolulu or something? Wouldn't I be in a slow jealousy-fueled burn? Yeah, I would." Amanda looked up at me as if she were sensing that I had fallen into one of those thinking holes—like the astronomer who had so lost himself in gazing at the stars that he had fallen into a fertilizer pit, make that a shit pit." Here Amanda paused and deposited her own version of fertilizer, which I dutifully scooped up into one of the biodegradable poop bags. I guess in the end we're all just fertilizer or maybe not. I thought about my buck. He lives on in memory and maybe more than that.

Exasperated that I wasn't paying more attention to her and to the cold pellets of sleet and rain falling from above, Amanda shot me a glance that said, "You fool, we need to head back home where it's warm and comfy. I'm ready to curl up on your bed and take a little nap."

When we got back home, Amanda and I entered through the garage so we could dry off first. Rachel was reading an article on breast cancer. I guessed she was just doing some in-service training, Cassie was talking on the phone, and David was playing some video game in which he could fantasize being Ronaldo and scoring hat trick after hat trick. The whole scene lulled me into a sense of calm and complacency. "Maybe it's the lull before the storm," I mused.

I took a quick trip down stairs to check on my buck's skeletal remains—at least the ones I had retained. Opening the box, I had hoped for some insight, but all there was nothing so dramatic, just blank, hollow eye sockets and jawbones closed tight—no message, no nothing. Not even some mystical, ambiguous pronouncement that I would be likely to misinterpret. Utter silence.

But then Rachel yelled down the basement stairs. "Luke, get up here. Your boss is on the phone and he doesn't seem to be too pleased. What went on there in Bishkek?"

My heart was racing when I picked up the phone. Instantaneously, my ears were blasted by Lou's screaming. "Get your ass into the office early tomorrow morning. We need to talk. You've got one hell of a lot of explaining to do."

I sat down at the table and supported my head with my right hand, my fingers drawing furrows along my forehead.

"Luke, what did happen in Bishkek?" Rachel wanted to know and she had every right to know.

I told her that I had sent an e-mail to Lou and to his counterpart at Exotic Adventures in London. The e-mail had explained my idea of PARTNER: Proud, Adventurous, Rooted in Tradition, Noble, Enigmatic, Regal. I explained to Rachel that I got the idea after interviewing a Kyrgyz woman of Russian descent. "Sophia is a professional, an engineer. She's divorced and wants nothing to do with some sleazy Buy-a-Bride scheme. But she would entertain some correspondence with a man, even a foreign one, who shared some of her same values. She said that 'First we talk, then we write, then maybe the man comes to Bishkek. Then we meet and see how it goes. If all goes well, then who knows what will happen.' Then I talked with young women—I think some of them were really girls—from the countryside. Did you know that the custom of *Ala Kachuu*, bride kidnapping, is still around. Sometimes it's all arranged by parents, but sometimes not. Anyway one young woman from the countryside not much older than Cassie, Leila explained that she didn't want to be sold like sheep. that she would welcome the chance to talk, write, and meet a man who would value her for herself. That's why I jettisoned Lou's whole Kyrgyz Kuties idea and dashed off the e-mails. I couldn't live with myself if I hadn't."

"No, I don't think I could live with you either if you hadn't. Do you think Lou will get over it?"

"I don't know. Maybe the only way he will depends upon how Exotic Adventures likes the idea. If they do, we're safe. If not I've got to go job hunting"

"Maybe you should start doing that now, just in case." Rachel was right. That night I started by updating my resume. "I wonder if I'll need a head-hunter?" I asked myself. And then I thought of that skull downstairs.

KAREN & CAMERON

I got to the office fifteen minutes earlier than I usually did. I expected to find the place empty as I was almost always the first one there. Not this time. Karen and Cameron were seated smugly and comfortably at their adjacent desks, busily pecking away at their computers as soon as they sensed that some other person was entering the workplace. Perhaps they had decided to come in early and do some actual work. Probably not, as both had the most fatuous, thin smirk on their faces. They both shot me a perfunctory glance and then riveted their attention to whatever it was they were typing. For the first time I took a long look at both of them. Cameron had a boyish look, a forty -year -old's boyish look. He had a clean-shaven face although I'm not sure he ever had to shave. He sported what used to be called a Princeton haircut, hair clipped reasonably short on the sides with just enough hair on top to comb over. He always wore long-sleeved shirts and, if he followed his usual habit, had on tan slacks with matching brown shoes. I couldn't tell as he was sitting down, but I have no reason that he had drifted away from his long-established uniform. Beside him, Karen sported a Cleopatra style hair do and, as far as I could tell, never deviated from that style. She customarily wore pant suits without any accessories, not even jewelry —no rings, no earrings, no bracelets, no necklaces, nothing else but monochromatic pant suits: yellow on Mondays (such as today), orange on Tuesdays, red on Wednesdays, blue on Thursdays, and black on Fridays. She dreaded and hated Fridays, the end of the workweek, since, as far as the rest of us in the office knew, she had no life other than work, which really wasn't work at all but a time to gossip and revel in other people's misery. Well, all right I was exaggerating and feeling sorry for myself. However, none of us—and that includes me, Miguel, Tony, and Lexie—could figure out just what the duo did other than write memos with the salutation "Hey, gang."

Lou thundered in next, slamming the door as he bellowed, "Luke, get your ass in here, pronto." I did, but only after exhaling and whispering a prayer as I made my way over to Lou's lair. Karen and Cameron made a show of not making a show, their eyes riveted to the keyboards in front of them at least as long as they weren't sneaking furtive glances at me. I imagined the two sneaking over and gluing their ears to Lou's door once I had closed it, but that effort wouldn't have been necessary as Lou was screaming so loudly that his words and curses and ridicule echoed even in the hallways that led to our office space.

"Just what the hell were you thinking? I send you off on an all-expense –paid trip to exotic Kyrgyzstan to interview lovely ladies and you turn the whole thing upside down by some dumb-ass moral crusade. All you had to do, dumb-ass, was to interview them to get some ideas on how to promote Kyrgyzstan Kuties. That's it. Here you go and come up with some dumb-ass PARTNER acronym and act as if you're on some damn relief mission, some kind of crusade or something, to help these gals." Here Lou stopped to catch his breath, but he was far from finished. "And then to top it all off, you go over my head and e-mail the whole lame-brained idea to our client, Exotic Adventures. First principle of work: Don't piss off the boss by going over his head. The second principle is: Have your resume ready because you're going to start a job search if you do something as dumb-ass as piss off the boss. You've been around long enough to know how it goes. Just what the hell were you thinking? Don't answer that. I don't want to listen to any bullshit explanation. Get the hell out of here."

I did an about-face and took two paces towards the door. Just as my hand grasped the handle, Lou ended his rant by bellowing. "The only reason I didn't fire you yet is that I haven't heard from Exotic Adventures yet. Once I do, I'll tell them that the dumb-ass who came up with the idea is, as they say, 'no longer with us.' Maybe, just maybe there's an outside chance that they won' think you had been drinking too much of the local joy-juice Ciao, dumb-ass, and don't bother me."

When I opened the door and strode out into the office air, I glanced at both Cameron and Karen, who both sat at attention, their eyes fixed at the screen in front of them and their fingers frenetically pounding away at the keyboards in front of them They both made their point with a thin, tight-lipped grin that told me that they were having the time of their lives hearing me getting reamed out by the boss, their near and dear relative.

By this time, Miguel had walked in as glumly as I had. He, too, was beckoned with Lou's peremptory command. "Miguel, get your ass in here, pronto." Miguel, too, exhaled, and probably whispered a prayer. "Miguel, what the hell were you thinking? Why the hell didn't you stop Luke from gumming this whole job up with some dumb-ass PARTNER idea?"

"Lou, I did my job. I got you photos."

"And the only reason I'm not canning your ass is that the photos are so damn good that I'd want to hire one of those Kyrgyz Kuties for myself. All right, get the hell out of here. At least we've got some damn good photos for Exotic Adventures. We can always get somebody to write the ad copy and the ad copy that I want. Stay away from Luke while you're at it. He's gone psycho or something."

Miguel exited and immediately ignored Lou's advice. "Look, Luke, I'm sorry."

"You've got nothing to be sorry about. Lou was right: you did a great job on those photos. You always do. As for me, I took a chance. Maybe it was stupid, maybe not, but I'm the one who did and no one else."

"Still, Luke,"—

Here I cut him off. "Don't worry about it. As they say, 'It is what it is.'" The rest of the morning resembled a picnic in which people looked up every few seconds at the dark clouds hanging above. Everyone exchanged seemingly pleasant glances, but their eyes told a different story. People were waiting for the thunder to roar and the rain to drench them. Clearly, the whole crew wanted to gossip while Lou sat secreted in his private lair and I was trying hard to conceal my own fears by working frenetically. So, at lunch I uncharacteristically left and let Miguel handle the thousand questions that none dared ask me, starting with, "Just what happened in Bishkek?" Of course, I had no way of knowing precisely how Miguel handled the questions, but from the responses I got when I returned from my uncustomary lunch break, I got a general idea. I owe Miguel.

"No good deed goes unpunished," Tony tried to console me.

"Here comes our Don Quixote," Lexie added.

"Thanks, I just did what I thought was right," I replied. Miguel must have embellished our story a bit. At least, he didn't try to throw any blame on me. But we all realized that Lou and his small company needed this contract with Exotic Adventures. We needed any contract we could get. No one was being coerced. The women who agreed to "correspond" or "date" relatively wealthy men did so of their own free will. But what choice did they have? Being kidnapped or living with a drunk or just living a lonely life. Well, we're all lonely in our own ways. I need to pause here. Yeah, we're all lonely in our own ways, but that doesn't mean we live in isolated cocoons. Sometimes we have to extend beyond ourselves. Maybe that was what my buck had done moments before his death. "Here" he said or seemed to say. What that cryptic one word meant eluded my feeble mind. I don't know. All I can do to live with the consequences of my own decision.

Then at 3:30 I got a call from Rachel. "I've got to go," I told Miguel as I hurriedly left the office. I'm sure I gave Karen and Cameron something to gossip about for the rest of the afternoon.

"Sure, no problem, Miguel responded. "What's wrong?"

"It's Rachel. She needs me right now."

"Oh, no," Miguel moaned. He must have known what was wrong.

When I got home after a drive that saw all the images of our life together flashing by: the first time we met, our wedding, the birth of Cassie, and then the birth of David, all the holidays we spent together, that visit out West to hike along the Colorado trails, all our lives. Thankfully, traffic was light that early as I was more than a distracted driver.

When I got home, Rachel was sobbing. "I should have known, I should have known. I work with cancer patients for forty hours a week. Now I'm one of them." I tried to hug her, but she was too absorbed in her grief. Then with red swollen eyes, she turned to me and said, "Luke, I've got a small lump in my breast. I've got a biopsy scheduled in a week. That's the soonest I could get one. But I know, I know the results. They may as well schedule a mastectomy now. But the biopsies needed for the insurance. What are we going to do?"

"Rachel, what do you tell your patients?"

"I know the routine by heart. But now the words seem to be just dust in the wind blowing through a desert. I'll be all right. Just give me a minute. What do we tell Cassie and David?"

"The truth. That's what you'd advise your patients. They'll figure it out soon enough, but we need to sit down and discuss it with the two of them. Is there any chance that Cassie will eventually face the same problem later in life?"

"We won't know until we get the biopsy results. I already had a mammogram and from the results I knew I'd need a biopsy."

"When did you have the mammogram?"

"Last week, I didn't want to worry you."

"But don't you routinely have a mammogram?"

"Yes, but this time I knew there would be a problem. I was just hoping I was wrong."

Suddenly, my issues at work seemed to be sucked down a dark hole. But all we could do was wait.

I didn't even sound enthusiastic when Tom called. He contacted me twice a year: at the beginning of deer season and at the beginning of turkey season. What many people don't realize, especially about turkey season, is that most of it consists of a lot of waiting. It's true, we sound out a lot of turkey calls, but mainly we wait. Rain or shine, we mostly wait for the turkeys to come in range.

DAVID

That night, Rachel and I sat down with Cassie and David and explained as best we could what my wife, their mom, would be facing. David's reaction stunned us. "A guy in my class told us that his mom had breast cancer. He said she had an operation that left her with tubes sticking out of her sides and then she had chemo and radiation. He said she cut her hair real short right before she lost all of her hair and started wearing scarves and turban-like stuff as a hat, so she wouldn't look too weird. He said she got a little sick from the chemo but then got some medicine so she wouldn't heave. But now she's all right and back to being a mom again. So, I guess we can help out a little and things will be OK in the end."

"So, David, you know all about it?" I asked. As I think back, I realize that my reply was more than stupid. Maybe I had prepped myself for some kind of semi-grand father-knows-best kind of explanation. I shouldn't have shot back that smart-ass question. David was doing his best to think that there'd be some hard times not only for Rachel but for the whole family. I guess I was being a little too self-centered.

David's reply to my question showed only how stupid I was in asking it. "Well, I don't know everything, just the big things. I know we'll all have to help Mom get through all this. It sucks."

Cassie didn't say much. I wonder if she had been wondering if she were in store for a similar fate when she was older. After a lull in the conversation, she finally broke down and almost begged for an answer. "But, Mom, you did everything right. You don't smoke; you hardly drink any alcohol at all except maybe a glass or two of wine every now and then.

You exercise. You're not fat, at least not for your age. It just doesn't seem right."

Rachel started to laugh. "Well, Cassie, I'm glad that you don't think I'm too fat for someone of my advanced age. You're right, though, about the risk factors. But that's all they are: factors. Even if a person avoids all of the risk factors, there's no absolute guarantee that a woman won't get breast cancer. Obesity and drinking alcohol can increase your chances of developing cancer, but that's all we know. Despite all of the advances in medicine, we still don't have all of the answers. Our best educated guess is that a complex mix of genetics and environment can cause cancer. What that mix is we don't know."

"Mom, did your mom ever have breast cancer?" Cassie asked, apparently fearing the genetic factor. She was downcast, nervously shuffling her fingers.

"No, my mom didn't. One of her sisters did, though, but you never met that aunt. The majority of people diagnosed with breast cancer don't have a family history of the disease."

Cassie still didn't find that very consoling. So, Rachel continued. "There is a blood test to detect whether or not a person carries the BRCA gene, but let's say the test results come back negative. If they do, great, but you may still end up with a cancer diagnosis later in life. There's no absolute guarantee. But we do have excellent treatments. They're no fun, that's for sure, but the mortality rate—the death rate—has really gone down over the last twenty years. So, it's super serious, but it's not a death sentence. Maybe by the time you're as old as I am, we will have come up with even better treatments. Do you feel any better now, Cassie?"

"I guess so. It's just a lot to take in all at once."

"Well, we'll take things one step at a time. That's all we can do."

"I guess for once my younger brother David is right. All we can do is help you get through all of this."

At this comment David seemed pleased with himself, a thin smile breaking across his face. For once, he was no longer just the meddlesome, mischievous younger sibling. He was starting to grow up—but only starting. He was still a boy.

And I was still an employee just hanging on to my job. I had to admit that it would be far less painful to get another job than it would be to undergo cancer treatments. Still the next few days at work sped by quietly. Lou stayed sequestered in his office; the rest of us went on with our work or with gossip. I wondered if Karen or Cameron were hoping to replace me. "Not a chance," Miguel reassured me. "Then they'd have to work. Come on, we've got to the promotions out for the boat show coming up. Everybody's focusing on the future and the end of the winter doldrums."

Miguel was right. I'd just have to handle the immediate tasks at hand, and let the whole Kyrgyz thing slide for a moment. Apparently, we still hadn't heard from Exotic Adventures. Whether that was good or bad, I didn't know.

At home, Rachel was prepping for the biopsy, but she thought the results would be a foregone conclusion. " Luke, I can handle the biopsy thing on my own. It's no big deal, and I am almost positive I know the results. If I'm right, and I'm sure I am, I'll need lots of support for the double mastectomy that will soon follow. If you have to take time off work, save it for then." So, Rachel faced the biopsy alone. "I won't get the results until after the weekend, so all we can do for now is wait."

On Saturday morning, I took David to a tryout for a select soccer team. He had played well for the local church team, so he thought he might have a chance to play at an even more competitive level. I guess the tryout at least took our minds off a situation neither of us could control. And David was acting so uncharacteristically considerate that he was driving Rachel crazy. "Luke, in the kindest way you can, just let David know that I'm not dying at least for a while. Let David be David and annoy his sister and me in his own patented way. Please, take him to the tryout if for no other reason than to give me some peace of mind."

So, on Saturday morning, off David and I drove. The soccer park fields lay only about a twenty or thirty minute drive away, but David wanted to get there early. It was a blustery late winter day with a few snowflakes blowing in the wind. Before we left, David reluctantly donned the sweatpants both Rachel and I told him to take along. "You can take off the sweats as soon as you finish warming up," we both told him.

"Mom, Dad, none of the other kids will be wearing sweats over their shorts. I'll look like a wus."

"Put them on before we leave. If we get there and none of the other players are wearing sweats, you can take them off in the car so no one will know. It'll just be a secret between the two of us." I replied, trying desperately not to show any desperation.

Rachel gave David her best and hugged him before we left. When we got in the car, David commented that, "The two of you treat me like a baby." Once again I held my tongue. In some respects, David acted older than his years but in others younger. Since traffic was so light at that time of day on a Saturday morning, we arrived early. "Can I take the sweats off now?" David whined.

"Wait until you see the other player." In ten minutes other cars filled the parking lot and out of these vehicles jumped boys aged twelve to eighteen. Most of them sported matching green sweat suits with the logos of a white leopard leaping. The older boys, almost young men, also had their last names on the backs of their sweats. These older boys soon began stretching, still clad in sweats. The younger ones followed suit. David sprang out of the car door, yelling simply, "I've got to go." So, off he went. He knew most of the stretches already but not all of them. After ten or twelve minutes of stretching and an easy run, the boys, including David, took off their sweats. At first David looked around. He was one of about five new boys who didn't sport the green warm-ups. Soon the boys formed impromptu circles of six with one boy in the middle for a keep-away drill. David found his age group and joined in. Because the other boys already had played for the Leopards the year or years before, David was designated "It" for the first round. The first three or four passes deftly eluded David. But he soon caught on, intercepted a pass, left the center, and joined the circle while the player ignominiously assumed the role of "It." Then the whistle blew, and one of the coaches swiftly formed scrimmage squads. The coach, a slim older man of perhaps forty—he had closely cropped white hair—didn't have to assign positions as the experienced players immediately assumed them. He then gave out sheets of paper with a number on it. Each new player was instructed to pin that numbered sheet on his back. David drew number three. The odd numbered players were assigned to one squad, the even numbered to the other. "You there, number three, what's your name?" David shouted back a response, perhaps a little too loudly as a few of the experienced players were stifling a laugh. "OK, David, Number Three, play left wing fullback." David filled that spot.

As soon as the other players got their assignments, the coach blew another whistle and the scrimmage began. At first, David felt lost as he didn't know how his teammates played. He sent one errant pass that the opposing squad intercepted. David recovered, tackled the opposing player cleanly, and delivered another pass. This one, a blast that switched the play from the left side to the right, almost screamed as it blew across the field As the scrimmage proceeded, David played his usual steady role, nothing spectacular but a solid, error-free performance. After thirty-five minutes, the coach sounded his whistle three times to indicate a break in the action. Then he shuffled players around, but he kept David as the left wing fullback. At the beginning of the second half, David stole the ball from the opposing winger, and raced down field until he drew ten yards away from the penalty area. The opposing goalkeeper raced out to meet him as David had outpaced the opposition. Then David blasted the ball towards the right upper corner of the goal. It just missed, barely skimming over the top of the crossbar. Even though David didn't score, his wide smile indicated that he felt he had made his point. So, too, did many of his teammates, who yelled out, "Great play."

After another hour of play, the coach blew the whistle and called all of the boys in a huddle. Here he made an announcement loud enough so that parents and other spectators on the sidelines could hear him. "You all did a great job. I'll post the names of those who made the team on the bulletin board next to the concession stand. Nobody is a loser here."

But the boys knew better. He'd carry only eighteen boys on his team, maybe nineteen. Twenty-three had tried out. Seventeen of those twenty-three were veterans from last year's squad. All of the veterans had played well. They knew each other's moves beforehand, so passes cruised along on target. The newcomers—the ones who weren't donning the green sweat suits of experienced players—hung their heads as they had already guessed their fate. Nevertheless, they hung around, still hoping that there might be a chance that they had made the team. David beamed as one of the veterans, slapped him on the back and said, "You've got it made, bro. Nice play."

But, when the coach posted the results. David's name was missing, so were the names of four of the five newcomers who had made the trip out there on a dreary, blustery early Saturday morning. He was crushed.

"Dad, I don't get it. I played better than I ever had. I almost scored. I didn't screw up except at the very beginning. It isn't fair."

Any consolation I could offer would seem lame, just another adult cliché that offered little consolation. Then I took a second look at the roster. The only newcomer who made the squad was a goalkeeper. The coach would clearly want to have a second keeper on hand in case the first-stringer got injured or otherwise couldn't play. So, I offered this consolation. "David, did you notice that only one newcomer made the squad and that kid was a goalkeeper?"

"Yeah, so what?"

"All right, put yourself in the coach's shoes. He needs two keepers, right?"

"Right," David mumbled.

"And he knows the other players, right?"

"Yeah, again, so what?"

"So, would it be easier to cut an experienced player or a newcomer?"

"Yeah, Dad, but that's still not fair."

"No, it isn't, but that's the way it works. You know Michael Jordan?"

"Yeah, well he got cut his sophomore year of high school. But he didn't quit."

"Who said I was going to quit?"

"David, most of the time all you can do is your best and just face whatever comes your way." I think both he and I were thinking the same thought. Rachel had done everything right, but she still came down with breast cancer. Maybe that was some of what my buck was telling me when I heard that word "Here." The oracle might portend life as well as death. I didn't know.

Still, in the back of my mind, I was wondering what we'd do if I got "cut" from work.

RACHEL

The weekend following the biopsy found all four of us acting like clumsy ballerinas dancing around the one issue that concerned us the most. Cassie shut herself up in her room, claiming that she had work to do on an English paper; David went outside when it wasn't pouring down an early spring / late winter rain and practiced his ball skills. As for me, I acted overly solicitous, fetching Rachel coffee and offering to do the weekly grocery shopping. "Thanks for the offer, Luke, but you'd probably buy all the overpriced stuff we don't need. I'll take care of it. I'm still able-bodied, you know."

I fumbled around for a response, fully realizing that it's possible to be too helpful, to kill or at least wound with too much kindness. So, I mumbled something stupidly noncommittal like, "I guess you're right." Instead, I went outside to bother David as he was juggling the soccer. Cassie had already told me that she didn't need my help on her English paper. She could do it all herself, thank you. When I could see that David was just letting me "help" him as a filial duty, I went downstairs to once again look for some answer as I opened the wooden box and stared at my trophy / nemesis / relic. I recalled that many Native Americans prayed to the spirits of those animals they had killed for food. They would pray, asking forgiveness as the death of one being was necessary for the food of another. So, I begged forgiveness. I don't know if I was a fool or a heretic or just a man seeking answers to those forces he couldn't control.

I have no idea if my prayer was answered or even if my prayer was heard or made any difference. I went up the stairs and looked at Amanda, who seemed to have some canine sixth sense and knew the worry that was afflicting her so-called owners. We went for a walk, as the weather was still deciding whether it would look back to the cold of winter or to the warmth of spring. Amanda knew our usual walk, so in reality she was walking me and not vice-versa. She stopped to sniff some of the first sprouts of jonquils and daffodils that were popping into the open air. Maybe I read too much into that simple act, but I felt as if the dog was teaching me that out of the death of winter emerges the beauty of spring and new life. While that thought might have been consoling on some grandiose scale, in the microcosm of my world it didn't offer much consolation. What if the biopsy turned out to be positive? What would we do? Rachel felt she already knew the answer and I feared it. I knew what she would do. She'd follow procedure and prepare for the surgery as best she could. I'd help, of course, but other than that I felt lame and useless. What would the kids do? Cassie must fear that the same fate would await her even if her mother had advised her that most breast cancers are not hereditary. As far as our medical knowledge has come, we still don't know so much. And David must wonder, too, what it would be like to have a life without the person who had nurtured him from birth. Maybe he'll be a bit more empathetic to the boy in his class who had lost his mother. Maybe. I don't know. Then I started feeling sorry for myself, wondering how I'd fare as a single parent. At this point, Amanda stopped sniffing, turned to face me, and shot me a look that seemed to say, "Get on with it, man. And whatever happens, happens. Don't feel sorry for yourself. Just accept your fate and help Rachel and the children as best you can. There's nothing else to do."

Of course, there was nothing else to do—except question my own sanity. Talking to the skull of a deer and to my pet? I must be crazy.

On Monday morning, I walked into work, early as usual and soon lost myself in a thousand minute details. Miguel came in next, soon followed by Lexie and Tony. They all seemed shy about intruding on my thoughts. Finally, Lexie came up and asked if we'd need any help. I responded that we wouldn't know anything, at least not until late afternoon or tomorrow. "Don't be shy asking for help, you know, if you need it." She patted me on the shoulder and left. Miguel said he'd cover for me if I had to get some time off and so did Tony. Even Karen and Cameron wiped those customary fatuous grins off their faces. "Did everyone know?" I wondered. Did Lou know? I dreaded going into his office and asking for some time off if the biopsy results thundered that ominous word "Malignant." I might as well be proactive and ask for some consideration in advance if I were to need it. So, fearing the worst, I e-mailed him and asked for an appointment. In such a small office, normally e-mailing Lou for an appointment wouldn't be necessary. Lou was out and about the office so he could keep abreast about our progress or lack of it. Lately, though, Lou strode into his office, not looking at any of us but intent on getting past us and secluding himself in his private office.

Lou responded immediately. "Sure, come on in." When I knocked twice on his door, he bellowed, "Get your dumb-ass in here." That wasn't exactly the tone I wanted to hear, but Lou continued, still poring over the spreadsheets in front of him.

"Look, Luke, we both know why you're here. You're gonna ask for some time off if you need to help Rachel, right?" I nodded a "Yes." You're still a dumb-ass, but I'd be a worse dumb-ass if I didn't let you. I just want you to know that I'm doin' this not for you but for Rachel. She's a nice lady. How in the hell she married you I'll never know. But what I said before—about canning your dumb-ass if we lose that contract with Exotic Adventures—still holds true. I haven't heard anything from those guys. Whether that's good or bad, I sure as hell don't know. I know that you've got some of the best people in the world pulling for you. Lexie, Tony, and Miguel all volunteered to take on some of your workload if you need the time off. But right now you don't know anything, right? So, get your dumb-ass back to work."

I slowly opened the door and walked even slower back to my desk, thankful that that burden was at least off my mind. I went up to everyone in our office—to Lexie, Tony, Miguel, and even to Karen and Cameron—and thanked each one of them. Still, how could word have spread so fast?

Late Monday afternoon, Rachel called me and let me know what she had already foreseen: the tumor was malignant.

Several more weeks would elapse before the bilateral mastectomy. The exact number of weeks I forget, for they all coalesced into one experience. When she wasn't working, Rachel busied herself with making sure that Cassie and David were well taken care of and with preparing for her recovery. She told David and me to bring the recliner in the family room upstairs to our dining room. "I'll have to sleep in the recliner until the drains are out, and that will be anywhere from one to three weeks. I'll also need a few shirts that button in the front. I can borrow some of yours, Luke, but I think I'll have to buy a couple closer to my size. I'll need a shower seat or maybe I can get by with that old stool we have downstairs. No, I'd better get one with sidebars so I can steady myself with my hands. Oh, yes, and a shower apron. I might have to content myself with sponge baths for a few days; but, as soon as I can, I want to shower. Otherwise, I'll just feel so dirty. Don't you agree, Luke?" I wanted to say, "Whatever you say," but I held my tongue and just nodded assent to the rhetorical question. "Since Cassie can drive, I'll take her grocery shopping so she can learn how to save a little money. We will be OK, financially, Luke, won't we?" This question almost floored me as my stomach, heart and soul almost dropped to the floor. I turned away so that I wouldn't betray my fear. "You said that Lou is so understanding that he'll let you take some time off while I recover. Now that's the advantage of having such an understanding boss. Not all bosses would do that." My mind was spinning: how close to that deep precipice of being unemployed was I? "Well, I'll put in some extra hours—the hospital is short on staff--- and get some overtime, just in case, you know."

And so it went. Cassie felt so grown up when her mom took her grocery shopping and taught her all of the tricks of the trade. "Some sale items, advertised as twenty percent off aren't really sale items at all," Rachel explained. "Be sure to look closely at the cost per unit. And there's no sense in buying in bulk if you have to throw away a good portion of the food because it spoils before you can cook it. Look over the ads. Sometimes you really can find a bargain. But, if you buy something just because it's on sale and then don't use it, you're just throwing money away." Unfortunately, I couldn't offer much advice to David, who would assume a few more duties while his mom recuperated. I don't suppose that showing him how to load a dishwasher for maximum efficiency counts for all that much.

On the day of the surgery, Rachel and I got up early. We really hadn't gone to sleep as we tortured ourselves by constantly staring at those red numbers beaming at us from the alarm clock. Cassie got up with us. She wanted to go, she explained, so that she would get a better idea of what to expect if "You know, later on I have to undergo this." David would go to school because there was nothing he could do other than wait through an operation that would take four to six hours. Rachel had decided on reconstructive surgery so she could still wear a swimsuit and some of her other clothes. She had heard stories of how "falsies" would suddenly pop out and she wanted none of that. Before we left for the hospital and waited in the car for Cassie to join us, Rachel asked me, "You'll still love me, won't you Luke?" I thought of responding for "better or worse" but I checked myself. Rachel was feeling bad enough already, so I just leaned over and kissed her on the cheek and said I'd always love her. Cassie joined us and off we went. We all pretended that we weren't worried even though we all must have had that terribly empty feeling in our stomachs.

Just before Rachel went to surgery, Cassie and I kissed her and told her we loved her and then an orderly wheeled her over to a surgery "It's so cold, "Cassie said.

I hazarded why. "It's to reduce the risk of infection." Even as I said that, I reflected that surgery has to be cold emotionally. To cut into a person requires intense focus on the task, a focus so intense that to do it, you must rein in all distractions—even emotions. This point became even clearer when the surgeon walked, introduced herself to me and then checked yet once again with Rachel to make sure she was having a bilateral mastectomy and then used a marker to outline the incisions. I thought of the old carpenter's axiom, "Measure twice and cut once." I kept that comment to myself. I've learned to suppress most of the first thoughts that come to my mind. While the surgeon discussed some more matters with Rachel, my thoughts wandered over to a passage in *Lord of the Flies*, the one describing the enormity of that first blood-letting. Even a pig on some remote island is a living, breathing, animate being. Then I envisioned once again that majestic buck, whose remains I kept not only in my memory but also downstairs. He exuded a majesty that I still can't fathom. I had to admit that I knew so little. Then I wondered what life would be like without Rachel. How would Cassie and David fare with a single parent? But, I had to shake myself free of such thoughts. Right now, I just had to support Rachel as much as I could. Just before the orderlies and nurses wheeled Rachel into surgery, I kissed her and told her I loved her. Then I took small steps back to the waiting room where I had another job to do.

Cassie hadn't been allowed in the pre-surgery room, so she waited anxiously and tried to distract herself from all the thoughts that tumbled through her mind. She had brought her physics book and dabbled a bit at solving some of the problems she had been assigned to make up for missing the class. She hadn't solved any of them. So, then we hugged and waited. Finally, out of boredom, we both simultaneously and somewhat reluctantly took out our laptops and began to work. Cassie had her physics homework, and I e-mailed Tony, Lexie, and Miguel about promoting a boat show and then in another month a car dealership's tent show. All three of them were kind enough not to ask about Rachel; they knew it was too early.

At eleven o'clock, Cassie and I broke the monotony of just sitting in the surgical waiting room and slowly found our way to the hospital's cafeteria, where we ate something, not much, to supplement the apples and snacks we had brought. The cafeteria food wasn't bad; it was just cafeteria food. Rachel had advised us to eat healthy and not pour quarter after quarter into the vending machines. "That stuff is so loaded with preservatives that it would last for several centuries," she warned us. And we both laughed as we recalled the caution. Then Cassie laughed even more when she told me that she and David appreciated the bag lunches that Rachel and I had prepared for them. "Dad, do you remember back in fourth grade when David cried because he forgot his lunch and had to eat the school food—they mystery meat fried hard as a hockey puck and watery apple sauce?" I replied that I still remembered. So, then Cassie asked, "Dad, you still take your lunch to work, don't you?" I once again nodded and Cassie paused for a moment. "Maybe life is just a succession of bagged lunches." We laughed again and walked back to the waiting room a little faster than when we had left it.

Time passed slowly, once again as I just sat and stole glance after glance at the clock. "When will Mom be out?" Cassie asked, once again worried.

Almost on cue, the surgeon walked over to us. "You must be Cassie, she said. "Your mom is so proud of you." Then she turned to me so she could address both of us. "Rachel came through the surgery well and is in Recovery. You may see her briefly once she is moved to her room. She's a strong lady."

So, we waited again, only this time without as much anxiety. I texted David, who might be on his lunch break. He was. "Mom's doing well and is in the Recovery room. We'll see her in an hour or two." In his usual laconic manner, David typed back, "Good." That's all he replied, but maybe that's all he had to reply.

Despite all of the preparation that Rachel had done, the recovery proved more difficult than the surgery. The drains, in particular, proved to be a strain physically and emotionally. "I feel like a freak," Rachel moaned, "like some kind of alien insect-thing with multiple arms or legs or whatever." I helped in whatever small ways I could. David kept asking, "When will those tube-things come out? When will Mom be Mom again?" Finally those dreaded tubes did come out. But that wasn't the end of the recovery.

Rachel still had chemotherapy and radiation to undergo. She had prepped herself for the expected nausea of chemotherapy, but the anti-nausea pills spared her the worst of that agony. She even joked that at least she might lose some weight. But radiation proved a different matter. "I feel as if I'm being burned alive," she lamented after the first round. "But I'm still kicking. Here I am."

And she was stronger than ever. I wished I had her strength. When she said, "Here I am," I thought back to my buck.

AMANDA

With Rachel recovering, I assumed most of the responsibility of walking Amanda. Cassie or David would sometimes take Amanda out, but they had become immersed in all types of adolescent distractions to assume what they might regard as a burden. Cassie did, though, do the grocery shopping and did so responsibly, checking prices and staying within the boundaries of our customary food budget. And she did this even though David constantly tried to persuade her / goad her into making additional purchases of such items as Deli meats and candy sweets. David did some of the housework, such as vacuuming, but rather reluctantly and slovenly. He soon adjusted, though, when Rachel ordered him to do the whole job over again and not just run the vacuum over the central corridors and forget the rest. So, we had established a new house order and routine. . I tried to help Rachel out as much as I could, but she was determined to shower on her own and to attend to as many household tasks as she could, explaining that I did a half-ass job of folding the laundry, a statement that I couldn't deny. In reality, I knew that I looked forward to an excuse to get out of the house. Walking the dog became a bit therapeutic for me. I suppose that's a bit selfish of me. Besides, putting myself in Amanda's place, I realized how I would react if I were restrained so that I couldn't go to the bathroom more than twice a day, once in the morning and once at night. So, I wasn't totally selfish in wanting to walk Amanda as much as I could.

In reality, though, Amanda took me for the walk. She knew our customary path so well that the leash seemed superfluous except when another dog ventured into what Amanda had considered her turf, that is, the entire neighborhood. Or when a squirrel ventured a little too close to us. As a puppy, Amanda had pulled hard against the pressure of the leash so that she could break free and pursue the squirrel up the tree. She soon learned that Nature had imposed certain restrictions: dogs can't climb trees no matter how hard they try. So, now Amanda had matured and yanked me only when some forgetful squirrel scurried out too far from a tree and could be viewed as fair game. And then there were the molehills, tunnels of upraised dirt that she would sniff intently and, when the smell of mole became too strong, she would dig furiously, intent on a quick kill. Most of the time her frenetic mining ended in nothing. She would take another deep breath and realize that the mole, as well as the squirrel, had its safe zone. Still, the predatory instinct remained strong even in so domesticated a being as Amanda, who could lounge for hours, content to be petted and informally groomed. Sometimes I even thought that she was the one holding the leash, leading me around to wherever she wanted to go as my mind wandered aimlessly in a thousand different directions.

Amanda wasn't the only predator who led me around. Lou was still fuming at work as I retreated up some metaphoric tree or down deep into the earth like Amanda's squirrel and mole. Taking advantage of a few days off from work, I put in my eight hours plus at home as Rachel was recovering from surgery. But after a few days, Rachel told me to go to work. "Luke, I'm not an invalid, so stop treating me like one. Besides, your version of keeping things clean differs from mine. When you do something, I just have to do it all over again. So, do what you do best: fix the meals, walk the dog, keep the basement and garage from becoming toxic waste dumps, and go to work." Later, when Rachel was undergoing chemo and radiation, I drove her to the first few visits of chemo, but she soon tired of me and insisted on going alone. She stressed once again that she was no invalid and needed some time to take care of things on her own.

So, I went back to work, pretty much on the same schedule as I had before. And pretty much on the same schedule as before, Lou would bellow at me. "Dumb-ass, why the hell is it taking Exotic Adventures so long to cancel their contract so I can fire your dumb-ass? They must be concocting some exotic ways torturing you for being such a dumb-ass. You know like ripping your entrails out, stretching you on the rack, hanging you until near-death and then when they got tired of flogging you, delivering the final blow of beheading." Lou must have been keeping me around so he could indulge his sadistic fantasies. But, despite his bombast, my best bet is that he couldn't bring himself to fire me when Rachel was so sick. Besides, the company was enjoying a lot of black ink and profits were rising. The boat show had gone well. Tony had seen to that. Lexie had coached a roofer and a plumber so well that their TV spots on the local station attracted some notice and brought us several more clients. As always, Miguel had mastered all of the technical details so well that all went flawlessly—even when technical problems arose and they often did—Miguel could address the problem and fix it. As for Karen and Cameron, well, they remained where they always were seated, pecking away at the keyboards, doing who knows what. The office was running so smoothly that I had something else to worry about: becoming superfluous and, therefore, disposable. I wondered if Rachel felt the same way at home. Perhaps that's one of the reasons besides my unsatisfactory job performance that she insisted on being as independent as possible. So, I worked harder than ever, became even more scrupulous than ever. In short, I was becoming a pain in the ass for everyone. Miguel took me aside, and offered some friendly advice. "Take it easy, man. You haven't been fired and the longer we don't hear from Exotic Adventures, the better it is for you. Hell, Lou will keep you on as the designated whipping boy if for no other reason. You're driving the rest of us crazy with your over-the-top exactitude. You're not only dotting *i*'s and crossing *t*'s; you're measuring precisely the size and placement of the dot and the cross. You're under a lot of stress. We all get that. But you're wound so tight, you're gonna spin off the table and collapse on the floor."

So, I took Miguel's advice and the next Saturday after David's soccer game, I took Amanda for a stroll in a nearby park. A chilly, blustery late winter / early spring wind, combined with high humidity made it seem colder than the forty degree temperature, but Amanda could have cared less. She was in her element, enjoying a thousand (or more) new sniffs. As the trail wound past a playground, she stopped every few feet to add her drops of urine to that of other canines in a form of instant olfactory messaging. How dogs could exercise that amount of control over their bladders amazed me. She seemed to know just how much to add at each spot. When I go, the stream flows until its reservoir empties. Maybe I lack the self -control. I know I lack that heightened sense of smell. Maybe humans and dogs bind because they complement each other. Humans' greater stature gives them an expanded range of sight while canines'—built lower to the ground—utilize their greater sense of smell to become aware of realities that humans overlook. The playground remained empty probably because of the bone chilling cold. Still later in the day when the sun would rise higher, I felt sure that some parents would take their young children out. As the trail wound past the playground, Amanda paused to mark less frequently either because fewer dogs ventured beyond the playground or because she had already emptied herself of all that she could. I didn't know and never would. So, we ventured on, just skirting the perimeter of a lake. The waters, ruffled by the wind, exercised a strange invitation. They appeared both alluring and threatening, especially since only a few trees had begun to recover their leaves. The landscape still retained winter's grasp: stark and bare tree branches above and below brown and yellowish vegetation. So, we continued for a quarter of a mile or so. Then the sky broke forth with a majestic sight. A bald eagle soared overhead and blew past us only some thirty or so yards ahead of us. Amanda and I both froze in fascination. Then the eagle swooped down and carried off some careless fish and carried it to its tree house on the other side of the lake. The eagle's nest was so huge that Amanda and I could have curled up inside it and still have had room to spare. Every year the nest grew larger. Another predator, we thought, and nodded in its presence.

We moved on. The trail meandered away from the lake's perimeter and wound into the woods. Here Amanda lowered her head and took small intense sniffs, obviously picking up the trail of some creature. An onlooker of my age or older would have laughed to see the two of us. We must have appeared like the intrepid Elmer Fudd and his trusty Fido, bumbling their way in pursuit of the "Wascally Wabbit." I guess in many respects, I was an Elmer Fudd, blundering my way through a maze resolutely, but deceived time and again by that old trickster. After forty yards or so, Amanda lost the scent or lost interest in it. So we marched on

As the trail wound deeper into the woods, we passed a low lying area where a thin sheet of ice still blanketed the pool. A large tree trunk, probably from an oak tree that had fallen, lay in the pool. All around, there remained the brown and blacks and grizzled yellow reminders of winter except for a small mound that rose on the far side of the pool. A lone dogwood tree broke the darkness with a sprinkling of a scattered few white blooms, all the more intensely white because of the winter's darkness that still framed it. We stopped or I should say I stopped to take in the scene.

Amanda was pulling in the opposite direction and pulling hard. She had sensed the presence of some prey and the old predatory instincts rose in her. So, we doubled back in the graceful winding of the trail until my eyes spotted what Amanda's nose had detected. A huge buck had approached the very edge of the trail. He had long since lost his antlers, but he still stood majestic and aloof. He turned to look at us casually. Then, assessing that we posed little threat rambled back slowly into the deeper woods as if we mattered little to him. When Amanda had been younger, such a sight would have triggered her hunting instinct, but over time she had grown more cautious. She sensed that any show of aggression—a loud bark, a galloping headlong attack—would be futile for two reasons. First, a human held her by a tight-fisted rope and would not unleash her; second, even an antlerless deer posed a threat. If attacked, the buck would rear on its hind legs, ready to shred a lone dog to shreds with its front hooves. That's why canines, whether dogs or wolves or any other of that kind-- even rifle-less humans-- would attack in packs. The front attackers would distract the quarry while others would come from behind to cripple and then kill. Nature can be very cruel as well as majestic. This time it was majestic.

The remainder of our walk served only as an anticlimax to what we had seen: three awe-inspiring visions: a dogwood bursting out in its first bloom of the year, an eagle soaring and in the sky and then swooping down into the cold waters, a lone buck reigning as the uncrowned ruler of the woods. We had been blessed.

When we returned to our home, all seemed normal and unmoved. Cassie was on the phone, David was watching a Premier League soccer match on TV, and Rachel was working remotely from home. Soon she'd return to work full-time; she had already gone in for a few hours to keep abreast of things but still wasn't strong enough to work directly with her patients. As I entered, Rachel advised me. "Luke, you had two phone calls while you were out with Amanda. Lou called and then so did Tom."

"Thanks," I responded, my heart dropping below my knees. "I'd better get the worst out of the way first and see what Lou wants. The voice on the other end of my call fumed with a slow burn. "Listen up, Luke. Are you hiding something from me?"

"No," I responded a little too loudly.

""Well, you damn well better not be. I couldn't get any sleep all night wondering why we still haven't heard anything from Exotic Adventures. Are you positively sure you haven't heard anything?"

"Absolutely positive, Lou."

"All right, but, once you do, you let me know. I don't care what time of day or night it is. You call me, you hear."

"Will do, Lou."

"What was all that about, Luke?"

Still reluctant to cause Rachel any more worry, I replied calmly—or at least tried to. "Oh, Lou's having one of his periodic rants. That's all"

"Just a periodic rant, huh? That's all."

"Oh, the whole Kyrgyz thing is still rattling him. It takes time to do international business and he's eager for an answer."

"Well, Luke, you're good at a lot of things, but there are two where you aren't: first, you're an abysmal liar and second you're not exactly an expert in international business after one trip overseas."

I turned and gulped. Rachel was right. I wondered how much she really knew.

So, I changed topics. "I'd better return Tom's call."

"You do that."

I punched in Tom's number. "Hey, old man Luke, are you ready?"

"Ready for what?"

"Don't give me that BS. It's time for turkey season, bro. Let's get with it."

TOM

─────────◆─────────

I hadn't forgotten about the coming turkey season; the thought of it just had to take a more distant place in the remote corners of my mind. But Tom's call rerouted me a bit. Rachel was still undergoing chemo but had avoided the worst of the side effects so far, claiming that the early stages of pregnancy had been much worse. For all of the advances in medical procedures, we could be thankful. Still, the treatment regimen was imposing. She had only two more sessions left before she would begin radiation and was strong enough to return to work and resume some household duties. Since she complained that I at best did a half-ass job of keeping the floors clean, she assumed that duty. She also hated the way I made the bed—perhaps I was still reacting against the stringent regime of boot camp some twenty odd years ago. My sergeant also complained that I did a half-ass job of making my bed. At least I didn't have a colonel come by and in disgust pick up the mattress and throw it at me as one hapless recruit in another unit had experienced. I have to confess, though, that that story might well have been apocryphal, part of military folklore. Still, the gist of it contained some truth. Some people, including me, just don't have a knack for certain types of mundane chores. Now as for cleaning the toilets, there I shone, but I'm not sure that's much to boast of. In any event, Rachel was gaining strength every day and didn't enjoy any part of being a semi-invalid. She might have even welcomed me being gone for a morning or two over the next few weeks.

Turkey hunting differed from deer hunting in several ways. Both involved a lot of sitting and waiting, but turkey hunting demanded perhaps a little more patience because it required more "seat" time although I'd never say that to a deer hunter who would sit for hours in a tree stand. In deer season, we all donned some hunter orange, so we wouldn't become the object of an over-eager hunter shooting before he or she had clearly seen a deer. In turkey season, we'd wear a bright orange hat out to the spot we had picked out but then don camo outfits to try to blend in as well as we could because turkeys, even "tom" turkeys are extremely wary and sensitive to any outlier in the environment. And then there's the matter of noise. During deer season, we'd steel ourselves to silence and try as much as possible to remain downwind of our prey. In turkey season, we'd try to "call" the tom turkeys in by using friction calls, which mimicked the sounds hens make: a yelp, a cluck, and a hen cut. The yelp consists of five to six notes of an "ee-yuk" sound; the cluck, well, sounds like a cluck; and the hen cut resembles a kind of Morse code like cluck. Tom, that is Tom as in my hunting partner not as in tom turkey, had worked out a rotating arrangement in which we'd take turns calling in a gobbler: the one making the calls would let the other one take a shot should a gobbler get called in. Once a hunter had claimed his daily limit of one, then he would be the caller so that the other guy could also fill his tag. The arrangement worked out fairly well over the years although there were some years when only one of us bagged a gobbler and other years when neither one of us did. Perhaps that's good because lately turkey populations haven't been as robust as deer populations. Many deer hunters shoot at one hundred yards, sometimes more, but turkey hunters must wait until the gobbler is forty yards or less away. Beyond that distance, any shotgun blast is far more likely to wound a bird if it even does that. No true hunter wants any animal—deer, turkey, even a squirrel—to suffer. I know that some people claim that hunting is cruel and barbaric, but so is killing any animal, and killing at a slaughter house is no less cruel and barbaric as cows are hammered on the head into oblivion.

Hunting may seem to some to be more cruel and barbaric, but I think it is even worse to distance oneself from the killing. We have all bought packaged meat in the supermarket. Sure, there's a little blood left, but not that much. We then see a product, not a living, breathing animal. When we view the meat as only a product, a commodity, we distance ourselves from it. And, when we do so, we devalue it. Many Native Americans would pray for forgiveness to the spirit of the animal that they had killed for food; they would take one life to sustain another. That's not barbaric; it's simply a practical necessity. Nature exists in a delicate equilibrium. Kill too much prey and you will kill yourselves in the process. When we don't recognize the lives of the animals we eat, we devalue them and assume a displaced arrogance. We humans may be at the top of the food chain, but it's just that, a chain. Any break in the links affects the whole chain. No doubt, there have been and unfortunately still are instances of outlandish killing for the sake of killing: killing to extinction the passenger pigeons that at one time filled our skies, driving our native bison to the brink of extinction just for the convenience of the railroads, slaughtering rhinos just for their supposedly aphrodisiac horns, and far too many other instances of killing for the sake of killing. Hunter and hunted are not all that different from each other, but sometimes we overlook that and indulge ourselves in fantasies of humans being different in kind and not only in degree. We all—humans and animals-- depend upon each other. Not all of us need to be hunters, but all need to recognize the lives that once were when we eat our processed hamburger or rotisserie chicken. Maybe that's why I still treasure the skull and antlers of "my" buck and keep them locked away in my basement.

On the morning of the first day of our hunt, I picked up Tom at 3:30 am on Saturday morning. Before I left my house at 3:15, I kissed Rachel lightly on the cheek. She briefly awoke and surprised me with a simple statement. "I'm glad of one thing," she whispered, still half asleep.

"What's that?" I asked, totally expecting some response such as "I love you" or "Miss you." I'd be home for lunch as the best time for hunting usually starts at daybreak and ends around ten in the morning. Still this would be the first time I left Rachel home by herself on the weekend.

"Instead, she whispered something totally unexpected. "I'm glad we live where we do."

"So am I," I added, still puzzled by her statement. "Why do you say that?"

"Because if we lived in a state where it'd be legal to use electronic turkey calls, you'd have to bag two turkeys a year for fifteen years straight to even break even on the cost. Those electronic gizmos start at $300 and the cost goes up from there. Have fun and take your boots off before you come into the house."

"Will do," I chuckled. Rachel had anticipated any argument that my hunting put meat on the table. If it did, it'd be awfully expensive meat. The permits, the camo clothes, the turkey seat, the shotgun, all those costs add up. No, I was hunting for the sport of it and for that chance to once again reconnect with a Nature at once cruel and kind.

With those thoughts still simmering in my mind, I picked up Tom at 3:30 a.m. and off we went, cruising through the mostly empty streets and then the somewhat busier Highway 44. At this hour, many but certainly not all truckers had pulled off the road for some rest. Still, we began the typical leapfrog game, passing trucks on the uphill and then being passed by trucks on the steep downhill. For the first twenty minutes of our ninety- minute drive, Tom was dozing. Then he blurted out, "Hey, Luke, you stopping for some breakfast?" Of course, this really wasn't a question but an indirect way of declaring that we would stop for breakfast. I would have preferred to keep driving, but stop we did, but only at the drive-through window of some fast food joint. "Hey, Luke, aren't you ordering' somethin'?" I shook my head but then added that I'd probably order a small coffee. "Yeah, have it your way. As for me, I'll be chowin' down on the Big Breakfast."

"Tom, if I did that, I'd end up spending half my time peeing and pooping."

"Don't worry. I've got you covered."

"How's that?"

" I brought along tons of huntin' TP, you know, the biodegradable stuff."

"That's good to know, Tom. We've got about another hour to drive before we stop. Will that give you enough time to finish off the Big Breakfast?"

"Plenty. Hey, do you got some extra ammo. I left mine at home."

"Yeah, I've got a few spare shells. Take three. We'll probably need only one each."

"Awesome. Back to breakfast."

Of the crowd who went deer hunting in the fall, only Tom and I did the spring turkey hunt. You couldn't shoot more than one turkey a day, so we'd spend two consecutive early Saturday mornings on hunts from about dawn until ten. If we hadn't had any success and the mosquitos weren't too bad, we'd stay until the end of the hunting day, one p.m. Then we'd pack up and return. The only downside to the spring hunt was the likelihood of rain. We had spent many an hour sitting in the rain with our ponchos on, just waiting and trying to call in a gobbler. Still, the woods exerted a strong pull in the spring. Vegetation remained still a little sparse. In two months, the woods would be overgrown with all types of low bushes, but now the forests seemed to glow with all types of spring wildflowers and blooms: white-flowering serviceberry, wild plum, flowering dogwood and hawthorn, pink red bud, and others. Of all the blooms, I'm drawn to the dogwood the most, but by this time in the spring only a few dogwoods still retained their brilliant whites. After we parked, we'd still have at least a half-hour trek through the woods through the darkness of the predawn sky. We carried flashlights, but we had traversed this same trail for many years. Still, it took us closer to forty minutes than to thirty to reach our favorite spot. I guessed that maybe age had been creeping up on us.

We set up our spot and donned our camouflage outfits to blend in with the woods as much as two lumbering middle-aged guys could. "Hey, Luke, how do I look" asked Tom. He preferred to use face-paint over a camo face covering because, he claimed later in the morning he'd get hot. Actually, I thought Tom did so because of a boyish glee in painting his face. Most adults shun getting their faces painted even at fairs or other festive events (with the possible exception of Halloween), but most children up to a certain age can't wait to sport a face all decked out in multi-colored paint. Adults and teenagers will apply paint only under some other pretext like the black paint would reduce glare or, in this case, help to conceal oneself in a hunt or in combat. By six am, we were ready to start the long, sometimes tedious process of calling in gobblers and then just waiting.

As Tom was still digesting his over-sized breakfast, he volunteered to act as the call guy first. For all of his shortcomings (almost as many as mine), Tom was one of the best yelpers you could ever find. He could emit an "ee-yuck" sound that would bring in any lascivious tom turkey in a quarter mile radius. After fifteen minutes a gobbler, hazarded into shooting range, about thirty yards away, but I couldn't get a clean shot until he had cleared a stand of oak trees that stood between us. So, Tom yelped away.

By now the gobbler stood a little more than twenty-five yards distant and in range for a clear shot. I fired and the once strutting male lay prostrate on the ground. I soon did a quick field dressing and tagged him.

Since the blast from my twelve gauge had probably scattered any remaining gobblers in the area. We traveled on to our second spot, about a half -mile away. For that march, we both sported bright orange hats so that no overeager hunter would mistake us for turkeys moving through. In forty minutes we had reached our second hunting spot. Here I yelped and clucked and made that cut sound for over an hour before a gobbler strutted into range. Tom took two shots to finish the bird. By then our killing session had ended. We had taken our daily limit. Tom was exultant. "I've got me a young tom, great for frying. As for you, Luke, well, you'd better slow cook the old bird you got for a long, long time." I nodded in agreement and thought that at least Cassie would be happy. She loved slow-cooked wild turkey although for some reason she hated venison. Maybe the turkey reminded her of Thanksgiving.

We went again the following week, but all we did was wait and sit in one of those heavy April rains for three hours before we gave the hunt up. As for me, I was grateful that I could still look forward to a warm Saturday night meal—unlike many previous generations who would have to make-do with spinach and turnips and maybe some early strawberries or other early ripening plants. "Well, I could stand to lose some weight," I consoled Tom. He agreed. Still, the hunt was disappointing. Nature had no guarantees. Maybe that's why we treasured our brief moments of victory so much.

On that Sunday evening, I got another indication that there are no guarantees outside of Nature as well. Lou had dashed off a curt e-mail" "We've got an answer from Exotic Adventures. Come to the office early on Monday. We'll talk."

I went down to the basement to visit the relics of my buck. "Sooner or later, I'll be joining you, my friend," somewhat melodramatically trying to console myself. I didn't dare tell Rachel or the children what I feared had happened—not yet. There was still an outside chance. Maybe.

LOU, REVISITED

That Sunday night I couldn't sleep, not even succeeding in making a pretense of it. "What's wrong, Luke? The way you've been tossing, turning, getting up and then jumping back into bed, you must have been doing some kind of wacko cardio workout."

Figuring that Rachel already was weighed down with her own burdens, I didn't mention anything about work, just the usual BS about a churning stomach, probably caused by too much hot sauce on the meatloaf. I couldn't be convincing, not even to myself. Rachel guessed it immediately. "Troubles at work?" I nodded. "Sorry to keep you up. I may as well get up and get dressed and let you sleep. "Luke, it's two, fifteen in the morning. Can't you at least get a few hours of sleep in?"

"OK, I'll try again." I did lie down, but all I did was to stare at the red numbers on the alarm clock. 2:15 took an eternity to pass into 2:16. The transition from 2:16 to 2:17 was just as excruciatingly slow, but I figured that I'd at least have to wait until Rachel had returned to a sound sleep before I could slip out of bed and shower. I'd use the basement shower to remain as quiet as I could. In less than ten minutes, Rachel had transitioned from a light doze to a deep sleep, so I gently pulled back the cover and sheet, swung my legs to the floor and eased out of bed. Slipping on my robe, I ever so gently headed downstairs, with Amanda giving me a brief glimpse as she wondered about the strange behavior of humans. By stealth, I had secured a minor victory. Sometimes we all have to take delight in whatever victories we can secure.

The downstairs shower consisted of a small area curtained off from the rest of the basement's grey concrete floor. David used it when he came back from a soccer game all splattered with mud and I used it when I returned from a particularly muddy hunt. We also used it to clean off shovels and other tools besmirched with dirt and grime. But, most of the time we used it to bathe Amanda, who would occasionally take great pleasure in rolling in the mud. She didn't do so often; but, when she did, she did so well, coating herself from snout to tail. Right now anxiety, not mud, had coated me from head to toes. So, that basement shower seemed the perfect place to wash away my troubles for a few moments at least. Since the shower rested only a few steps away from the box that housed my buck, I thought I'd take a look. The skull had that bleached white look of dried bones—no worries there. The antlers opened up as if they embraced me. "Great," I reflected after a few seconds, now I've gone from anxious to insane." But I hadn't, not really. I took my shower in peace, dried off quickly, and then stepped slowly upstairs. "What will be, will be" didn't offer much consolation, but I'd have to accept what I couldn't change. I went back upstairs and eased myself back into bed as if nothing had happened. Sleep came easily now, only to end when the alarm blasted.

"See, Luke, you did get back to sleep. You almost always wake up a few minutes before the alarm and turn it off. Today the alarm beat you to it. I guess we both better get up and dress for work if not for success." Rachel hadn't missed much work lately. As soon as she had regained enough strength to work with patients, she was back on the hospital floor. She lamented the fact that sometimes she'd have to call for help if the strain of moving a patient was just too much. She had to leave early for some of the radiation treatments, but no one begrudged her that concession. In fact, most of her colleagues covered for her if she just couldn't do a job that she had done easily prior to the surgery. Soon she'd be requesting time off in the morning to get in her radiation treatments. Still, Rachel preferred to work. "If I stayed home, all I'd do would be to worry."

So, I'd have to go back to the office and, as they so often say, face the music. Rachel was right. No sense in worrying over what you can't control. I wondered what tune Lou would be singing—probably some heavy metal blast.

As had happened earlier—but doesn't happen often—Karen and Cameron had beaten me to the office and were dutifully pecking away at their computers, all the while exchanging "knowing" glances at each other. Something in between a smirk and a gloat. Clearly they had sniffed out something. So, I trudged over to my desk and did the only thing I could do: finish the ad copy for a local plumbing company. Maybe plumbing is what makes us human. It's hard to create much of a civilization without good plumbing to bring water in and sewage out. I wondered if the history of civilization is really the history of plumbing. I thought back to *Lord of the Flies*, where the beginning of the end of civilization starts when boys got caught short and fouled the drinking water. "Oh, well, I guess I can expect some foul language flowing from Lou's mouth."

But Lou strode into the office without a word to any of us. This behavior could portend either good or bad, but probably bad. I e-mailed him since he had slammed the door to his private office and gave the impression to all of us that he didn't want to be disturbed. And he wasn't. Around ten-thirty, he responded to my e-mail request for an interview. Lou's message was both cutting and curt: "Get your dumb-ass into my office ten minutes before lunch."

"So that was how he was going to handle it," I guessed. "He's going to fire me just before lunch so I can clean out my desk during the break and leave before they all return from their break. No fond farewells, no final handshakes, just be whisked away." I fell into a deep self-pity, which I disguised by intently focusing on my work. If Lou wanted to can me quietly, I'd honor his wishes if only to save me some embarrassment. The thought of Karen and Cameron smirking as I left the office in disgrace motivated me to at least act stoically. Still, why did I care what the undynamic duo felt? The real test of character would come when I had to face Rachel and Cassie and David and own up to my failure. Amanda might not mind. I'd be home more to take her on walks. Perhaps there'd be an outside chance that I could turn the tables around and get another job, perhaps an even better one with a better salary. Still, Lou had gone out of his way to let me work at home so that I could offer Rachel more help when she needed it the most. Maybe he, too, was floundering around, trying to figure out how to salvage the business he had put so much time, energy, and money into. Well, in the end, we're all just floundering about. We all might think of ourselves as invincible and immortal, but we're not. And, in case we delude ourselves into thinking otherwise, we get curt reminders of our vulnerability. Maybe that's what my buck was telling me. So, in the end while pretending to work doggedly all morning, my mind was churning around hundreds of thoughts, none of which centered on the work I was supposedly and outwardly doing.

Periodically I'd steal a glance at the clock that hung just above the exit door, an act totally pointless. My laptop gave me the time, calibrated perfectly right up there in the upper right hand corner. All I had to do was just barely glance at it while I continued the ruse of being the ever-faithful employee. For some reason, that time listed on the computer lacked the gravitas of the old, outdated, oversized behemoth that hung above the exit door. In any event, the minutes ticked away into hours, and at eleven-fifty, I exhaled and whispered to myself, "This is it. My judgment day has come. What am I going to tell Rachel and the kids?"

Still, I kept up appearances, stepping over to the door to Lou's private office as nonchalantly as I could. I knocked twice. A gruff voice answered. "Get your dumb-asss in here, Luke."

So, I did. "Sit down. I need to finish up reading this contract before we talk." Down I sat, and there I waited for perhaps two minutes although the delay struck me as lasting two eternities.

Finally, Lou set the papers down and wrote something down. Glancing up at me, he said as matter-of-factly as he could his judgment. "Well, dumb-ass, you stumbled your way into not getting the ax. Their Board of Directors thrashed through your ideas and then, in the end, decided to adopt the broad outlines of your plan. I got a call and an e-mail last night that confirmed the call and had an attachment that outlined their new contract with us. It seems that they really like your idea of linking the dating business to their whole exotic adventures business. Even if the romance didn't work out, they could still offer some lonely guy an adventure of a lifetime, one that the poor slob would never forget. You also won over two members of their Board--a woman and a man—who had previously objected to the very thought of going into the Buy-a-Bride business. There's just one change they want to make."

Loosening my rigid posture in the chair, I almost slumped but asked nonchalantly, "What's that, Lou?"

"Well, in that whole acronym thing--you know—the PARTNER business—they wanted to change the *E* to *Exotic* to work in a link to the title of their business. So now, that acronym *PARTNER* stands for "Proud, Adventurous, Rooted in Tradition, Exotic—not Enigmatic--, and Regal.

Their Board accepted the whole proposal as outlandish as it may seem. It took 'em a while, but they handed us a new contract, a little fatter than the initial one. I got the call last night when it was early morning in Bishkek as Exotic Adventures sent someone there to complete the details with some Kyrgyzstan officials. Zamir sends you his best wishes probably because he's going to cash in on the deal, too."

Assuming the whole ordeal was over, I started to stand up.

"Sit down, dumb-ass, I'm not finished. Don't get too cocky. You owe a lot to two Kyrgyz ladies, Sophia and Leila. Sophia—she's the one with the Russian background--right?"

"Right."

"She contacted Exotic Adventures and said you and Miguel treated her so professionally. She had gone to another dating service before and they had treated her as little more than a whore. She said you two guys made her feel at ease that this wasn't some sort of international human trafficking thing. She also said she wouldn't agree or even listen to any other dating agency. You owe her, Luke. Without her letter, you'd be out on your ass. You owe her at least a letter."

Once again, I started to stand up.

"Sit down, Luke. There's a second lady you've got to thank, Leila. She's the native Kyrgyz one, right?" In response I just nodded yes.

"Well, she also wrote Exotic Adventures. I guess she had Zamir or someone fluent in English help her. Anyway, she thanked you and Exotic Adventures for offering her the hope of escaping something called All Cashews."

"It's called, Ala Kachuu, Lou. There's a movie about it."

"No kidding. Well, anyway, when the Board of Exotic Adventures read her letter, it was a moment, as they say, that became transformational. Instead of exploiting women, the company could save them. The real truth probably lies somewhere between exploiting and rescuing. Anyway they then become sold on the whole idea with only that minor change from *Enigmatic* to *Exotic* that I told you about."

For the third time, I started to stand up again, and for the third time, Lou bellowed in a tone at once both gruff and pleased. "I've got more to tell you. They said if I ever got tired of seeing your dumb ass that you could move to London and work for them. Well, they didn't really say

179

dumb-ass—only I can do that. But they did throw in that offer. Now I suppose I'll have to give you a raise or something. Now, get out of here and enjoy a lunch on me. Here's a gift card to just about anyplace you want to go. As for me, I've got to think of a way of rewarding Miguel. He took some great pictures. I guess you two were on the same wavelength, huh."

This time I stood up to accept Lou's gift card. My brown bag lunch could wait until tomorrow.

"Luke, before you leave, tell Miguel to see me after lunch."

"I'm on it, Lou."

As I reached for the door handle, I was having second thoughts. I knew that Karen and Cameron would have zeroed in their vision on Lou's door the millisecond it swung open. As I look back, I suppose I was being petty, but I couldn't resist. I sculpted my face to conceal my glee. Instead, I hung my head low and rubbed my forehead with my right hand. Stepping slowly, ever so slowly, I made my way over to Miguel's desk, looked up at him, winked, broke into a broad smile that only Miguel could see, and then said a little too loudly, "Miguel, Lou wants to see you in his office right after lunch." More than eager to be in on the game, he slunk back in his chair in apparent despair. Then, he recovered slightly and asked if I'd be sharing my brown bag lunch with him. "No," I replied, "Lou "invited" me to leave during lunch."

"Oh, I see, Luke, so that's the way it is."

"Yeah, Miguel, that's the way it is. Maybe we can go out for a beer after—"

"Yeah, Luke, maybe so.—"

"You know what they say about misery."

"Yeah, I've heard that line, along with many others, too many times to count."

Karen and Cameron were bursting with glee. They could hardly contain their oh-so-obvious delight as they raced out of the office to take their lunch break, which really wasn't much of a break because they never did anything anyway. As Lexie and Tony were about to express their best wishes and fond farewells, both Miguel and I dropped the mask of self-indulgent sorrow and pity and broke into a wide grin. Miguel addressed their bewilderment right away. "We'll tell you guys all about it, but for now we're just playing a little game." With a furrowed brow pulled down in utter perplexity, Tony looked ready to blurt something like, "Why can't you let us in on the joke?" But Lexie sensed right away which of their co-workers were to be the object of our little game. "All right, you two, we'll play along with your little game, but you've got to let us in on the details before we go home for the day. Miguel and I shrugged our shoulders and nodded in agreement.

After Lexie and Tony left, I turned to Miguel and said, "I've got to get out of here and walk off all that frenzy that's been building up inside of me. I can't eat anyway. My insides stretched to the max, just ready to burst."

"I get it, Luke, but we're still going to stop for a beer when the day is done. What do you think Lou has in store for me?"

"I don't know, but whatever it is, you'll like it."

I raced out of the office and did some speed walking for twelve city blocks, six out and then six in. I saved the gift card for a time when Rachel and I could celebrate together.

After lunch, Miguel rose from his desk and walked at a funereal pace towards Lou's office. All eyes were on him, especially Karen's and Cameron's. A few minutes later, he walked out slowly, head hung low.

Neither one of us could continue the game much longer. As it turned out, we didn't have to. Ten minutes later, Lou sprung open the door to his office and called out. "Ladies and gents, gather round. I've got some news for you. In this business, sometimes you've got to take risks to get ahead. Sometimes you win and sometimes you don't. Thanks to some smart thinking, some technical expertise, and a little bit of human empathy, Luke and Miguel took a risk and it paid off—big time. There'll be bonuses for everyone and some special gifts for Miguel and especially for my favorite dumb-ass, Luke." With that said, Lou did an abrupt about-face and slammed his office door not in anger but in celebration.

After work, Miguel and I shared that beer and then left for home to share the good news.

When I arrived back home, Rachel was sobbing. "I thought I could handle the radiation on my own. The chemo wasn't quite as bad as I had feared, but, Luke, right now I feel that I've been burned at the stake. I didn't tell you anything because I thought it would be no big deal. I was wrong. I'll be all right in a little while. Just give me some time."

Our celebration would have to wait.

LUKE AND RACHEL

Rachel continued with radiation. She didn't experience as much pain and discomfort on subsequent visits or so she said. I suspected that she had determined to tough it all out and not burden anyone else with her sorrows. At least, the worst of the treatments would soon be over. Still, as for any cancer patient, there lingered that troubling fear that remission would remain only a temporary vacation from cancer. For all that's wrong with the modern world—the depersonalization, the lack of community, the loss of respect—at least medical practices have improved so that cancer is not always the death sentence that it once was. Still, Rachel's experience demonstrated a truth that we often overlook: we're all just sojourners here on earth. We speculate about what happens when that sojourn ends but even the most fervently faithful have their moments of doubt. Many different religions offer explanations for that spirit that seems to dwell in all living beings, but we still harbor doubts. I just can't escape that sense, though, that the spirit does somehow survive. It may be the only factor that gives us grace, dignity, and at times a sense of majesty. At least, that's what I sense when I look upon the remains of my buck. Even the supposedly apex predator of the animal world—humans as dominant as they supposedly are—ultimately become the prey. Rachel hadn't reached that stage yet, nor had I. But we all would. As that physical reality is consumed or rotted away, perhaps our spirits live on. In different ways, in different cultures, we all celebrate that one mystery.

But, now winter had yielded to spring, but not without a fight. In mid May, just as we had all assumed that winter lay behind us, a sudden cold front screamed in from the north and we woke up to three inches of snow, not a vast amount but just enough to remind us how fickle and transitory life can be. At least, as wet and heavy as that weight of snow was it wouldn't last long. Those who owned and maintained peach orchards did their best to spare the fragile blossoms from harm. But, as quickly as the cold front came, it left. Soon we had sunny skies and gentle breezes.

So, we decided to celebrate both spring and the end of Rachel's radiation. Early on Saturday morning Rachel and I packed strawberries, a strawberry-rhubarb pie, which I'd like to claim as being home-made but it wasn't, fried chicken, a salad of mixed greens and tomatoes, and grapes. Our ancestors would have made the pie themselves, but there was no way they could have enjoyed the grapes, which came from distant Chile. The tomatoes hailed from southern California and Arizona. Our supermarkets offer us qualities and quantities of food unavailable to our forebears—although I had to confess that my grandmother would whip together mouth- watering pies that no supermarket could reproduce. For every season, there was a pie or cobbler. In the spring, she made strawberry-rhubarb pie; in mid-summer, peach cobbler; in late summer blackberry pie; in early fall, apple; in mid and late fall, pumpkin and pecan pies; even in winter, she'd make mincemeat pies and meat pies. As she prepared the filling for the mincemeat pie, she'd have her own celebration: two tablespoons of brandy for the filling and two tablespoons of brandy for her. The supermarket pies are economical and convenient, but they do perhaps lack that personal touch, the one that gives them a spirit, too.

So, off we went, Cassie sleeping in the back and David fixated on some video game. Our dog Amanda was the only one enjoying the ride. And she did so in typical canine fashion. With the window cracked open, she breathed in the passing air with gusto. She reveled in the moment. But at least we were traveling together as a family. I suspected that David and Cassie agreed to go along only because they thought that doing so would make Rachel happy. Both had pitched in to help when their mother was feeling too weak to maintain the frantic pace of daily work both at the hospital and at home. Cassie did the grocery shopping for four weeks and, despite an occasional splurge, stuck to the list we had worked out. However, when her three weeks were up and Rachel resumed her the chore of shopping, Cassie felt relieved. "I never knew it took so much time and thought to do the grocery shopping. I guess I assumed that Mom just went to the store and filled the cart with whatever she wanted. I never knew that she and Dad worked together on the list and prepared it in advance. Dad did the cooking so he actually planned out the meals in advance. And Mom knew all about the best deals on food. It takes a lot of work to shop. I always had thought that shopping was fun." David did his part, too, in running the household—at least in his own small way. He managed to keep his room clean for a month, a feat amazing in itself. He also helped with the laundry, but he never could fold the clothes, and I tried but never did master the art. At least, we didn't have to do much ironing except when our efforts at folding were pitifully pathetic.

In an hour we arrived at our destination, a state park along the Meramec River. Local legend maintains that the Meramec is the River of Death, but our hour's drive had distanced us from the downstream areas where most of the drownings had occurred. And, unfortunately there had been many despite fences and multiple signs downstream warning of the danger. Like all rivers, the Meramec can be treacherous, but outwardly it appears to move slowly, tranquilly along, concealing the deep pools beneath where the water swirls in deadly contortions. Upstream, though, about fifty miles away, the river runs more moderately, the shallow waters glistening over the rocky bottom, resembling some pristine trout stream. But trout aren't indigenous to our state. But smallmouth bass are and the upper Meramec far from the deadly pools downstream offers some fine smallmouth fishing.

But we didn't travel this far to fish. "Dad, do I have to fish," Cassie moaned on the drive down. David complained about having to get up so early when Saturdays were reserved for sleeping in except when he had an early soccer game to play. As soon as we arrived, Cassie, who had worn her swimsuit beneath an old shirt and some baggy jeans, raced over to the waters. After a long winter, she longed to plunge into the waters, Here the spring sun warmed the rocky beach—we all had our "creek shoes on—and the shallow waters, where tadpoles and minnows abounded. Years ago, when Cassie was younger, she loved to play catch and release with these small creatures. Now, though, she longed to refresh herself in the cool waters. Here, distant from urban centers, a thousand springs fed cooling waters into the Meramec. Cassie would have appreciated these cooling waters much more in later summers when the temperature rose to the 80's and 90's. In spring, the air temperature neared 70, while the water retained some of the winter's cold grasp. Nevertheless, Cassie plunged into waters perhaps four feet deep and registering perhaps a water temperature in the mid 50's. Rachel and I both knew what would follow. Cassie shrieked, ran over to the beach and huddled inside a warm towel. Later she would content herself by dipping ankle deep in the shallow waters nearby. Amanda lay next to Cassie, just soaking in the sun and allowing her forepaws to rest in the waters. David threw in a fishing line. I wasn't even sure that he wanted to catch anything. He sat in the shade of a large willow tree on the bank of the river and lounged in the shade. When lounging about grew too tedious even for him, he tried his hand at other options. Occasionally, he'd get bored and try his hand at skipping rocks across the river to see if he could land one on the other side. In any event, both of our children just luxuriated in the warm glow of spring. The muffled grumblings and complaints about having to get up early on Saturday morning and not wanting to go they either forgot or suppressed. I wasn't sure, but I thought that perhaps they had learned to follow Amanda's example.

But Rachel did want to fish, though. She enjoyed the challenge of snagging a smallmouth and then bringing him in and releasing her catch back to the river. She also relished the idea of one-upping me. She always landed more fish than I did, having an almost instinctual ability to know just where to cast her line where there would be smallmouth. In an hour, she had caught three smallmouth although one of the three might have been one she had netted earlier. As for me, I caught two bluegills that had unfortunately come across my hook. I could claim no skill in catching them. For me, it was all a matter of luck.

Perhaps my luck had extended to meeting Rachel. As I leisurely cast a line in the direction of what I assumed was a deeper pool of water, I thought back to the first time I had met Rachel. It was on a day like this: early spring, with the sun warming the earth and the river water and the two-dozen people who had gathered there. Rachel's hospital had sponsored the trip and I had just happened to be there, too. While most of her co-workers were relaxing in beach chairs at the edge of the river, sipping cool drinks and dipping their feet in the water, Rachel had walked upstream of them and had begun fishing. At first, I just admired her skill from afar, but then I strolled over and introduced myself. "You've landed some nice smallmouth. Maybe you can teach me some tricks, for I haven't even had a nibble let alone a bite."

"You're trying too hard," Rachel responded. "You're approaching this all too aggressively, just cast in a good spot, wait patiently for a few moments before you reel it in and look elsewhere. You're whipping that line out too aggressively and scaring off the fish rather than tempting them to bite."

"Am I being too aggressive now?"

"There's a time and a place for all things."

I extended my hand, "I'm Luke."

"And I'm Rachel." She didn't take my hand, but did extend an invitation. "Why don't you come with me? I'm sure no one will mind if you share some of the sandwiches and chips we brought." That was a nice way of testing me out. She wouldn't commit to anything and wanted to extend our conversation but only in the safe confines of her crowd. For all she knew, I might have been some depraved river rat monster, ready to pounce on any unsuspecting female.

"So, Luke, what brought you here? Were you on the lookout for any fishing lessons?"

"It was a nice warm spring day and I wanted to get away from work and just take in the sun."

"So, you came by yourself?"

"Yup, I drove here out alone."

We soon reached the crowd on the beach. Most of them had brought a date or a spouse or a friend. Rachel hadn't. She was right. No one cared if I ate a small sandwich or two or munched some of the chips. They were just hanging out enjoying the spring.

One of Rachel's co-workers wanted to sniff out just who this newcomer was, eyeing us from afar. Rachel responded proactively, "Angela, this is Luke. He came here looking for some fishing lessons."

"Well, you came to the right place or, perhaps, I should say the right person. Rachel's the queen of fishing among us. Besides being sorely in need of fishing lessons, what else do you do?"

I knew that Angela was conducting a little fishing of her own. "I'm in advertising, working for a small firm. You might have seen some of our ads on TV, the ones for Johnny Newman's Chevrolet dealership."

With that answer, Angela had almost all of the information she needed. She figured that I had a college degree but probably not from some prestigious university. Otherwise, I would probably have landed a job with one of the better known ad agencies, the ones that pay more.

Rachel wanted to shut her colleague Angela up. After all, she had landed him, not Angela. In the back of my mind, I wondered if I would be tossed back into the river or if I was a keeper. I guessed that for the afternoon at least I'd be a keeper.

"Luke likes to fish too, so he introduced himself as a fellow fisherman." Then turning to me, Rachel said, "Luke, why don't we try our luck downstream?"

"That sounds like a good idea," trying a little too hard not to come off as overexcited. I thought that both she and I wanted to move out of Angela's eyesight.

Now, two decades later, Rachel and I were still fishing together.

But the waters ran calmly only in brief stretches. My thoughts ran over to the deaths of first my parents and then of Rachel's. At least by modern standards, my father had died relatively young, at 63. The life expectancy for an American male lies somewhere in the late seventies. Of course, that figure is only on average; the fate of individuals remains a mystery. He had worked hard all his life and yearned for just "five good years" after retirement. He never got them. After a few years my mother followed my father. During her long illness—she had a heart condition and COPD— Rachel would do whatever she could to make her comfortable. I'd go over and try to keep the house where I had grown up in decent condition. Rachel and I were juggling a host of responsibilities then: trying to raise our own children, maintaining our jobs, keeping house, and ministering to our sick parents. At about the same time, Rachel's parents fell ill. They, too, need assistance. So, we did what we could. I wondered if our children would do the same for us. I suppose I was being a bit self-centered in thinking so. Besides, there are no guarantees. I might not make it until sixty-three, nor might Rachel. The cancer seemed to be in remission. Maybe it would remain so. But it could flare up again somewhere else in our most temporal bodies. What would I do then? How could I help Cassie and David with that loss? Well, there's a time for everything. Right now, we were enjoying the moment, a simple pleasure but one we could recall years later.

David broke my riot of emotions. "Dad, when are we going to eat?" Amanda seconded David's question with her deep brown eyes just pleading for treats. She knew her begging would prompt David to slip her some of the chicken under the table. Cassie would do the same, so would I, and probably Rachel as well. Amanda's eyes could beg so longingly that none of us could deny her.

So, we feasted and reveled in the moment. Overhead, a red-tailed hawk flew, surveying the land for any careless prey—a self-absorbed squirrel or rabbit, perhaps or field mouse that had ventured too far in the open. Farther down stream a murder of crows rang out their raucous caws. I guessed that after we had left, they'd feast on the remnants of our small feast.

The drive back home found us quiet for the most part, smugly satisfied with the food and sunshine. After twenty minutes on the road, Cassie broke the silence. "Mom, Dad, can we come again in the summer when it's hot enough to swim?" David seconded the request. All this while, Amanda just stuck her snout out the window and felt the air rushing against her and with her.

"We can arrange that," Rachel replied. And so we did.

SIMON

At the end of September, just when the August heat had surrendered to the first cooling breezes of autumn, the eight of us who had hunted the previous November drove down to Salem. Our supposed reason for doing so was to talk with Simon and make sure he knew we were coming so he'd be ready to process our deer later in November. We also said we'd scout around and look for any sign of deer: hoof prints hardened in the mud, trails, scat, those sorts of things. And we did. But we also went for another, more powerful reason. We longed for that connection with the woods. A few of the leaves were just beginning to turn into the bright oranges and reds and rusty browns of the fall. So the eight of us—Mark, John, Mike, Gabe, Matt, Seth, Tom, and I—set out for the woods at first raucously, but after a few hundred yards we all fell silent as if on command. We headed off to the west towards a small creek. On the still muddy banks of the creek, Mark and John spied the ground looking for the double convex tracks with pointed tops. These telltale signs of deer eluded them for twenty minutes, but a low-lying muddy area all churned up with the hoof prints of many deer lay just ten yards off a slight turn in the creek. That bend produced a deep pool that even in the late summer heat would have supplied drinking water for a herd. While his two friends were hunting for tracks, Tom scoured the ground, spying for deer scat, which he found in abundance just beneath some scrubby undergrowth. Then, we reached the ravine where I had seen my buck. Nothing was there. High above, some birds—probably turkey vultures—soared. They would catch the wind and let it carry them. Then ever so slowly, they'd make a mid-flight correction, make a wide turn and then circle back again Occasionally one of the six scavengers would flap its wings but otherwise all seemed tranquil in the blue sky. On the ground, though, turkey vultures look every bit the scavengers they are. Their bald, red head glows demonically and they plod on mechanically. Repulsive as they appear, they act as Nature's garbage collectors, ridding the earth of rotting flesh. Still, my limited perspective found them emblematic of the ambivalence of Nature: majestic in the air, repugnant on the ground. As our heads turned upwards we could detect a slow, inevitable change.

The air was turning colder, and so we returned to meet with Simon, traipsing back like reluctant schoolboys just headed back to the classroom after recess. "Hey, you boys find what you were lookin' for?"

"Yeah, Simon, there's enough deer shit out there to fertilize forty acres," Tom hollered back.

"Yeah, well, they say there'll be plenty of acorns out there to fatten up the deer, gobs of them."

"Gobs of what, Simon?" Mark yelled back.

"Acorns and deer," Simon retorted. "The one feeds the other. Say, you guys lookin' to buy some ammo? I've got plenty to sell: .30-30, .270, .308, .243, and 6.5 Creedmor. I've also got plenty of knives, some camo outfits, hunter orange vests and hats. In fact, I've got just about everything you could think of, even some trail mix and jerky for when you're out in the field feelin' hungry."

Without any conversation or consultation, we all had privately shared the same thought. We probably owed Simon some business. He always had treated us with respect. So, we shuffled around his store. Mark, John, and Matt all bought orange hunter caps for about the same price—maybe a little higher—than they'd find them at Wal-Mart. Mike and Gabe picked ups orange vests. "That's a smart move," Simon commented. "You don't want nobody mistakin' you for a deer and blastin' away at ya. Some guys get so hyped up on the idea of killin' that they just shoot anything fairly big out there in the woods. That's a shame. Shouldn't be that way but every once in a while it is. A lot of times I wonder if deer aren't smarter than humans."

Tom bought two boxes of .30-30, boasting that he needed only two bullets to hunt with—one for each of the two deer he was allowed to take. "Yeah, that gives you thirty-eight rounds to practice with. Ya don't want any deer to suffer. One an' done is what I say. You make sure you practice real good with that ammo you bought. You be ready to do the right thing." A bit chastened by Simon's caution, which was really more like a command, Tom promised to make good on his boast. Seth took his time, finally deciding upon a set of three wool socks. "I hear it's supposed to turn cold early this year," he explained.

"Yeah, that's what the Almanac says," Simon observed. "Anyways we got a long winter to contend with and nothin' keeps your feet warmer than wool socks. If your feet are cold, your whole body shudders."

I wandered aimlessly through the half-dozen aisles of Simon's small store. I didn't really need anything, but felt I ought to buy something. Finally I decided upon two bags of trail mix and three packages of deer jerky. Rachel and Cassie and David all liked-- trail mix. Amanda would chow down a little jerky, and so would Cassie although she swore she couldn't stand the stuff. As for me, I could eat just about anything. All of my friends had already paid for their purchases and walked out. Tom sat on an old wooden rocker on the porch of Simon's store. "Go ahead and take your time, Luke. I'm in no hurry. In fact, it feels pretty good out here."

Before Simon rang up my tab, he looked at me intently. "You're the one who last year brought in that prize buck, right."

"Yes, I did." My response didn't swell with pride, just a mix of perplexity, awe, and a little sorrow.

"Come on back here, Luke—that's your name, right?" I nodded a response. "I've got something to show ya." He headed down some steps to his cellar. Then he headed over to a table and opened a large wooden box. "Looks kinda familiar, right."

I beheld a skull and antlers identical to the ones of my buck, even the bullet hole in the forehead. I shook my head in bewilderment.

"I got this one thirty years ago. I think mebbe on the exact same day as you got yours. And that bullet hole lies in the exact same place where mine does. That's why I knew you were the one when you just sorta quietly asked to keep the skull and antlers. I'll bet you haven't shown them to anyone else, have ya?"

"I shook my head.

"I didn't think so. I think maybe Nature's tellin' us something. I've been trying to puzzle it all out for thirty years, but I still don't have an answer. But I got a glimmer of an idea. It's sort of simple, but sometimes people take themselves too seriously and forget that we live in a here and a now from moment to moment. Sometimes we're all Nature's predator and sometimes its prey. A lot of times we're no better than a pack of feral dogs fightin' over some bone or just fightin' to see who's gonna be top dog. We're all lookin' for that edge, but we're really just hangin' on the edge of a cliff, ready to fall off. But then there's a few graced with—I don't know—mebbe you'd call it a sense of majesty. And all that means is doing' the right thing at the right moment. And when we do fall off that cliff, something happens. Not either one of us killed that buck. He lives on in ways our simple minds can't' begin to understand. All we can do is to make the best of each tiny moment in that here and now. Well, anyway that's all I got to say. Take it for what it's worth, which probably isn't too much."

I did and still do.

Printed in the United States
by Baker & Taylor Publisher Services